DESPERATE DAYS

THE JUDGE

MATT PRESS

This is a work of fiction. All names, characters, places, and incidents portrayed within are the product of the author's imagination or are used with fictitious intent. Any resemblance to actual persons, living or dead, events, or locales is entirely coincidental.

Copyright © 2018 by Matt Press

All rights reserved.

No part of this book may be reproduced in any form or by any electronic or mechanical means, including information storage and retrieval systems, without written permission from the author, except for the use of brief quotations in a book review.

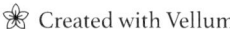 Created with Vellum

ACKNOWLEDGMENTS

I would like to give my heartfelt thanks to all who helped turn my personal indulgence into something that I hope is worthy of sharing with the public.

This book would not exist without the many years of storytelling and camaraderie I shared with those who joined me at the weekly gaming table in Bloomington, Indiana, including: Art, Simon, Erica, Russ, David, Keith, Nathan, Matt, Tom, Chris, Brenden, and Julie.

Desperate Days would not be worth reading if it were not for the heroic efforts of my very patient and skilled beta-readers. Many thanks to: Art Lyon, Russ Dalton, Amy Cornell, Elizabeth Press, and Irwin Press. A special thanks to Mike Cagle, for his double duty as a beta-reader and secondary editor.

I would like to tip my hat to Carl Mefferd, for the fantastic design work he did on the book cover, and to

Stace Wright at Eureka Cartography, for his gorgeous, spot-on rendering of the New Eden map.

Finally, this book went from an amateur hobby to professional grade work with the invaluable input and guidance of my primary editor, Britta Friesen. Hire this amazing woman.

I dedicate this book to my parents, Gloria Press and Irwin Press. You gave me life and you shared your energy, wisdom, and love with me. I am profoundly grateful for all that you've done for me and I love you both.

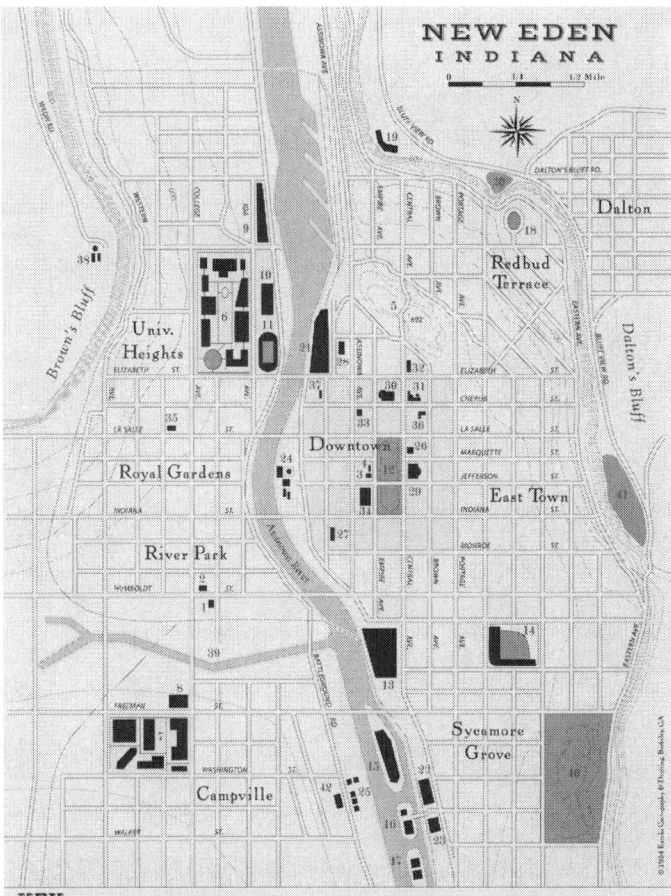

NEW EDEN
INDIANA

KEY to points of interest

1. Henry Hollis Residence
2. Jeanette's Diner
3. Browne-Lyon Building
4. Odeon Hat Building
5. Council Oak Mound
6. New Eden University
7. Harvey College
8. Good Works Hospital
9. St. Elizabeth's Hospital
10. University Fieldhouse
11. Memorial Stadium
12. Monument Park
13. Union Station
14. Sportsman's Park
15. Shockessey State Hospital
16. Victor Ordnance Works
17. Old City Power Plant
18. Pelley Square
19. New Eden Home for the Elderly and Infirmed
20. Children's Park
21. Atlas Steel Company
22. Red Arrow Motors
23. Victor Ball Works
24. New Eden Standpipe
25. Trenchville
26. Easey Hotel
27. Crazy 8s
28. Port-o-Call Restaurant
29. City Hall
30. County Courthouse
31. Central Police Station
32. New Eden Athletic Club
33. Grosvenor Mansion
34. Robertson's Department Store
35. State Theater
36. Redbud Grill
37. Council Oak Tavern
38. WEDN Radio Tower
39. Southwest Diversion Canal
40. New Eden Zoo & Botanic Gardens
41. Riverview Cemetery
42. Lee's Superior Pawn

CHAPTER 1

First Entry:
Monday, May 28th, 1934

My name is Henry Hollis and my life took a turn recently that I didn't see coming. The easy way to say it is that I got a job offer, but that doesn't do justice to the situation. Maybe they should have told me the job would get me tangled up with mobsters and space aliens. Maybe it wouldn't have mattered. Times being what they are, I took the job, and every day since has been just this side of madness.

I've met powerful men. I've been on the receiving end of death threats and bribe offers, and just yesterday, a .38 caliber slug to the leg. I've conversed with a 400-year-old child, beaten a perfectly decent man into unconsciousness at his request and been mistaken for a vengeful angel from beyond the veil. It's been quite a carnival ride, and I don't expect things to slow down any time soon.

After some reflection on the situation, I've decided to keep a journal of my experiences on this runaway train I'm riding. I have a few reasons for keeping this account of events and I can't say as yet if I'm being smart or stupid for writing it all down. Maybe this will all be nothing but a waste of good paper, but I'm following what you might call an educated hunch. I hope you'll forgive the coffee stains.

On a recent Monday morning, I took my usual one-hundred-foot stroll from my third floor tenement apartment at 821 West Humboldt Street, in New Eden, Indiana. My destination was a window booth at Jeanette's Diner, across the street. I take some pride in keeping the rent paid on my digs, but my cupboards are not exactly stocked with the necessities of life. I treat myself to coffee and eggs at Jeanette's most every morning. For company, I usually pick up a copy of the *New Eden Gazette*.

For those of you who are not fully familiar with New Eden, Indiana, it sits on the map just about midway between Chicago and Indianapolis. The city straddles the banks of the Assinowa River and is home to about a hundred and fifty thousand mostly-upstanding citizens. There's more to the place, of course, but I'll keep the exposition short and sweet, for now.

Part of the attraction in my morning ritual at Jeanette's Diner is taking in the view from the window booth and watching as the world walks, drives or stumbles by. That particular spring morning, I was treated to the sight of an immaculately cleaned and polished silver Stutz DV-32 sedan pulling to a stop across the street, in front of the humble building I call home. The DV-32 is a personal favorite of mine – long and classy, but still athletic – not that I had ever been in one. I set my paper down and took it in like it was a Rembrandt on wheels. The scene was made even more remarkable when the driver's door swung open and a man climbed out. He was a specimen of the gender to make Atlas quake in his sandals. His suit was dark and stylishly cut, and contained enough fine wool to swaddle a rhino. The man had skin like deeply tanned bookleather, a jaw fit for splitting wood, and topping the whole affair was a tightly wrapped indigo turban upon his massive head. I had never seen this fellow before, but to my astonishment, I was almost instantly certain who he was.

The man in the turban came around to the rear passenger side of the car and, as he opened the door, I found myself muttering the name, "Mohinder." He glanced about briefly and nodded to the much smaller man who climbed out of the car. This fellow was in a distinctly more conservative gray suit and had the slumped shoulders of a man who had done far too much worrying in his life. The way I see it, worry is just about the most useless of all the emotions. My advice is stick with anger, fear, desire or even happiness, if you can manage it.

My amusement at the scene in front of me was cut

short as the two men made their way to the steps leading up to the tenement that I call home. They both scanned the front of the humble painted-brick building and conferred. The little man sported a particularly dubious look on his face. After exchanging shrugs, the two gents mounted the steps and disappeared behind the front door.

I gazed on for a bit, but my attention eventually returned to my newspaper. After a couple minutes, I caught a glimpse of movement out of the corner of my eye and again I looked across the street. The two men were back outside, standing and chatting with a woman in a pale blue robe, whom I knew to be none other than Mrs. Szymanski, the wife of the building's superintendent. She was nodding intently and pointing in the direction of Jeanette's. The two men were soon following her directions, heading across the street.

I watched as they entered Jeanette's Diner and made a study of the morning assemblage. My natural inclination in life is to keep a rather low profile, and I'm generally not a paranoid sort. My reward has been very few occasions like the one I had that morning. Sitting there, at that moment, I knew they were looking for me. I didn't avoid their gaze. I didn't make for a back exit. I simply waited for them as their eyes settled on me in my window booth. The smaller man looked to his companion for reassurance, and, with a nod, they walked over.

The gray-suited man came to a stop just outside of

arm's reach from me and tipped his hat. "Mr. Henry Hollis?"

"Yeah, that's me." I offered him that much to keep things simple, but the look I sent his way kept my words ice-cold company.

The little man shifted uneasily and again cast a gaze seeking moral support from the much larger gent, who stood silently with an expression that gave away a grand total of zero information. Disappointed in his colleague's response, he returned his attention to me. "Mr. Hollis, my name is Abner Dodds. My associate, here, is Mister... uh, Mohinder."

I am a generally fit man, but I rarely instill fear in strangers. I was struck by how this fellow, Dodds, seemed to be almost shaking in my presence. The fabled Mohinder had no such affliction.

The nervous Mr. Dodds fumbled in a jacket pocket and, after several missed attempts, produced a business card, which he proffered to me. "My employer," he said, pointing at the face of the card, "is the honorable Judge Arthur D. Lockwood, and he is very keen to meet with you."

He surprised me with that and I let it show. "What are you? A bail-bondsman?" I said. "Look, I'm sure you hear this a lot, but you've got the wrong guy." I straightened up my back and leaned in toward him for effect. "I'll give you fair warning. It just so happens that I actually know a thing or two about the local county court system and I don't recall a Judge Lockwood."

Dodds placed the card gingerly on the edge of my

table and darted back to the safety of Mohinder's shadow. "Well, to be precise, Judge Lockwood is not currently a presiding judge – and his bench was in Hartford, Connecticut."

I raised an eyebrow at that bit of news. "Yeah?"

The little man held up a finger, begging a moment of indulgence. "The judge recently returned to private practice, and has set up a new firm here, in New Eden, Indiana."

None of that made any sense. "Why'd he do that? Got caught with the Hartford mayor's daughter sitting on his lap?"

Dodds took that poorly. "Look here, Mr. Hollis, Judge Lockwood is a very good man. He is making a great sacrifice for his country by moving to this little burg and putting up with people like you!" he said in a heated whisper, furrowing his wispy brows at me for a moment – and then, he suddenly recoiled, clearly regretting his choice of words.

"Serving his country, huh?" I mused. "So, you want me to serve my country, too?"

Dodds stared down in the vicinity of his shoes and coughed. "I think it would be best if the judge spoke with you about that."

"When does the good judge want to have this meeting?"

"His strong preference would be soon... well, rather... now."

I glanced up at Mohinder. "I've heard tell of you.

But the way I hear it, you work security for Charles Victor. Is that old news?"

I expected Mohinder to confer with Abner Dodds before responding, but he seemed to be making a point when he took a half-step forward and offered up his own response. "I am still employed by Mr. Victor – and no one else."

I saw that as good news, actually. "I've met your boss a few times," I said. "He's a stand-up man in my book. Does he know you're driving around with dusty law clerks in that gem of a car?"

"He does," Mohinder offered, with the barest hint of amusement in his deep voice.

"Well, if Charles Victor is okay with it, then I suppose I am, too." With that, I tossed some change on the table and grabbed my hat. "Lead the way, gentlemen."

Ten minutes later, I found myself on Empire Avenue in downtown New Eden. The Stutz sedan turned off the street and drove through a stately limestone portico that was the private garage entrance for the Bowes-Lyon Building, a new Art Deco showpiece overrun with pricy law offices. My two companions were polite but not very chatty on the elevator ride up to the tenth floor. It seemed that their marching orders did not include small talk.

"Mr. Hollis, please follow me," Abner Dodds said, gesturing toward a door with overwrought wood details and smoked glass that was being stenciled with a new name even as we approached. Once inside, we were met by a flurry of activity, as a new office was clearly being set up.

A dour woman of about fifty with a very tall and rather severe hairdo stopped in mid-bustle and exchanged knowing looks with Dodds. "Please be seated, Mr. Hollis," she instructed, then glanced around to discover that no chairs were within sight. Slightly flustered, she offered, "Just a moment, please, gentlemen." With that, she handed off a cardboard box to a workman and made for the mahogany double-doors at the rear of the reception area.

"That's Miss Amelia Knobloch," Dodds volunteered in a whisper. "You may have future dealings with her."

"Does she always look like a third-grade school teacher about to grab a kid by the ear?"

"Yes, well, do keep in mind that she has also been uprooted from her comfortable existence in Hartford and thrust into the rustic Midwestern charms of New Eden."

"Another patriot serving her country?"

Abner Dodds winced again. "Um, yes, I suppose."

"What's your job, here, anyway?" I asked.

"Senior staff attorney for the judge."

"Senior?"

"Well, *only* staff attorney, for now," he said, sheepishly.

The double-doors soon swung open and Amelia Knobloch stood on the threshold, pointing one arm stiffly behind her. "Judge Lockwood will see you now."

The three of us entered Lockwood's office, which was in a much more complete state of affairs than the reception area. The mahogany desk at the far end of the room was ornate enough to be a museum piece and so grand that it defied both the laws of logic and physics as to how the flying-buttressed behemoth made its way up to the tenth floor. An equally grand man sat behind its formidable bulk. He stood as we entered and offered up a smile that was both professional and warm.

"Mr. Hollis? I'm Arthur Lockwood. Thank you for coming on such short notice. I'm grateful that you could accommodate my invitation."

As Lockwood spoke, I became vaguely aware that my escorts had left my side. Dodds slipped back out the double-doors. Mohinder remained in the room but melted into the shadows of the floor-to-ceiling bookshelves that surrounded us like a primeval oak forest. It was then that I also noticed the two leather chairs in front of the desk, one of which was already occupied by a dark-haired man in an expensive suit. Lockwood motioned to the empty chair. "Please do take a seat."

I sat back in the chair with my eyes glued to Lockwood. He sported a bald, round head perched upon a thick-boned body. Silver-framed spectacles adorned keen gray eyes. I made him out to be nearly sixty, but his ready stance and straight back spoke of a man who still had a bit of fight left in him. I also took him to be a man who had rarely lost a fight – in any arena of life.

"Nice to make your acquaintance, Mr. Lockwood," I offered.

"It's my understanding that you two already know each other," Lockwood said, redirecting my attention to the man sitting in the other chair.

I looked over and studied the other fellow. For several seconds, I stared in confusion. Then, the memories came flooding back. "Captain Charles Victor?"

"I'm not a captain anymore," the man said with a smile, "and, you can call me Charlie."

I laughed and thumped the arm of my chair. "Seeing your man Mohinder should have been fair warning." We both extended hands and shared a hearty shake. "It's a certified pleasure to see you again."

"Pleasure's all mine, Henry."

We exchanged a few more pleasantries and then entered into a slightly awkward moment of silence. Lockwood cleared his throat and gained our full attention. "Charles Victor is one of the main reasons you're here, actually, Henry."

"Oh? I'm not sure I follow. He and I crossed paths over fifteen years ago, and only for a couple of days. We were barely more than kids back then." Charles Victor and I had met near the end of the Great War. In the intervening years, my life had followed one path while Charlie's life had followed quite another. If my understanding of the story is generally correct, he spent the decade following the war living an adventurous and sometimes scandalous life on his wealthy father's tab.

The elder Victor had been the founder of Victor Industries, which was – and still is – a major builder of aircraft, ships and rail stock. After the Great War, Charles Victor senior became a political player and something of an activist for world peace. Two years ago, he and his wife met a very untimely end in a fire at their summer estate on Lake Michigan. The story made for front page national headlines. Their deaths also made the younger Charles the sole heir of the family fortune and the family business. The way I hear it, he took on the more sober role of company president much better than most folks expected.

Arthur Lockwood continued. "Well, it seems that you made an impression on Charles. And, to be frank, Charles Victor's opinion on this particular matter is taken very seriously indeed by some very important people right now." He nodded to himself. "To be even more frank, those important people have been looking for someone like you, Henry." He tapped a finger on a small stack of papers in front of him. "This is a file on you that I've put together over the past month or so. It contains your military history, employment history, family history – the usual things. It also contains the transcripts of interviews conducted with people who know you, collected as part of our due diligence. I have found, as an attorney and a judge, that a person is almost always best judged by what others say of him. You, sir, have made more of an impression on people than you may realize."

I enjoy flattery as much as the next man, but I

knew my resumé didn't add up to what this gent was flaunting on his ten-ton desk. "I'm a little confused, Mr. Lockwood," I said. "If you don't mind me asking, did your due diligence tell you that I haven't held a steady job in close to four years?"

Lockwood nodded and smiled. "Yes, Henry, it did."

"I admit that I could use a few extra bucks, but I really don't need to be buttered up by a man in a hundred-dollar suit just so he can offer me a job cleaning toilets for a nickel an hour." The words hung awkwardly in the air.

Lockwood and Charles Victor exchanged glances. After a few moments of reflection, Lockwood spoke. "Mr. Hollis, I hope you'll indulge me a little while longer so I can describe to you why you appear to be just the man for a rather important and unique position. And, might I add, a well paid position."

The way he said those last words very much caught my attention. "Sure," I agreed. "Go ahead. I don't have anything better to do today."

"Thank you." Arthur Lockwood glanced once again at the file in front of him. "You were born here, in New Eden, in 1896. Your parents are both alive and residing nearby. You are a graduate of New Eden University, class of '17, magna cum laude. You volunteered to join the United States Army immediately after graduation and served in various roles during the war and after, including military police, until 1921. Your military record shows several commendations and your service reviews are universally glowing. There are two unsolicited letters in your service record attesting to your qualities as a soldier and also as a stand-up gentleman; one of them being from a certain Captain Charles Victor." Lockwood smiled and nodded at Charlie. "Within months of re-entering civilian life, you were walking a police beat in Chicago. Once again, commendations filled your service record. In 1924, you made detective and spent almost seven years setting the standard for the position. Your arrest and conviction record was nothing less than breathtaking. And then..." Lockwood paused.

I took a deep breath. "And then?"

Lockwood shifted nervously for a moment then continued. "This is where the conversation gets a bit difficult."

"Don't sweat it," I offered. "Just spit it out. I've heard it before. I can take it."

"Your record shows that in 1927, you met and married one Evelyn Fabré. In 1929, a daughter – Charlotte – was born." Lockwood paused again and looked up at the ceiling before speaking again. "In November of 1930," he said, lowering his eyes back to the document in front of him, "your wife left you, taking the little girl with her."

I let out a long breath. "They disappeared, without a trace."

"There was a note, according to the police report."

"It was a fake." I felt a sensation in my chest much like a sink-hole opening in the earth, swallowing everything that lay within its dark, clawing reach. Lockwood had given me advance warning but it made no difference.

He gave me a sympathetic look, but continued on. "It was in her handwriting, according to testimony at the time provided by none other than you."

"I've been looking for my wife and daughter for the past three and a half years, but so far I've come up with a big, fat zero. If a guy like me spends that much time looking for someone, they usually get found – dead or alive."

For several heartbeats there was silence in the wood-wrapped room. Then, Charles Victor spoke up. "Terribly sorry to hear that, Henry." Charlie looked at me and seemed truly pained by the news. "My parents were taken from me two years ago and I still feel their ghosts every day," he said. I nodded in silent appreciation.

"Yes, my condolences, Mr. Hollis." Lockwood offered. He shook his head gravely. "I hope I haven't offended you by bringing up this painful part of your history."

"Don't sweat it, Mr. Lockwood," I said. "It's a package deal with me, now. If you think it's important to know what I'm made of, this is pretty high up on the list."

"Yes, very true..." Lockwood agreed, then cautiously started in on his monologue again. "In the months that followed, you resigned from the Chicago Police Department, moved back to New Eden and eventually took up a career as a freelance journalist."

"Freelance bum, more like," I offered, with a dark laugh.

"This little bit of your history almost slipped by me and my people, but it seems that your writing career goes back more than a decade, with you doing occasional work as a freelance journalist and dime-novel author, under various aliases."

"A man has to pay for his bad habits some way."

Lockwood smiled. "Our brief survey of the *New Eden Gazette* and several Chicago papers show no less than fifty articles penned by you in the past ten years, most of those pieces being in-depth investigations of the people and issues in question, not just the telling of lurid tales. These articles were almost always trying to shed light on some injustice or righting a wrong."

"I had an inside scoop on most of those stories," I admitted. "Broke a lot of departmental codes, but..."

Arthur Lockwood gave me a piercing look. "But, it seemed like the right thing to do, didn't it, Mr. Hollis?"

"Maybe."

"Your dime-novels and short stories are better than they need to be, by the way," he observed. "I skimmed several of them. Not my taste, but more than competent and no doubt a pleasant distraction on a train ride or day at the beach."

"That's the goal, I guess. That, and the paycheck, which incidentally ranks somewhere below panhandling."

Lockwood snorted a laugh at that. "Well, I think I can offer you something of a bump in your paycheck."

He leaned forward. "Mr. Hollis," he started to say, but I interrupted.

"How about you just go ahead and call me Henry."

The man behind the desk nodded. "Henry, a small but influential group of likeminded individuals – including some within the US Government – has given me the task of putting in place resources to undertake certain investigations here, in the New Eden area – discreet investigations."

I raised a hand. "Don't the Feds have a Bureau of Investigation under that Hoover fellow to do that kind of work?"

Lockwood seemed briefly uncomfortable. "Yes, but... *that Hoover fellow,* as you call him*,* is a bit of a wildcard at times. He is very good at his job but his priorities don't always align with ours – and he has built quite a little empire over there at the Bureau. His men are, to be frank, more loyal to him than they are to the Attorney General, or the President, for that matter. He is also a man with a street-level mentality, not always able to grasp the bigger picture. That big picture view is important, as the investigations that we want to undertake are rather more – how should I put it? – esoteric, in nature."

Arthur Lockwood took a deep breath, then continued. "I think it is important that I be clear with you about our relationship with the United States Government. I don't work for the government and neither will you, if you accept our offer. Our government connections run deep, but our work is not – for the time being – sanctioned or supported by the US Government."

"So," I mused, "this is all some sort of grand conspiracy?"

Lockwood's response took far too long to arrive. "There are secrets and conspiracies much deeper and more dire than ours at play these days."

I raised an eyebrow at that. "If I'm not mistaken, treason is still a hanging offense."

"I am not a traitor to my country, Mr. Hollis. Are you?" Lockwood's eyes flashed with a brief moment of anger.

"No sir, I am not. I don't wrap myself in the flag to make a show of my patriotism for people, but it just so happens that I really do buy into what our Constitution is selling. I don't expect I'll be changing my stripes anytime soon."

Lockwood shifted his gaze to Charles Victor before continuing. They nodded to one another. "Henry, as I've alluded to, there are people in high places, both inside and outside of government, who have some measure of insight into events that are changing our world even as we speak. These men and women also share a deep love for justice and the rights and dignity of all humanity. Few people currently recognize the truth of what is happening just yet, but there are grave threats looming, more dire than my words can fully express. And they will affect the entire world, putting the people of all nations on a perilous cliff edge. These are desperate days, Henry. The world just doesn't know it yet."

Lockwood paused again and took some time to gather his thoughts before continuing. "These threats are coming from many directions, but they often seem to be connected or even coordinated, yet without obvious links between them."

I held up a hand. "What kind of threats, exactly?"

"Political killings, for example," Lockwood explained. "Violence is becoming more common any place you look, these days, but in the last twelve months, there have been more than two hundred and eighty murders around the world, where the victims were either politicians, diplomats or prominent members of organizations – all sharing sympathies for democracy, pluralism and openness. Another fifty or so mysterious deaths fall into the same category." The judge sighed. "There has always been hate in the world, but these political killings are happening at a pace never seen before."

"Bad time to be a politician," I said, nodding.

"The list of the dead includes four of my colleagues, by the way," he said, looking down briefly, before continuing. "There have also been other things happening – events that are hard to explain or understand. We've collected tales from around the world, of encounters with strange creatures and highly unusual people. There are stories of ordinary and generally decent men and women becoming possessed by some kind of madness that turns them cruel or unrecognizable or simply devoid of all memories. There are reports of fantastically advanced devices and weapons being found or offered up to certain individuals and groups and even to governments. My associates and I have in fact received several such *gifts*. It's like the world is being armed for a coming battle."

"You've been reading too many pulp novels, Judge."

Lockwood shook his head and smiled. "Not at all. I've been reading crime reports and newspaper clippings and diplomatic cables. I see the threads of these stories building and spreading out and connecting. The invisible threads also have a way of crossing again and again, passing over the same ground, in such places as New York, London, Berlin, Tokyo. Not much surprise, there. But, tellingly, and much more surprisingly, those threads also have a way of repeatedly crossing and passing over a few other places of a distinctly lower profile – including New Eden – and we want to know why. Important things are happening here, more often than luck or fate or chance would ever dictate. Something beyond our current understanding is afoot."

"Now I think you've attended a few too many séances," I said.

He shook his head. "My associates and I are convinced that there is something very special about this place."

"You mean the smell from the brewery?"

"Funny you should mention the smell of the place," Lockwood said, giving a brief smile. "It's what visitors often mention about the place, lately. I've interviewed dozens of them in the past few weeks – people arriving at the train station, climbing off of buses. They have a hundred reasons for coming to New Eden but, when I dig into their reasons, a common refrain keeps coming up: There is something about the place – in the very air, they often say – that stimulates them and attracts them. They often talk about taking a deep breath as they step off the train and feeling a burst of energy course through them."

"That's some pretty funny nonsense," I said, cracking a smile.

"Think back, Henry," Judge Lockwood urged. "I would bet that sometime soon after your wife disappeared, you made a brief visit to New Eden, perhaps to visit your parents."

"Yeah. So?"

"When did you decide to leave Chicago and move permanently back to New Eden?"

I stared blankly at Lockwood, not speaking.

"It was on that train platform, that very day, wasn't it?" he said, with some urgency.

"Yeah... it might have been."

"There was suddenly something very important – even urgent – about being here. It was more than an intellectual decision, it was a decision that was passionate and immediate. It hit you hard and filled you with a sort of excitement that coursed through your entire body."

I sat a bit slack-jawed at his words. "Yeah, something like that," I said cautiously.

"It happened to me, too, Henry, the day I arrived in town. Something is happening in New Eden. There's been something in the air for a few years, now, and whatever that is, well, it's drawing people here, like bees to honey."

"So, you're here to smell the spring air?" I said.

Lockwood laughed. "It's not the one and only thing that brought me here, but it is part of a larger trend – many threads are crossing in New Eden."

"It's an odd little town, I'll give you that. So, what's your job, here, anyway?"

"I'm here to observe and report, and to intercede if necessary. But my skills are not suited for all occasions. We need a discreet and capable man on the ground to do the things that I can't."

"Someone like me..."

Arthur Lockwood rose from his chair and strolled around the side of his desk. He almost loomed over me as he spoke. "Mr. Henry Hollis – Henry – we would be profoundly in your debt if you would accept this most unique job offer."

I pushed my way out of the leather chair, as did Charles Victor. "What's the job title again?"

This time Charlie answered. "No title would do the job justice, Henry, but I would like to think of you as a freelance investigator of all threats diabolical and fantastical, from sources both worldly and beyond."

"Worldly and beyond?"

Charlie did not answer, but nodded while sporting a devilish grin.

Lockwood chimed in. "What's your answer, Henry?"

I rubbed my chin. "Anything would pay better than what I've got going right now," I said, laughing to myself. "Sure, I'll take it – on one condition." I looked over to Charlie.

"Yes, Henry?"

"I get a ride back home in that silver Stutz sedan of yours."

"Any time, Henry, any time!"

CHAPTER 2

The next day or so was a bit of a blur, but it included me getting the keys to a very small office in the basement of a building next door to the Bowes-Lyon Building, where I had first met Judge Lockwood. The Odessa Hat Building is a much more humble four-story dark brick affair. It's been home to many transient and fast-failing businesses. Half of the building sits vacant and the other half changes hands about every other month. The halls smell of cigars and slow burning despair. The one amenity that I truly appreciate is Finnian's Feast Cafe, just off the front lobby. I recommend the meatloaf.

The office they assigned me had small windows high on the back wall that offered a wonderful view of automobile tires, trash cans, shuffling feet and the occasional stray dog passing through the alleyway behind. Abner Dodds gave me the nickel tour.

"This is just your temporary office, until we can

arrange a more appropriate work space," Dodds explained.

"More appropriate work space?"

Dodds nodded. "A desk and a file cabinet won't cut it for very long. You will need more space soon."

"For what?"

"The New York Field Services staff work out of a building that covers an entire city block."

"New York Field Services?"

Dodds shuffled his feet. "Yes, well, I'll let the judge explain that to you."

After that awkward moment, I was also given the keys to a very lived-in looking Ford coupe, which was parked in the alleyway. The highlight of my setup, though, was a tidy cash advance that Abner Dodds handed over for office and personal expenses.

"Spend it at your discretion, but try to keep things reasonable," Dodds instructed. "Officially, you are self-employed. All funds we provide to you will appear in our paperwork as consulting fees or as payments for contracted services. We aren't trying to hide our association with you as such, just making it a little more challenging for the casually curious to follow the breadcrumbs back to Judge Lockwood and his colleagues."

"So, what do I tell people when I go nosing around in their affairs?"

Dodds adjusted his collar. "You've spent a decade acting as a freelance journalist and pulp novelist, delving into all manner of subjects, correct? Every assignment that you undertake on our behalf will no doubt be either newsworthy or rich fodder for your... prose. Not that we want to see any of it print, however. Judge Lockwood would like to have – let's call it *editorial control* – of any information that you gather while working on an assignment for us. If it's of some solace to you, there may come a time when he and his colleagues will call on you to document your experiences."

"Sounds reasonable," I said, pocketing the cash. Dodds handed over a box of business cards, and I pulled one out to examine. "My own personal telephone line?" I smiled. "When I want someone to call me, I usually hand them a matchbook from Jeanette's Diner and ask them to leave a message."

Dodds shifted nervously, as he did in response to most things I said. "Some of your contacts may respond well to that. Others may prefer the card."

Later that morning, Amelia Knobloch made a pilgrimage down to my temporary office. Arthur Lockwood's office manager presented me with a stack of files. "Mr. Lockwood has asked me to provide you with some of the files that we have gathered to date. We have more, which will be made available to you when necessary."

"Thanks. Go ahead and drop them on my desk. It was looking too clean, anyway. I'll take a look at them after lunch."

Amelia didn't budge. "I'm sorry, Mr. Hollis, but these files are not to be simply left on your desk. When you're not using them, they must be locked safely away." Then, much to my surprise, she walked to the rear wall of the office and stood in front of an old coal chute whose metal door had been welded shut. She pulled on the rusted handle and, with a groan, the door fell forward, like an undersized ironing board. This revealed a sparkling new strong-box, the door of which measured perhaps two feet by three feet. There was a combination lock and pivoting handle on the right. She deftly spun the dials and then turned the handle. Once open, the strong-box revealed two levels, with a metal shelf bisecting the space. "This, Mr. Hollis, is where you will put documents and other items germane to your investigations."

I nodded in approval. "Nice piece of work."

"We take this work very seriously," she said flatly. "I hope you will do the same." She placed the folders in the safe and pulled the top file from the stack.

At about noon, I made my way back up into the sunlight and headed north on Empire Avenue to a place called Cafe Roma. The lunch plan for that day was to dine with Charles Victor's security man, Mohinder. I had enjoyed my ride home in the Stutz the day before and Mohinder was surprisingly good company on the trip. When he got me to my place, he surprised me with the suggestion that we meet for lunch the next day, which suited me just fine.

I got to the restaurant and found Mohinder wedged into a booth, nursing a hot tea. "Must take a lot of pasta to keep you fed," I said, extending a hand.

"I usually get a double-order of the mushroom bolognese," the big man explained, smiling.

I took a seat and glanced over the menu. A waiter saw me and glided over to the table. I ordered a meatball sandwich.

"What's it like working for Charles Victor?" I asked, thinking I was making small talk.

"It has lately become a rather dangerous vocation," he said.

"Oh, yeah?" I said, raising an eyebrow. "Should I expect the same from *my* new vocation?"

"You were Mr. Charles Victor's first and only choice for the job, and not simply because you have the skills for it."

"What else makes me a good hire? Crippling debts?"

Mohinder grinned. "Heart and a moral compass, Mr. Henry," he said calmly, stirring his tea. "When Mr. V. urged Judge Lockwood to hire you, he did so because he trusts you to make the right decisions at moments of great stress and confusion."

"I'm afraid he's set himself up for disappointment," I said with a grim smile.

"I highly doubt that. He is a man who shares a smile with a stranger quite freely, but his trust is most hard-won and he very rarely gives it to others. I am my own man, Mr. Hollis, but I am loyal to Charles Victor because of the trust he has placed in me. He seems to believe that you are worthy of that same kind of trust. It is a most rare thing, indeed." Mohinder smiled broadly. "I hope that you will come to value that trust, as I do."

"You seem to be a good guy, Mohinder." I said warmly. "Sorry if I caused any offense."

"No offense taken, Mr. Henry. And, I gladly offer you my friendship because, well, it would seem that we are now fellow batsmen on the same cricket team."

I laughed at that. "We play baseball, here."

"You should consider your new position as being like the game of cricket: something new and unfamiliar to you and with much for you to learn, and yet with many hints of things you know very well. I take you to be a sporting man, Mr. Henry, and in this game you will do well, but the time for learning is short, and this is a much more difficult sport than you could ever imagine."

With that cautionary note ringing in my ear, I turned my attention to my meatball sandwich, which was top-notch. We kept the rest of the conversation more on the lighter side of things and about an hour later, I walked back to the Odessa Hat Building, to prepare for an afternoon meeting with my new boss, Judge Arthur Lockwood.

Back up on the tenth floor of the Bowes-Lyon Building, Arthur Lockwood's outer office was looking ready for business – whatever that entailed. Miss Knobloch wordlessly pointed me to one of the new chairs, in which I dutifully sat. A few minutes later, she pointed to the double-doors. Amelia's air of barely-contained hostility bordered on the theatrical. I struggled to stifle a laugh as I passed by her desk.

Lockwood was pacing in his office as I entered.

"Good afternoon, boss."

Lockwood looked up and smiled broadly. "Strangers call me Mr. Lockwood. My friends call me Judge. My enemies call me Your Honor. Pick one and we'll see if it sounds right."

"Thanks for letting me know, Judge."

Lockwood nodded in approval. "I see Amelia gave you the file. Are you ready to get to work?"

"Absolutely," I said, as Lockwood gestured for me to put my backside in a chair. "I glanced through the file, and, near as I can tell, you want to find out more about some vandalism to a statue in a park. Seems like a pretty small deal to me."

"Yes, but as you no doubt suspect, there's more to it." He found his way back to his desk and flipped open a file. "Have you heard about the incident?"

"I think I read something about it in the paper, maybe a week ago. Didn't pay much attention. I grew up in this town but I can't say I even remember the statue."

"Not surprising. It's not much to look at, frankly. Perhaps all of four feet tall. Just a dingy bronze statue of a small child staring down at his hands, which he's holding out in front of him, plaintively. It resides – or, rather, did reside – in Children's Park, which doesn't get much traffic. It is host to a few benches, some sparse trees, and a lovely view of the city from its location on Dalton's Bluff, but nothing to attract children, ironically. Did you get a chance to study the photos?"

I nodded as I pulled three photos out of the file. The first was an undated photograph of the park, as seen from across the street. As described, there were a few benches, some stunted trees, and a small statue of a child, off to one side. The second photograph was of the statue itself. It looked rather rough and even slightly abstracted in its design. The eyes were what stood out: large and downcast and pleading. The third photo was again of the statue, but this time as it lay on its side in the grass.

In this third photo, the statue's feet were still firmly planted on the limestone base, but the rest of the bronze boy lay on the ground a short distance away. The lower legs had been bent and mangled violently, until the metal had given way. Someone had also taken the time and effort to cave in the statue's face and crush the outstretched hands. The whole effect was surprisingly disturbing and reminded me more of a homicide than an act of teenage vandalism.

"That statue sure rubbed somebody the wrong way," I said. "It would take a sledgehammer to do that kind of damage."

"Yes, indeed. And I think I had something to do with its demise."

"Oh, yeah?" I asked. "How's that?"

Lockwood drew a breath. "I think I asked the statue one too many questions." He smiled as he spoke.

I decided to bite on the joke. "The statue was one of your informants?" I said, trying to be clever.

"One of my best, actually," Lockwood replied, sounding distinctly more serious.

I had tried to keep an open mind at the beginning of the conversation, but now I was starting to feel dumb. "Alright, Judge, I'm not sure I follow you. What's the story here?"

"When I first arrived in New Eden several weeks ago, I set about delving into the history of the area, looking for patterns. I did the usual – I read old newspapers, visited the historical society, talked to a few senior citizens at a coffee shop – and made some progress, but I wasn't satisfied. The record and the memories become scant for anything or anyone prior to about 1880.

"On a wild hunch, I visited the New Eden Home for the Elderly and Infirmed. There, I was allowed to speak with residents who had gathered that afternoon in the solarium. Their caretakers said that the sun stimulated them and made them more cheerful. I made the rounds of the large room, asking questions about historical events both great and small. They enjoyed the questions, and their advanced age was certainly helpful, but their memories were often dim.

"One bushy-browed old man, however, promised to provide me whatever local historical insights I wanted. He introduced himself as Archibald Flood and his offer seemed very sincere and earnest. He asked me to write a question on a sheet of paper and leave it with him. Intrigued, I tore a page from my notebook and scribbled down a question about local immigrant communities in the 1860s. The old man promised to have an answer for me by the next morning. I chatted with a few more residents of the Home and then departed.

"As instructed by Mr. Flood, I returned the next day. He presented me the same piece of paper I had given him the day before, but now with an answer written on it, below my question. The answer was, as far as I've been able to discern since, accurate. I marveled at the response's detail, in fact, given the obscure nature of my question. Once again, he offered to take a question from me and provide an answer the following day. Again, I obliged, partly to humor him but equally out of an eagerness to have answers to my questions. All told, I visited him for five consecutive days.

"On my fourth visit, I noticed two things: the first being that my elderly informant had tremors in his hands, which, to my mind, precluded him from being the author of the hand-written responses to my questions. The second thing I noticed was that the sheet of paper he presented to me that morning was slightly damp and mottled, the ink spreading through the fibers. This immediately made me recall how I had been awakened in the pre-dawn hours that previous night by crashing thunder and howling winds as a storm front moved quickly through New Eden. I felt a sudden certainty that the note had been out in that brief deluge. 'Why?' I wondered. It seemed very unlikely that this little old man had been walking about in a spring storm in the small hours of the morning while waving around a sheet of paper.

"I wrote down one more question for the old man – this one a very specific question about certain crimes committed more than fifty years ago – and I promised Mr. Flood that the question would be my last. He seemed genuinely disappointed at the news but assured me that he would have one last answer for me on the following morning.

"I stopped at the nurses' station as I was leaving the facility and used my newfound familiarity with the staff to strike up a conversation, steering the friendly chit-chat such that I could ask about the old gentleman's habits. Did he have other visitors? Did he call people on the lobby telephone? Did he leave the property? They shared with me that he had no visitors and made no calls. They did mention, however, that he took a stroll most mornings after breakfast, and then again after dinner, leaving the grounds for about thirty minutes at a time. Dinner, they told me, was served promptly at six every night. I made my good-byes and left, but returned later that evening, parking a discreet distance down the block from the Home.

"It was then that I had the novel experience of sitting in my car on a stakeout. I watched the comings and goings at the retirement home, waiting for a glimpse of my new friend, Mr. Archibald Flood. I don't envy that part of your work, Henry, but it did prove effective. The old man shuffled out the front doors of the home at about 7 PM and took to the sidewalk fronting the building. As you no doubt know, the retirement home sits on the long, high bluff that runs to the east and north of downtown New Eden. I exited my car and began a leisurely stroll about fifty yards behind my quarry. He soon stepped off the sidewalk and followed a well-worn path along the bluff edge. His walk continued along the bluff for a few blocks, and then, as the sun was setting spectacularly off to the west, he turned from the path and entered a small park. I watched from some great distance as he approached a small bronze statue standing off to one side in the park. The old fellow loitered there for a few moments and seemed to pull something out of his pocket. Soon enough, Archie turned and strolled back to the path, forcing me to retreat. He paused again and enjoyed the view for several minutes, then made his way dutifully back to the Home.

"And that was it. He simply walked to the park, admired the sunset, and returned home again. I had assumed that he must have been given the answers to my questions by someone, but, if he made no phone calls and had no visitors, then the walk to the park must have played a role somehow, but what role, I could not guess. I retraced my steps back to the park, just as the last of the light was fading from the sky, but saw nothing enlightening. Then I approached the statue and examined it. To my great surprise, there in the bronze child's hands was the very sheet of notepaper I had given the old man earlier that day. It was held in place by a red apple.

"I stood there in front of the statue for some time, pondering what it meant and what I should do. The park itself sits apart from homes and businesses, isolated on a slight promontory on the high bluff. Children's Park has a lovely view of the city but, to be honest, it's a rather lonely place. I briefly entertained the idea of keeping vigil that night in a dark corner of the park and watching for someone to come for the note, but one stakeout in a day is quite enough for me. I was reminded in that moment how much I needed to bring in someone like yourself, Henry. In the end, I simply went home.

"The next day, I returned one last time to the New Eden Home for the Elderly and Infirmed. My aged friend Mr. Flood was reading a book on the large veranda when I arrived. I greeted him and pulled up another chair and sat down.

"As he had on the previous days, Mr. Flood made short work of pleasantries and handed me the sheet of paper, with a reply penned in below my question. I thanked him, but then hesitated for a moment, which prompted Archie to ask if something was wrong. At long last, I plunged in and questioned him on his source. He gave a surprisingly sly smile and replied obliquely that his source was 'a friend.' I asked if I could meet his friend directly, as a way of speeding up my research. He grinned again and said that I was welcome to visit his friend any time I wanted and ask any question I wanted, so long as I was willing to bring his friend a bit of a snack in trade. He cast a conspiratorial eye about and then leaned in close to me.

"'Truth is, I've never met this friend face to face as such,' he confided. 'I was born and raised just a few blocks away, up here on Dalton's Bluff, Mr. Lockwood. I've seen the comings and goings in this part of town for just about eighty years. I've seen the good and the bad, pretty much in equal measure. I've seen a lot of common, everyday things around here along the way, but I've also seen some uncommon things and heard a few uncommon stories – stories that make me wonder about this place – and one of those stories is about my friend.'

"I encouraged Archie to continue his narrative. He briefly feigned reluctance but then agreed. The bushy-browed old man explained that he had first heard of his informant years ago, when things started to go missing from porches and sheds in his neighborhood. The thief skulked around Dalton's Bluff, taking small things, but he always leaving something behind in a trade of sorts. A stolen pie, Archie explained, might be swapped for a finely whittled toy; a hammer would be replaced with some wild blackberries, and so on. Sometimes, a thing would go missing and be replaced with a note. The notes were not simple thank-yous; they were brief but detailed and very personal insights and pearls of wisdom for those from whom he had taken a small item. People started to like the notes, and they began leaving small gifts of food for the bandit,

Desperate Days

along with notes, asking often very private questions. It wasn't long before people started calling him the Oracle of Dalton's Bluff."

I held up a hand and brought Judge Lockwood's story to a brief stop. "So, you're saying they had a neighborhood thief who moonlighted as an advice columnist?"

"Yes, a sticky-fingered advice columnist with an affinity for a little bronze statue."

"Yeah? How's that?"

"Archie went on to describe how this had gone on for some time, but after a few years people slowly stopped leaving things for the Oracle, and he was eventually forgotten. But then, a few years later, a story began circulating that a young man had penned a note to Cupid, professing his unrequited love for a particular young lady, and then left the note and a half-finished bottle of wine in the hands of the statue in the park. He returned the next day to find the bottle empty and a very detailed response written at the bottom of his letter.

"News of that encounter started a new round of neighbors leaving notes and gifts of food for the Oracle, this time in the hands of that little statue. The *New Eden Gazette* even caught wind of the story and published an article about the Oracle. That, in turn, drew a surprisingly strong response from someone high up in city government. The park was cordoned off and declared off limits to the public for an entire year – complete with a 24-hour police presence."

Arthur Lockwood nodded to himself as he reflected on his story. "I was struck by the old man's tale, Henry. It was nonsense, of course, but then again, it was these very kinds of stories associated with New Eden that caught our attention in the first place and thus brought me here."

"It's a doozy of a story, Judge," I agreed.

"There is one last bit to the story, though," the judge said. "Just before I parted ways with the old man, I asked when he had first heard of the Oracle of Dalton's Bluff. He scratched his chin for a moment and then guessed it must have been around the time he returned from his stint in the army, in 1872."

"That's more than sixty years ago!"

Judge Lockwood nodded. "But that's not where my part in the story ends." He held up two of the notes. "I spent a few days digesting what Archibald Flood had told me and busied myself with following up on other matters, but, eventually, I couldn't help but dwell on his tale. Finally, I succumbed to my curiosity and penned another note, then dutifully drove to Children's Park and placed it in the pleading hands of that little statue, along with a deluxe ham sandwich, prepared by Miss Knobloch and wrapped in wax paper. Out of an inexplicable deference to the unknown Oracle, I refrained from staging an all-night stake-out and simply returned just after dawn the next morning. There, under a rock, was my note now inscribed with a reply, and a compliment on the sandwich. That night I wrote one more note, and got another useful reply the following day. That was one week ago. The following night was when the statue met its savage end. A final note I penned vanished along with the statue's dignity."

"Did you try to speak with Archie about it?"

The judge bowed his head a bit. "Yes, but it seems he has taken the statue's demise rather personally and refuses to talk to me or even let me visit him." Lockwood paused for a moment of reflection. "I do feel rather bad about it, truth be told."

"So, what now?" I asked.

"You tell me, Mr. Hollis," he said with a smile. "This is where you get to start earning your pay. Your first assignment is to find out what you can about the destruction of the statue and then look into the mysterious Oracle. Your job is to gather what information you can and my job is to pass judgment on the results."

"Sounds fair," I said. "Now, two questions."

"Yes?"

"How fast do you want answers?"

Lockwood tapped his chin or a moment. "No later than one week from today. And the second question?"

I squinted at one of the photos of the statue, scrutinizing the inscription on the statue's base. I turned the photo so that Lockwood could see it. "Who is OLAM ESHTAW?"

"I have absolutely no idea."

CHAPTER 3

I spent the rest of my afternoon going over the various notes and files that Arthur Lockwood's office had given me. He and his staff had been busy getting to know New Eden's history and I was in need of a refresher. I pushed back from my desk around 4 PM and called it a day, then headed upstairs and out to my company-issued Ford coupe parked in the alleyway. I drove back to my apartment on the west side of town, which was a novel experience for me, and, other than smelling like a gym locker, the car got the job done just fine.

I got home alright, but then, just as I was walking up the sidewalk to the tenement building, something caught my attention. My years as a Chicago police detective gave me the habit of sweeping my eyes methodically across the scene in front of me but not lingering too long in the process. The habit has stuck with me, and it usually pays dividends, even now, years after leaving the force. There, as I was walking, I noticed – or, rather, sensed – a less-than-flashy car pulling into a parking spot up the block. It was a muddy black sedan with dented front fenders. I can't quite say what it was about that car that got the hair standing up on my neck, but it did.

I got to the steps for my building and went up. But then, rather than going up to my flat, I made a quick side-step to my left and entered the cramped alcove that served as the mail room. It also had a small window looking out onto the street. I put my back to the far wall across from the window and looked out, confident that the bright afternoon sun would obscure my presence in the relative darkness of that small room.

I could just make out the sedan parked across the street and down at the end of the block. Within a few seconds, the driver opened his door and stepped out. The fellow was a slouching little man in a thin brown leather jacket. He shoved a greasy, billed tweed cap onto his head and marched down the sidewalk while taking several long glances in my general direction. Mid-block, he cut across the street and made for the steps leading up to my tenement.

I watched from the mail room as the little man in the greasy brown leather jacket started up the stone steps. I moved to a spot in the cramped little room just to one side of the door frame and waited. Soon enough, I heard him enter. A moment later, he darted into the mail room, his back to me, as I pressed myself into the corner in the tight confines. We were barely two feet apart, but he was clearly unaware of me as he scanned the names on the mailboxes, running his finger down the row. His finger stopped at my box and he tapped my apartment number: 3A.

"He's not home," I said, loud enough to put a fright into a man fifty feet away. His instincts sent him crashing forward into the wall of tiny brass doors. He swung his body around to face me and, at the same time, those trusty instincts of his then kicked into high-gear and he put his little fist into motion, swinging blindly my way. I batted that ball of knuckles down with my hat and took a step to my left, adding some space between me and the red-faced little man hopping around the tight confines of the mail room, looking for somebody to punch.

I pegged Mr. Knuckles to be no older than about twenty, and he was several inches shorter than me, but he had a look in his eyes that I won't soon forget. Those were the eyes of a killer. "Take it easy, kid. I didn't mean any harm," I offered with a smile.

Mr. Knuckles puffed a few times like a pint-sized bull, but got himself under control, more or less. "People who play games like that get hurt, buddy!" he said between clenched teeth.

"No harm done, right? You looking for Henry Hollis?" I asked.

"What? – Uh, yeah."

"Well, congratulations. You found him. What can I do for you?"

"You and me, we've got business."

"Oh?" I said.

The little man cocked his head to one side, pointing the way out of the mail room into the entry hall. "Let's you and me head up to your apartment so you can listen to what I got to say."

"Not a chance, kid," I said, using my grown-up voice.

"Watch your mouth," he growled, puffing up his chest. He shook his head in frustration, then shoved his greasy mop of hair back into place with a little hand and settled his cap back on. "Fine. Let's take a walk."

"Sure. It's a nice day out."

Mr. Knuckles pulled his cap back on and trudged out the front door of my tenement building, casting frequent glances over his shoulder at me as I strolled amiably behind him. He descended the steps outside and nervously scanned our surroundings before shoving his hands deep into the pockets of his jacket. The kid then began pummeling the sidewalk with his angry little feet and left me trailing a few steps behind. He took a long glance back at me as we walked. "I got an offer for you," he said. "A cash offer."

"Yeah?" I said.

"I got a thousand bucks in my car right now and it's yours to keep, if you go back to your apartment and sit tight for the next couple of years."

"Oh, yeah? Well, a thousand bucks sounds real

nice," I admitted, "but my apartment is a pint-sized piece of crap and I'm not much good at sitting around."

Mr. Knuckles gave me his evil eye again. "Look, buddy, you can either play things smart or stupid. So, here's the deal, a little birdie's been keeping an eye on you."

"Yeah? Are you the little birdie?" I asked.

"Keep it up, smart-ass," he barked, before taming himself again. "You've been making friends with the wrong kind of people. That's gotta stop."

"Oh, yeah? Are you my new social secretary?" I said, "or, are you just jealous that I can make make friends?"

Mr. Knuckles didn't like that. He chewed on his cheek and spat on the ground. "All you've got to do is drop all this Judge Lockwood business and then you get a thousand damn bucks, cash, for your trouble. Say no to me right now and things get real bad for you, real quick." The little man stopped walking and turned to face me. "So, what's it gonna be?"

"You tell your boss that he can take his thousand bucks and shove it up your ass. But tell it to him with a smile, because I don't want to be rude."

The little man pulled a hand out of his jacket pocket and set a stubby finger against my chest. "I get a kick out of watching smart-asses like you cry." He pushed that finger harder on my sternum until I had to take a step back. His eyes narrowed. "You're gonna cry for your mama when I'm done with you."

Desperate Days

I smiled and nodded at him. "Go back to daddy, little boy."

Mr. Knuckles pulled his hand back and clenched his fist, pondering one last go at my chin, but finally thought better of it. "This ain't over." And with that he turned and pounded his little feet across the street and into Jeanette's Diner.

I must admit, a thousand bucks did sound pretty nice, but nobody tells me to sit on my couch and drink whiskey. I've got that job covered, already. Besides, I was getting too much of a kick out of making that kid mad.

I made my way back into my building, but instead of climbing the stairs up to my apartment, I ducked back into the mail room and kept an eye on the front of Jeanette's. Maybe ten minutes later, the little man exited the diner, glancing my way again briefly before hustling back to his dent-filled car. The sedan soon lurched away from the curb and clunked down the street.

I counted to ten and dashed back out of my building and across the street to Jeanette's. I found the diner empty, save for the eponymous Jeanette behind the counter.

"Afternoon, Henry!" she called out cheerfully.

"Afternoon, Jeanette. Say, the fellow who just came in here – did he meet someone or maybe make a phone call?"

She gave me a curious stare, then smiled again and

jerked a thumb toward the phone booth at the back of the dining room.

I picked up the phone, dropped in a nickel, and dialed for the operator. A very bored female voice greeted me. "Operator."

"Yeah, hello. There must be something wrong with the line," I said. "I was just on a call from this number and then all of a sudden, I was disconnected."

"The line is just fine, sir," she said flatly.

"Well, my call was cut off just the same. Could you reconnect me?"

"Yes, sir," the voice replied, now sounding annoyed. The line began to ring. A man with an impressively deep voice answered.

"Stardust Club –"

That bit of information was all I needed, and I immediately hung up the phone. I gave Jeanette a distracted wave and made my way back to my apartment in a daze. I paced the confines of my little flat for the next ten minutes, then retraced my tracks, back to Jeanette's. I had a couple very important calls to make.

After about an hour, I was back in my apartment. I spent some time getting ready for what I had a feeling was coming and then started my vigil. Just after sunset, I took a seat in my padded wingback chair, which was now pushed up against the back wall of my living room, just beyond my postage stamp of a kitchenette. I was a little rusty at this kind of game, and yeah, I was nervous, but I knew that once things started, I would be fine. I had a plan, and, with a little luck, I was going to be the hunter, not the hunted – but for that, I had to wait.

I usually take some pride in being a very patient man, but that night I was feeling something primal that didn't take well to waiting. My mind was racing and it decided to take me on a tour of the big gut-punch highlights of my life – whether I liked it or not. Fistfights on the playground were first up, soon to be replaced with the memory of a broken leg suffered in an auto accident near the end of my high school days. Up next was a real treat – a day of mortuary duty in France during the war, picking up ninety-one dead bodies of men killed by mustard gas on a field north of Paris. But, no trip down my own personal memory lane would be complete without a long, lingering stop on the day I came home to find my wife and infant daughter missing, just – gone. The panic came back to me, as I remembered how I ran from room to room with that damn goodbye-note in my hand. I could see the familiar faces of the men from the Chicago Police Department as they milled around my house. None of them knew what to say, even as a hollow, empty ache took up residence in my chest that day and stuck around for the duration.

I sat there for hours, staring at the door. A trip to the dentist would have been better than being parked in that comfy chair, waiting for trouble to come knocking. That's life sometimes.

It was maybe ten o'clock when I finally heard what I had been waiting for, the faint shuffle and scratch of lightly treading feet in the hallway. The sound stopped and I called out, nice and loud, "Door's open!"

I had a book on my lap but hadn't turned the page in two hours. The door rattled and swung open. A slouching, solitary figure stood in the threshold with hands planted firmly in the pockets of his dingy leather jacket, where I could see the faint outline of a snub-nosed revolver. My little friend from earlier in the day was back. Mr. Knuckles made a nervous glance over to someone on his right, just outside of my view. I guess he got the encouragement he needed because he took two tentative steps into my apartment and tried to puff himself up as big and tall as he could.

The little man rocked forward onto the balls of his feet and spoke, his voice rather high but full of bluster. "No funny business. You act stupid and you get hurt."

"I got it. You got a name, kid?"

That choice of words seemed to rub him the wrong way. He sprung across the room and held a fist in my face. "Get up!"

I obliged, slowly and calmly, with arms out to my side. He retreated a step and pulled his other hand from his pocket. "Keep those arms out and don't move a damn muscle!" he ordered as he started to frisk me. Once he was satisfied that I was unarmed, Mr. Knuckles took the opportunity to sucker punch me in the chest, which was his way of asking me to take a seat. It hurt just enough to get my blood flowing, and it reminded me that the line between hunter and hunted can sometimes get blurry real fast.

The little man looked quickly over his shoulder and called out, "He's clean."

Two more men walked into the room, shutting the door behind them and turning the lock. One of the men, a tall man with a knee that didn't bend, began nosing about the apartment, looking for other people or maybe weapons. Finding nothing, he reported his lack of success to the third man, a barrel-chested gent who seemed to be marginally in charge.

The big man turned his attention to me. "You and me, we gotta talk."

"Oh?" I said. I didn't add any of my usual sarcasm, for fear that they would get nervous and suspicious. I needed them to feel in charge for a while.

He nodded. "Yeah." The man stepped a bit closer and leaned down almost eye to eye with me. I could actually see my own reflection in his dark pupils. Those eyes swam below heavy brows and just above a meaty nose, all vying for space in the middle of his oversized dinner plate of a face. I got a hint of cigar off of his jacket and breath. He raised a meaty finger and pointed it into my face. "I'm gonna tell you something, and when I'm finished talking you are gonna say 'yes' to me in a way that convinces me that you mean it from the bottom of that shit-scared little heart of yours. Now, I've got orders to hurt you a little tonight no matter what, but how bad I hurt you is up to you, got it?"

I gave him the barest of nods.

Plate Face nodded back. "You put yourself on the

outs with someone today who makes for a bad enemy to have, you hear me? Now, you started keeping some bad company. But, as of tonight, that's over. If one of my boys ever catch you within a hundred feet of..." he hesitated, then turned to the tall man beside him, "what's the guy's name?"

"Lockwood," the other man offered.

"Yeah, Lockwood," he parroted. "You gotta steer clear of this Lockwood guy from now on. Completely. No second chances on this. If you see him coming down the sidewalk, you better run like hell the other way. Knock over a little old lady or jump in front of truck if you have to. I've got people everywhere and they'll let me know. After that, we hunt you down and we finish what I'm gonna start tonight. You understand?" He nodded to himself. "Right about now is when you say 'yes' to me in a way that makes me completely believe you."

This seemed like a good moment to take things in a different direction. "You're pretty new to town – from New York, right?"

"Look you little shit..." he started to say, raising a fist, but I cut him off.

"You work for Vincent Di Parma, right?"

That little question froze him in place. If Plate Face had been listening closely to anything other than me at that very moment – which he was not – he would have heard a key turning in the lock on my apartment door. The door swung open and in walked a thick-armed rhino of a man in an overly tight suit. He quickly made sure that everyone in my cramped living room knew he was sporting a Colt .45 semi-automatic. Right behind him came a rather tall, dashing fellow in a dark suit. He was whistling a little tune and swinging a key on a string as he entered, but the 9mm Beretta that he held showed he meant business. The man was going for the Rudy Valentino look and came passably close to pulling it off. "Good evening, Henry," he said amiably. "We were just down the hall, playing cards next door with your charming neighbor, Mrs. Kirschenbaum. I thought I heard your voice through an open kitchen window so we decided to drop by for a visit. Hope it's not too late."

"Not at all, Nick," I said with a smile. "Good to see you. Seems I left my kitchen window open, too." I stared around the room at Di Parma's boys. They were busy deciding how to react under the circumstances. The result of all that hard thinking was some red faces and not much else. "Gentlemen, this is a good friend of mine, Nick." I slowly rose from my chair. "Don't worry, gentlemen, he's only here to explain some things to you," I said in calm tones.

Nick flashed his winning smile at the assembled muscle. "Good to meet you, boys. Now, your boss, Mr. Di Parma, is in New Eden because he got the bum's rush out of New York last year. I heard a story or two about that, but I still don't know how your boss got the bright idea of coming here. Someone told me he likes the air here, but it's not really my business, seeing as *my* boss – the one and only 'Two-Ton Lou' Rosen –

gave your boss,Vincent, the okay to be here and set up shop at the Stardust. But if memory serves me right, Mr. Rosen said for you boys to keep quiet and stay out of his business. It just so happens that the health and wellbeing of one Mr. Henry Hollis *is* Mr. Rosen's business." Nick smiled and nodded my way. "So, imagine my surprise when I find you boys standing in the living room of my good friend, Henry." He put on a mock frown. "Now, I know that mistakes can happen, sometimes. You didn't know that this fellow was such close chums with Mr. Rosen, did you?" He glanced around at Di Parma's men, who shook their heads in confirmation of his assumption. "That's what I thought. Well, what you gents need to do now is stroll on back to the Stardust Club and give Vincent that very same bit of news." Nick gracefully waved his Beretta toward the door.

I took the opportunity to crack a wise-ass smile at the little man who had sucker-punched me. Maybe I should have let that whipped pup be, but something told me we were never going to be friends, no matter what. Fire flashed in his eyes, and that little fist came steaming my way again. Well, imagine how stunned we both were to see his high velocity little ball of knuckles come to a full stop, mid-flight. Like something out of a kids' cartoon, a hand about the size of my head materialized between us and completely enveloped that flying fist. Somehow, Nick's very large friend in the overstuffed suit had seen where things were heading and acted accordingly. After a couple heartbeats, I followed the arm back to its source and offered the man my thanks.

"Not a problem," he intoned from somewhere deep within his sternum.

Nick took that as a sign that we were done here. "Time to go home, boys. But on behalf of the good people of New Eden, welcome to town!" With that, Di Parma's men began heading for the door.

"Wait," I said, attracting the attention of the room. I pointed a finger at the little man in the greasy jacket and looked at his friends. "What's this guy's name?"

"That's none of your damn business," the little man growled.

"I'm a writer and I collect characters. I'm thinking my next book will have a character just like you."

"Yeah?" he said, balling up his fist again.

"Yeah. That character will end up dead in a ditch – because he's stupid. "

Plate Face stepped in between us, letting out a noise that was one part laugh and two parts snorting bull. But he let slip the name. "Ignore the jerk, Wilmer. Let's go. I need a drink."

I watched Di Parma's men file out of my apartment, and then I collapsed back into my chair. "Thanks, Nick," I said. "Give my thanks to Lou when you get a chance, okay?"

"Not a problem. The old man has a real soft spot for you, Henry. He says you should stop by more often."

"Tell him that I will."

CHAPTER 4

The slow burning fire in my gut flickered out and I wanted nothing more than to collapse into my bed, but I had my own boss to report to. I pulled myself out of the armchair and followed Nick and his friend down the stairs. They disappeared into the darkness in one direction while I hustled in another. My destination was the nearest pay phone, which at this time of night was at the back of a bar called The Alibi Lounge on West Indiana Avenue, a couple blocks north from my place. It was nearly one in the morning when I shuffled through the door. The second shift men from the Red Arrow Motors auto plant were well represented at the tables. I serpentined my way through the haze to the phone booth at the back. My first call was for a cab. My second call was to Abner Dodds.

"Evening, Abner."

"It's technically morning now, Mr. Hollis," he

reminded me. "Judge Lockwood has called several times. He's very anxious to hear from you."

"I know it's late, but I think it's important I see him in person as soon as possible, to tell him how things went. He still awake and willing to take a visitor?"

"I think that he would insist on seeing you tonight, Mr. Hollis. When can he expect you?"

"Cab should be waiting outside by now. Give me an address and I'll be there at soon as I can."

As I climbed into the cab, my thoughts were on what I would tell Judge Lockwood, but my street cop's instincts – for better or worse – stood vigil in the back of my mind. I became aware of something out of the corner of my eye, or perhaps just beyond, even – a figure standing in the deepest and darkest of the shadows down the block. It wasn't Wilmer. It wasn't some wino, finding a place to flop for the night. It was a shadow within a shadow. I got two brief impressions in that instant: first, whoever was standing there was short and was sporting a high-domed black hat with a very large brim, and second, he was staring intensely at me. Not just that, I also felt something beyond strange – what I can only describe as a finger touching my soul from the other side of the veil. I wasn't afraid. I didn't feel threatened. What I did feel was a powerful consciousness taking a walk through my mind, taking note of my every thought and memory. Whoever – or whatever – I saw standing there in the shadows had my number. He – or it – knew me, everything from my shoe size to the pranks

I pulled back in high school. Then, a second later, the cabbie was waving his hand in my face and asking for a destination. The moment ended and the shadow was gone.

I don't usually get much opportunity to visit the Essex Hotel in downtown New Eden. It's a sparkling new monument to the Art Deco style, and it has become *the* destination in town for well-heeled visitors. Long term accommodations can be had in the penthouses that make up the top two floors. That is where I went for my late-night chat with Judge Arthur Lockwood. As tired as I was, I still marveled at the intricate tile-work and bronze details that covered the floors and walls, and even crept onto the ceilings that I passed under as I made my way to the gilded elevator. I had to wake up the elevator operator before I could take a ride up to the penthouses, where I found the judge waiting in the hallway when I arrived.

"Come this way, Mr. Hollis," he said, pointing. "I have refreshments waiting."

I entered into the living room of his suite and whistled at the sight of the finery within. It was ablaze in yellow and silver – in the fabric adorning the furniture, the wallpaper, and the rugs as well. Lockwood offered me a seat on the couch, while he pulled up a chair. "Abner called me this afternoon and used rather dire tones in telling me that you were expecting some kind of confrontation tonight. He said you were cryptic about the details, but that it was very serious. What happened this evening, Henry?"

"Well, sir, I have good news for you, as well as some bad."

"Oh? And what would the bad news be?"

"It looks like you have enemies out there who are willing to put a lot of effort into putting your little enterprise out of business, and they hate you enough to tap the services of local mobsters."

Lockwood frowned and nodded. "Yes, that does sound bad, but I must admit that I'm hardly surprised. And, dare I ask, what's the good news?"

"Your enemies are cheap bastards and they tapped the wrong mobsters for help." I gave him a brief rundown of the evening's events. When I had finished, Lockwood leaned back in his chair and gazed into the hypnotic dazzle of the chandelier that loomed above our heads. He held that reverie for the better part of a minute.

Eventually, he said, "Thank you for your good work tonight, Henry. I've clearly hired the right man for this job." A grave look took over his face. "I feel that I owe you an apology."

"Oh, yeah? Why's that?"

"The forces arrayed against us are quite formidable, Henry. In all candor, I don't think I've sufficiently stressed to you just how formidable they are. These individuals and groups – and other forces – are truly global in reach. Some of them have vast resources at their disposal. Indeed, entire nations are poised to undo the very bedrock of human civilization." Lockwood put a hand to his brow. "People read the headlines of the daily newspapers and talk flippantly about evil in the world, yet they are utterly ignorant of the depth of the evil we actually face. At this very moment, most Americans are resting their heads in peaceful slumber, but the truth would shake them savagely awake and send them screaming into the darkness." Arthur Lockwood once again descended into a silent reverie, now staring out a window behind me and into the brooding night.

After a while, I decided that the silence wasn't working for me. "Not to worry, Mr. Lockwood. I can handle a few dumb mugs. They've had their wings clipped and they'll think more than twice before nosing into your business again."

Lockwood made a failing effort at a smile. "Thank you for the reassurance, Henry. I do have one more question for you, though: Why is Lou Rosen – the most prominent crime boss in New Eden, as you describe him – doing favors for you?"

"Don't get the wrong impression, Judge. I'm not mobbed up or in his pocket. It's... it's just that, well, when I was a kid, I was close friends with Lou's son, Abe. I was always over at his house, and Abe was a regular at my dinner table, as well. We were just two kids from the old neighborhood having fun doing kid stuff. Back then, Lou was generally respectable and quietly on his way up. Nobody warned me away from the Rosen family. They were nice people, from what I saw. Anyway, Abe and I stayed friends all the way through college. We both shared a passion for journalism."

"I guess that explanation will have to do," Lockwood mused. "Are you still close with Abe?"

I cast my eyes up to the chandelier. "Abe died in the war. He was an only child, so the Rosens took it pretty hard. It changed Lou. There was very dark edge to him after that, and he turned to food and violence as his drugs of choice. But he's kept a soft spot for me, underneath the layers of anger and fat. My guess is that I'm the closest thing to a son he has left, or maybe I just remind him of happier days."

"At the risk of placing you in harm's way, or on the wrong side of the law, might I suggest that you continue to cultivate that relationship?"

"That's strange advice coming from a judge, but I happen to agree. And besides, he's more Uncle Lou than Two-Ton Lou Rosen, as far as I'm concerned."

"Good enough. Oh, there's one other thing, Henry, if you'll wait a moment." Arthur Lockwood rose from his seat and retreated to a small desk in the corner of the room. He opened a drawer and pulled out an envelope. "This," he said, walking over to me, "is your first paycheck."

Even at two in the morning, I could appreciate a paycheck. I took the envelope and pried it open with a finger. The check inside had a nice, big number on it. I smiled at the sight. "This will make my landlord happy," I said. Then, inspecting the check a little further, I added, "So, what's with the name printed on the check?"

"The Wildflower Society?"

"Yeah, that."

"Why, Henry," Arthur Lockwood said with a tired but warm smile, "that is the name of your employer."

"Oh, yeah? You and your friends must really like wildflowers."

"Not particularly."

CHAPTER 5

I got a late start the next day, but, after some coffee, I was ready to earn my paycheck. Judge Lockwood had put me on notice that we were going to have bigger fish to fry soon enough, but I was fine getting up to speed in the job by investigating a little park vandalism.

It was clear from the pictures that the judge had given me that someone really had it in for that statue of the little kid in the park. It just didn't square with me that some drunken teens would put that much effort into beating a bronze statue to the ground and mutilating it almost beyond recognition. The old man at the retirement home had told a pip of a story to Lockwood, and, as crazy as it sounded, the odds seemed clearly in favor of a connection between Lockwood paying Archibald Flood a visit and the statue paying the price. Maybe bushy-browed Archie's roommate at the Home had been playing a joke on him; maybe there was some silver-haired lady who had taken a shining to him and this was her way of flirting. Maybe it was something else entirely. However the facts would play out, I had my marching orders and I knew my first stop was going to be the park.

I arrived in the afternoon, with the sun beaming cheerfully down on Children's Park. It was roughly triangular in shape, with a good portion of the park jutting out from the bluff on a promontory. The whole thing was maybe two hundred feet across. There were a few benches, a few clusters of trees, and a gravel path that ran around the boundary of the park. A long bed of newly budding flowers ran along one portion of the pathway, adding a dash of spring color to the scene. As I gazed about, I noted that there were indeed no homes or businesses within several hundred feet of the place. I felt surprisingly isolated, standing there. The park was bounded on two sides by untended trees that filled the upper reaches of the gullies running down the bluff, to the lower part of the city more than a hundred feet below. The other side of the park was bounded by Bluff View Road, and across the street from that was a long, low mounded rise covered in thorn bushes, grass, and scrub trees that had never been built on, so far as I could tell.

It took me a bit of looking to find the base of the statue, but I had the photos with me for reference, and I eventually triangulated in on it. I was surprised by how small it was – barely more than a foot across. The statue itself was gone, likely chucked into a parks department warehouse. I could see some flattened grass off to one side, but not much else jumped out at me. After that, I started a slow circuit of the park, along the gravel path.

I began to wonder about the final note that Lockwood had left in the statue's pleading hands just over a week earlier. Had the vandal – or vandals – taken it? What would they have done with that scrap of paper? The park had no trash bin and my circuit of the path had turned up nothing. I walked slowly up and down Bluff View Road for a thousand feet in each direction, but found nothing. With my options becoming limited, I returned to the park and strolled to the tip of the promontory, where a simple, rusting iron fence ran along the edge and came to a point. I stood for a moment, taking in the view of the city and gazing down the steep drop-off. About fifteen feet below me was a narrow ledge with a stand of holly trees clinging to it. The wind was blowing in my face from the west, as it usually does, and I suddenly had an image in my mind of someone standing on the bluff edge the night of the vandalism and taking in the same view. How did he celebrate the destruction of the statue and his disruption of Lockwood's communication with the Oracle?

I gazed along the promontory's edge as it ran back on either side of me and joined the main line of the bluff. I noticed that a small patch of grass off to my left that had been worn thin, showing where adventurous kids had made their way from the park down into the tree-choked gully. I walked over and followed the path into the trees. It sloped steeply down and soon opened onto the narrow ledge that I had seen running below the bluff edge. I steadied myself for a moment and made a tentative step onto the ledge. It was a solid, smooth, natural limestone shelf, bare of all growth except for the holly trees about thirty feet further along, ahead of me. I am not one for heights – particularly sheer drop-offs on cliff-edges – so my progress was slow and generally not my best showing of manly courage. I kept my eyes fixed on my shoes and covered the distance with a few minutes of patient, careful, white-knuckled persistence.

The holly trees were rooted in a patch of dirt about five feet across, where the limestone shelf had been fractured in ancient times and filled in with soil, likely blown from the plateau above. The ledge was wider at that point, and I was just able to slip in between the rock wall and the stunted trees. Immediately in front of my face was a holly branch, and within the clutches of those thorny leaves was... a scrap of paper. I plucked it free and immediately saw the tidy handwriting of my new boss, Judge Lockwood. It was maybe one quarter of the formerly whole sheet of paper but enough to convince me that a vandal had been on the ledge above and ripped up the note, then tossed it into the wind, only to have the pieces fall just below him.

After some diligence and more than one near-mortal scare on the ledge, I found another portion of the note. This piece was from the lower half of the page and showed no reply from the Oracle. That bit of information made me wonder if someone had been waiting at the park for Lockwood to show up, or maybe had even followed the good judge to the park. Either way, it meant that whoever was responsible for the statue's demise also knew about Lockwood and his keen interest in local history. My thoughts naturally wandered to Wilmer and his friends from Di Parma's gang of thugs, but I doubted they had ripped up the note. Sure, they were prime suspects for pounding the statue into submission, but my bet was the note was destroyed by someone else. Somebody was taking Lockwood's actions very personally, and that same somebody did not like Lockwood's game one damn bit.

A few minutes later, I was on my way back to my temporary basement office in the Odessa Hat Building. I had to admit that the Ford Coupe was coming in handy, even though it smelled like a drunken hobo was stashed in the trunk. I also appreciated the telephone on my army-surplus desk. Welcome to the modern world, I guess.

I had the beginnings of a game-plan in my head and I decided to get the ball rolling by using my new phone to call a couple of the largest pawn shops in town. I was going with a long-shot hunch, but at least this one didn't demand a lot of shoe leather.

It just so happens that about a year ago I did a few

biographical newspaper stories about the desperate straits that bring people into pawn shops. In those articles, I cut the shops some slack and didn't paint them as the villains, so no bridges were burned. This time around, on the phone, I spun a tale to the shop managers that I was writing an exposé on pawn shop success stories and I was looking for men who had recently gotten their stuff out of hock.

I assumed I would have to be on vigil at my phone for the next couple of days, but just two hours later, my old buddy Simon, at Lee's Superior Pawn, came through with a possible lead. My evolving theory was that whoever was responsible for ordering the destruction of the statue was also responsible for hiring Di Parma's men to give me the business. If that mystery man was still interested in making trouble for the judge and me, then he was probably still in need of muscle. He had just lost the services of the second biggest mobster in town, and the biggest local crew – Two-Ton Lou and his men – would be a no-go for this new thorn-in-my-ass Mr. X. So I made the leap that he would be hiring some freelancers, mugs from the street who would do a job for drinking money. These guys would be down on their luck, and if he hired enough men who were tight for cash, at least one of them would take their up-front money and go running to a pawn shop to get something out of hock. A lot of people have been pawning a lot of stuff the last few years, and it's pretty rare these days for someone to pull something back out of hock before it sells for pennies on the dollar. Simon gave me a heads-up on two men who had just come in flashing cash and looking to get some of their junk back. They had even come in together, no less.

I grabbed a notebook and headed to the south side of town, just west of the river. Lee's Superior Pawn on Battleground Road has a commanding view of what the locals call Trenchville. It's a strip of floodplain land maybe a hundred feet across and over a half-mile long that runs along the west side of the Assinowa River, penned-in by a new flood wall on one side and the water's-edge on the other. The last big flood – back in '27 – had made a wreck of the area. The devastation moved the powers-that-be to build the flood wall and to scrape the lowland clean of all structures. Just about the time the construction project was finished, the nation's economy went belly up. The growing homeless population of the city naturally gravitated to the vacant and rather secluded land along the river. City officials saw some advantage to this and quietly turned a blind eye to the tin-roof shacks and long rows of canvas tents springing up in the shadow of the new levee. Complaints from the historically black neighborhoods just to the west of the new encampment were met with institutional silence. The homeless camp soon became a de facto town in its own right, within the city. Food kitchens, charity infirmaries, dive bars, and pawn shops soon took up residence just beyond the wall. The city police department made some early efforts to keep an eye on the area, but eventually Trenchville was left to its own devices. Somebody should write a book about it. Maybe I'll do it when I have the time.

I found Simon sitting in his usual place, on a stool behind a tall desk that's placed just beyond a cage that functioned like a vestibule. The vestibule cage is not just for show. Simon told me he scavenged it right out of some zoo that had closed down. It's outfitted with two surplus prison doors, one at either end, and sports electromagnetic locks that Simon can operate remotely with a set of comically large buttons. He makes a habit of pounding them with his fist while making one of a small set of rotating stale jokes about being approved or denied entry or exit at his whim. The sawed-off shotgun propped up next to his knee is no joke. Sense of humor aside, Simon is a generally decent guy, working in a tough profession.

I pulled a notebook from my pocket as Simon pounded on the button letting me enter the inner sanctum of his shop. "What do you have for me, Mr. Lee?"

Simon leaned over to a file cabinet at the side of his desk and thumbed through the files. He deftly plucked out two files and handed them to me. "These guys came in together this morning and paid off in full on some items I was holding for each of them. They said something about them finding steady work with a new company in town. Sounds like the kind of story you're looking for, right?"

"Yep. Sounds like they fit the bill. Mind if I take a peek at those invoices?"

Lee handed them over. "They shouldn't be too hard to find. They were brothers. Really tall guys, both with dark hair slicked back. I think they used to work at the switchyard for the Monon Railroad."

Railroad men in New Eden are a close fraternity. And railroad men with a few spare bucks in their pockets tended to hang out at the same bar together.

I looked over the invoices. "Janos and Martin Stakowski... Maybe I'll find them over at the Council Oak Tavern."

"That would be my bet, Henry."

I nodded as Simon spoke, flipping through the rest of the invoices. The brothers had a long list of items in hock with Simon. They each had ponied up a hundred bucks cash to get maybe half of their stuff out of pawn shop purgatory. The important items for me were two Smith and Wesson .38 revolvers that got sprung – their conditions were both rated as "mostly functional/distressed." These were the gents I was looking for.

I gave my thanks – and a ten-spot – to Simon, and then headed back to my apartment so I could pick up a few items in anticipation of a stakeout. I knew this could be a long one. I'm not a complete masochist, so I planned on mixing things up a bit: 3 PM to 5:30 PM – on a street bench a few doors down from the Council Oak Tavern, with a copy of the Gazette as a prop; 5:30

to 8 PM – a window seat at Caslin's Soda Emporium across the street from the Tavern with a cheap detective novel to pass the time; 8 to 11 PM – a back table at the Tavern with a steak and a few drinks for company.

The Council Oak Tavern is actually a pretty nice place. I've been known to take my dear old dad there for a steak dinner on his birthday. They serve Hungarian food and American standards, along with enough beer varieties to give you a world tour from the comfort of your bar stool. The old men playing accordion tunes from the homeland I could do without, but they do draw a crowd.

My stints on look-out at the street bench and the soda fountain were a waste of time, but that's life sometimes. A steak at the Council Oak was fine consolation, though. I watched from my dim corner table as a crowd of railroad men slowly gathered in the main dining area over the course of a couple hours. Just as I was washing down the last of my steak with some fine Magyar wheat beer, I saw two very happy gentlemen make their way through the bar area. They were hailed by their rail yard comrades and soon the merriment began in earnest. It was clear that the Stakowski brothers had arrived and they were looking to share their good fortune.

I wasn't there to learn the life story of the Stakowski brothers. My job was to ID their new employer, Mr. X. In light of that fact, I felt that my evening at the Council Oak Tavern was done. I'd gotten a good look at Janos and Martin Stakowski's drunk mugs and that meant I could keep an eye out for them. If I was reading things right, their new boss would give them the job of tailing me, and Lockwood, as well. Knowing that they would be on my tail would actually make my life easier.

CHAPTER 6

The next morning, I started working on a question: who was Olam Eshtaw. That name was a new one on me, but I hoped the uniqueness of it would work to my advantage. Lockwood had already done some of the initial leg work on the topic. The fine folks at the historical society had been able to give him a date for the ground-breaking at Children's Park – March 16th, 1872 – but nothing on the name from the base of the statue. Lockwood then went to the county records office, but they were unable to offer up any clues into the child statue or the name engraved on it.

I decided to start by putting in a little time at the archives room in the basement of the *New Eden Gazette*. It isn't usually open to the public, but I had worked on enough stories at the paper to not raise any eyebrows when I showed up.

I was soon handed a copy of the *Gazette* edition from March 17th, 1872. I grabbed a seat and scanned the yellowed pages. Buried on the last page of the paper was a brief story about the ground-breaking. The mayor at that time had graced the occasion with his presence, as well as the public works director. No surprises there. Two other items in the write-up did catch my eye, however. First, the article stated that park was being built on city land but was being funded by a gift from an anonymous donor. And second, the article mentioned an attorney in attendance by the name of Ambrose Greene, of the law firm Greene and Colfax. The pickings were slim, but I scribbled down the name and set out on the short walk back to my temporary office.

That's when it happened.

As is my habit when leaving any building, I paused a moment to take in my surroundings at the top of the steps. My brain got to work developing a mental photograph, essentially. My instincts gave that photograph a once-over and, in another second or two, I got a report, so to speak. Normally I get the all clear, but this time I got a special kind of tingling down my neck and my muscles tensed up just a bit as I jogged down the front steps of the Gazette Building.

There, amidst the pedestrians making their way down the sidewalk, was a tall, underfed man leaning against a lamp post with his rumpled hat pulled low. There was something about him that might have tipped me off anyway, but I quickly pegged him as being one of the Stakowski brothers. That was fine with me. I was happy to play dumb for a day or so and let him and his brother get comfortable being on my tail.

I took my time walking back to the office, with a couple stops along the way for a newspaper and a coffee. The people passing me on the sidewalk told a story about New Eden. The businessmen in their dark suits were still part of the crowd, but almost five years after the bottom had fallen out of the global economy, most of the people walking by me that morning looked a little hungry or a little threadbare or a little scared. I was less than four days into my first regular paying job in nearly four years and I suddenly felt lucky – damn lucky.

Once back at my office, I pulled out the phone book and called a lawyer. Cornell McKim was an old family friend. He had retired from his law practice a couple years back, but quickly got bored with gardening and walks in the park. Now he only takes on clients that he likes and for whom he has sufficient patience. In his day, he had done just about everything a lawyer could do, including stints as a judge, county prosecutor, and defense attorney. He is also a walking encyclopedia of local legal history.

"It's a pleasure to hear your voice, young man!" McKim offered in his best courtroom baritone.

"Pleasure's all mine, sir." After exchanging a few more pleasantries and family updates, I cut to the chase. "Cornell, I've got a local history question for you. It might help me with a story I'm writing."

"Oh?"

"I came across the name of a law firm that used to operate in New Eden, but I have no idea what's become of them. I'm trying to track down some information, maybe a paper trail of some sort. But it's an old trail, going back to 1872. My only lead is the name of the firm: Greene and Colfax."

McKim whistled. "I haven't heard that name in about forty years. And you're looking for documents that were penned – what? – sixty-two years ago?"

"Yes."

"Hmmm... give me a moment." I heard him set aside the phone and then there were muted sounds of movement and Cornell muttering. This went on for some time. Finally, he returned to the phone. "As best as I can reconstruct the chain of custody, Greene and Colfax eventually became the law firm of Greene and LaSalle. Then, in about 1910, their client list was bought out by a firm we now know as LaSalle, Marquette and Brown. Misters LaSalle and Marquette are long gone, but I can report from personal observation that as of lunch time last Monday, Theo Brown was still alive and kicking."

I shook my head in wonder. "You are a genuine sleuth, Cornell."

"I have always valued a bookish clerk with well organized files over a dashing but disorganized master of courtroom oration."

"Aren't you the dashing but disorganized master of courtroom oration?"

Cornell McKim laughed deeply at that. "Yes, and

that is why I surround myself with bookish and well organized clerks."

"At the risk of putting my foot in it, could you arrange an introduction for me with this solicitor Brown friend of yours?"

"It would be my pleasure, Henry. I suggest a lunch, so as to avoid billable hours. Even lawyers have to eat."

CHAPTER 7

Cornell McKim was successful in setting up a lunch for the next day. Theodore J. Brown invited us to dine with him in the Frontiersman Room of the New Eden Athletic Club. I felt a small pang of guilt about one small aspect of my meeting: Though I genuinely had some questions that needed answering, I was also using both Cornell McKim and the honorable Mr. Brown as bait.

I wanted to give the Stakowski brothers something that was sure to send them running to their employer, Mr. X, and a meeting with the two senior barristers would fit the bill pretty well. The way I figured it, Mr. X would not want the scrutiny that would likely come his way if the Stakowskis played it too rough with these two old men of the bar. I gave myself a pep talk about my logic being solid, but I knew everything depended on just how smart – or stupid – Mr. X was. As the gamblers say, life is just an endless process of playing the odds and rolling the dice.

The next day at lunch time, I left my basement office and walked up Empire Avenue to Cherub Street. Within a block, I caught a glimpse of my tail. I couldn't tell you if it was Janos or Martin, but he was a good head taller than the average man on the street and that made it almost too easy. I also noticed that he had several patches on his faded trousers. This particular Stakowski brother tucked his newspaper under his arm and fell in behind me. I took it slow and, a few blocks later, led him to the front of the New Eden Athletic club. The club's name was emblazoned on a long blue canopy, which led into a garden area and eventually to the main entrance of the hulking limestone building. A man in an overdone bellhop uniform pulled the door open and ushered me in.

My life was quickly accumulating a series of firsts, not the least of which was lunch at the New Eden Athletic Club. Once inside the august halls of the club, I was immediately greeted by an impressively ancient gentleman in another overdone uniform. He took me as far as the Club Room, where men – and only men – were comfortably deposited in overstuffed leather chairs while they awaited their "sponsor" for the day. A waiter appeared from the mists of dark wood and cigar smoke and proffered to me a selection of whiskeys. After a brief hesitation on my part, the waiter suggested the Edradour 10-year-old single malt Scotch. My lunch was off to a very good start.

Soon enough, Cornell McKim shuffled into the Club Room and took a seat opposite me. "I would have suggested Irwin's Deli on Grand Avenue, but this will do in a pinch," he said with a grin.

"At least I would have known what to order at Irwin's Deli, but I'll try to make do here," I said with a crooked smile, raising my whiskey snifter to Cornell.

Cornell edged up on his seat and bent in toward me. "I should warn you about Theo Brown. He never gives anything away for free – advice, information, or even a kind word. He has no respect or patience for empty platitudes and he is quick to put you into one of two camps: a worthy equal or a useless member of the unwashed masses. Be a straight shooter with him and never let your confidence flag. Come to think of it, he'd rather be insulted by a cocky bastard than bored by a polite clergyman."

His cautionary lecture caught me off guard, and I was just in the process of nodding dumbly at Cornell when a stentorian voice boomed from the doorway. "Solicitor McKim, I thought I told you that I needed a month to recover from our last luncheon fiasco!"

The man filling the doorframe wore a mask of only slightly mock-rage. I instantly knew the kind of man I would be dealing with. During the Great War's closing months, I briefly chauffeured around a General who struck such fear and awe into his subordinates that they gave him the nom-de-guerre of General Punch-in-the-Nuts. I was clearly going to spend this lunch back in the trenches.

Cornell and I rose and approached Theo Brown. He was a few years past sixty, but stood well north of six feet and squeezed my hand like it was his mortal enemy. He barked out my last name like its virtues were somehow up for debate and then stared at me with the eyes of a predator. The testing had already begun.

"Pleasure to meet you, Mr. Brown," I said, withdrawing my wounded hand. "Cornell, here, suggested that I carry your books for you, but I don't see anything to carry. Not much of a reader, I guess."

Theo Brown shot Cornell a withering stare then boomed out a laugh. "Hah! This kid's got a little fight in him!" He then slapped my back with enough force to dislodge a lung.

McKim and I took a last sip of our drinks and followed our host to the Frontiersman Room. And what a room. The rich have a thing for dark wood and marble. This place found a way to put one or both on just about every surface. The room also had tapestries – tapestries of cowboys killing buffalo and Indians, and tapestries of trains. My initial survey of the place also informed me that several decades of well-fed life separated me from the next youngest man in the room. I haven't felt particularly young in the last few years, but this crowd made me feel positively kid-like.

We were seated at what I took to be Brown's regular table. No menus were ever presented. Instead, the waiter started to give us a verbal run-down of the offerings – until, that is, Theo Brown interrupted him and ordered for all three of us. The man knew what he liked.

We sat in a brief silence, until the wine was served. "Nice wine," I said, testing the conversational waters.

"Are you going to bore me to death with small talk, Hollis?"

"Call me Henry," I offered.

"I don't traffic in first names, Hollis, unless I'm talking to women or children."

I laughed, marveling at the brute force of his style. "Hollis it is, then, Mr. Brown."

Cornell McKim tutted his colleague. "Play nice, Theo. Our young friend is here to learn some local history, not how to take a punch."

It was clear from a brief exchange of glances between Cornell and Theo that had they been over this battlefield more than enough times in the past. A silent truce was called when Theo Brown nodded to his colleague. Brown returned his gaze to me. "Local history buff, eh, Hollis?"

"No, sir, not at all. But I make a living as a journalist. It's starvation wages, but the hours are flexible." I glanced between Brown and my lunch as I spoke, cutting through some iceberg lettuce with the Bowie knife they'd laid next to my salad. "Right now, I'm doing a bit of a history piece for the *Gazette*."

"You don't say?" Brown mused. "Any bit of history in particular?"

I coughed nervously. "I'm trying to write a piece

about a statue in a local park. The history of it – you know – the who, what, when, and why of it."

Theo Brown's face was a study in disinterest. "And why would I know anything about this statue?"

I set my serrated weapon aside and straightened up in my seat. "I'm not sure you do, to be honest, but I think your law firm just might."

Brown's look of apathy faded and was replaced by a hint of curiosity. "My firm? Are you looking for something in my client files?"

"Well, technically, yes."

"Technically?" he sputtered, leaning forward. "Have you spent your career writing for the comics pages? Any real journalist with a pulse knows that lawyers never hand over client files without a warrant and threat of violence."

"This situation is somewhat unique."

"Unique? How?"

"The document in question was written in 1872. My hunch is that anyone and everyone associated with the document is long gone and they won't care if you share it with me or post it on your front door or slice it up for toilet paper in your men's room."

Theo Brown laughed and leaned back, his own Bowie knife now stabbing the table. "1872? My firm is old but not that old."

"Greene and Colfax."

"What?"

"The law firm of Green and Colfax penned the

original document. They eventually became Greene and LaSalle. Ring a bell?"

The look on Brown's face was priceless. It was like watching two continents collide. The stalwart cliffs of confusion crashed against the rocky shores of enlightenment. "Oh... I see."

I described to him the statue in Children's Park and the anonymous gift that made the park possible, as well as the presence of an attorney by the name of Ambrose Greene at the ground-breaking all those years ago. The rest of our lunch was more mundane in nature, but I could tell by Brown's demeanor that the camel's nose of curiosity was wedged well under the tent flap. Brown was clearly smart enough to guess that there was more to the story than just a newspaper article, but exactly what, he could not yet discern. At the end of the meal, he casually mentioned that he would look into the issue, if he had time. I assured him that any help would be appreciated, but none expected. That last bit neither of us took at face value.

I also made a point of walking out of the New Eden Athletic Club with Theo Brown and then made a show of shaking his hand on the curb. Not far away, a Stakowski brother in his patched pants took it all in from behind a day-old copy of the *Gazette*.

Brown, McKim, and I parted ways, and I made as if I were heading back to my office. A hundred feet down the block, I stopped and took off my suit jacket, tucking it under my arm. I pulled my hat down a little and made my way back to the front canopy of the Athletic Club, just in time to see Theo Brown take a left, heading west on Elizabeth Street. I made it to the corner and just stopped and watched. Sure enough, Mr. Patches was shadowing Brown from the other side of the street, glancing a little too often in the old lawyer's direction. Another block on and Theo Brown came to a stately red brick home that had been converted into grand offices. It was the old Grovesnor mansion. Gloria Grovesnor had spent decades being the grande dame of the monied social scene in New Eden but had ditched the old family home about a decade back, when her husband, Edmund, had crossed over to the great beyond. She still throws parties, but has moved her soirees to other venues.

Brown entered the building and his tail was soon milling about near the door. For a moment, Mr. Patches looked unsure as to his next move, but, just then, someone else exited, and he took the opportunity to enter.

At about that same time, I made it to the sidewalk across the street where I was able to watch the man – whichever Stakowski brother it was – mounting the main stairs within the entryway. I had to hand it to the guy, he had guts. On the next floor up, I could just make out Brown through an upper window, chatting with someone in a hallway, and then he entered an office off to the left. I could also see that his tail was lurking in the stairwell. The tall man studied the stenciling on the door and then retraced his steps back out of the building. At this point, it became my turn to be the tail.

Once back on the street, Mr. Patches broke into a jog, which made tailing him a little harder, but I have my ways. I fell farther back for a few seconds and then also broke into a jog. People get tunnel vision when they run. If you don't want them to see you, just stay out of the tunnel.

Mr. Patches kept up the pace for several blocks, heading south. Mercifully, he came to a panting stop in front of Robertson's Department Store. Once inside, he made for the broad, sweeping staircases in the middle of the store, one large staircase going up and a somewhat smaller staircase going down. He went down.

I lingered as close to the top of the stairs as I could and listened. I had been down that stairway a few times myself. I was pretty sure that the landing for the basement level of Robertson's had three doors off of it: one was a set of swinging industrial strength double-doors heading into the bowels of the building, which was marked "Employees Only;" one door was a glass and metal affair, going into Madam Elsa's Hair Salon – which had a bell attached to the frame; and the last door was in fact a double-door, but this time stacked one half-door over another, with the lower half-door sporting a small wooden ledge. That set-up was for Scharf's Shoe Repair.

The heavy double-doors didn't swing and the bell at the salon didn't ring, but I did hear Stakowski's voice call out, "Hello, Mr. Offenbach. I've got something for you." That was followed by the sound of someone fiddling with locks and then the squeak of hinges, accompanied by a familiar voice saying, "Come in."

Details matter to me. Small things out of place feel like an itch that I can't scratch. My wife used to say I was "detail crazy." Whatever the name for my condition, hearing Olie Scharf's voice responding to the name Offenbach did not sit right with me. I edged my way down the sweeping staircase until I could see the door for Scharf's Shoe Repair. Both halves of the door were shut and a CLOSED sign hung from a peg. I went back up the stairs.

One side of the main floor of Robertson's Department Store is dedicated to men's clothing. That made loitering a bit easier on me. Truth be told, Judge Lockwood had mentioned something to me about upgrading my wardrobe. As I waited, I noted that pinstripes and wide lapels are threatening to make a comeback. Keeping in fashion is one aggravation that I don't need, and I doubt I'll be changing my stripes – or anything else in my wardrobe – anytime soon.

I was flipping through racks of suits when Mr. Patches trudging up the staircase, looking more than a bit anxious. He'd been given his marching orders and they weren't sitting well with him. This is why amateurs are rarely worth the investment. If there was some kind of global conspiracy at play in New Eden, it was evidently being financed on the cheap and orchestrated by a soft-spoken shoe repairmen, pulling the strings from his cave-like cobbler shop under a department store. I was feeling less impressed by the minute.

My tailing duties ended back at the Council Oak Tavern, where the Stakowski brothers were reunited on adjacent barstools. I went home, secure in the thought that they would remain on said barstools until they had pounded down enough Hungarian beer to float a Mississippi river barge.

As I lay my head on the pillow that night, I just couldn't get past the involvement of Olie Scharf in the whole affair. He was almost literally the last person on the planet that I could have envisioned being involved in anything nefarious. He was a middle-aged, myopic, bookish little man, without a drop of guile in his bones so far as I had ever seen. He wasn't exactly slow-witted but it usually took a few tries to get an even moderately complex point across to him. The man rarely caught the gist of a joke or the flip side of a double entendre. It just didn't make sense. I resolved to confront him the next day, after checking in with Lockwood.

CHAPTER 8

I awoke the next morning refreshed and ready to resume my work. I felt like I was ahead of the curve, and more or less making progress. For me, investigative work is a lot like being a scientist in a lab; I don't mind being confused by the incomplete results of a job half-done, as long as everything makes sense by the time I do my write-up at the end. I was still confused by most of what I'd learned so far, but I had momentum and the crumbs were leading somewhere. But the world has a way of changing pretty quick sometimes.

The knock I heard on my door that morning was a very special kind of knock – one that I had employed back in Chicago, during my years on the police force. It was four loud knocks, one too many for a friendly caller, but not frantic enough to make me grab my revolver from under the bed. So, I pulled on a robe and prepared to greet my visitor.

"Morning, officer. What can I do for you today?" I said as I swung my front door wide.

"Your name Henry Hollis?"

"Yes."

"I'm here to take you to police headquarters to answer a few questions. If you volunteer to come, I can give you a little time to pull on some clothes."

"That's real generous of you, officer, but I'm not much in the mood to go anywhere just now. What's this all about?"

"We're investigating the death of a man by the name of Janos Stakowski."

My jaw hung slack and for a moment my mind did a quick two-step between bewilderment and fear. "Look, officer, I have no idea what you're talking about. I don't know the guy and I sure as hell didn't kill him."

"Don't work up a sweat just yet. We know who killed him."

"Oh, yeah? Well, that's good," I said with genuine relief. "So, why am I about to volunteer for a visit to police headquarters?"

"Stakowski mentioned you before he died."

Things had just escalated in a hurry.

I was greeted at the police station by Cornell McKim, which surprised me, as I hadn't yet asked for a lawyer. It took a few heartbeats before I started putting things together, and, by then, I was walking into a detective's office. There, I found myself in the company of none other than Theo Brown. Theo was very casually dressed for the occasion – too casual for his liking.

His hair was a bit tussled and there was no hint of his usual self-satisfied smile on his now-ashen face. A knot started tightening in my stomach.

The detective asked me to sit down on the leather couch against the far wall. I didn't recognize the guy. He was evidently new to the department, but he wasn't exactly a fresh recruit, straight out of college, either. He'd earned his stripes and scars somewhere and had picked up on a recent job opening at the NEPD.

The detective turned his attention back to Theo Brown. He pulled a chrome-plated Colt .45 with a custom ivory-inlayed grip out of a small, ornate box. "This needs to be held as evidence while we complete our investigation."

Brown nodded. "I understand."

"Mr. Hollis," the detective said, returning his attention to me. "Thank you for coming down to the station. I'm Detective Aemon Bettis. I take it you know Mr. Brown here?"

I nodded. "Met him just yesterday, as a matter of fact."

"The name Janos Stakowski mean anything to you?"

This is where I had to start walking the information tightrope. A good detective can usually tell the difference between the truth and a lie right off the bat. My general policy is to avoid lying unless absolutely necessary, and since I was pretty sure that the criminal justice system didn't have me on the hook for anything at that particular moment, I wanted to stick with something resembling the truth. Don't get me wrong, if lying worked more often, I would abuse the privilege.

"I make my drinking money writing freelance articles for the *Gazette*," I told Bettis. "I have two stories I'm working on right now: one that involves Mr. Stakowski and another that brought me into contact with Mr. Brown." I proceeded to tell Bettis about the pawn shop article I had written and my follow-up idea that included my recent meeting with the owner of Lee's Superior Pawn Shop. I told him that I had been offered Stakowski's name as a possible client to profile. Once I'd covered that ground, I tiptoed into the territory surrounding my meeting with Theo Brown and the history of Children's Park. I left things a little vague as to exactly what information I was hoping to get from Mr. Brown, which the old lawyer no doubt appreciated as well.

"Well, Stakowski went to Mr. Brown's residence late last night," Bettis informed me. "He waved a revolver in Brown's face, demanding to know what your meeting with Brown was about. But it turns out that Mr. Brown is a believer in swift justice. Cool as a cucumber, he walks Stakowski to a bookshelf, telling him he'll show Janos what he's looking for – you know, in this little box – and then Mr. Brown pulls out this chrome and ivory beauty and puts two .45 slugs into his visitor."

"Holy Hell," I muttered.

"Mr. Brown tells me that he has no connection with Stakowski. Never met him, never heard of him before last night. I'm inclined to believe him. You ever meet with Stakowski?" Bettis asked me.

"No, I never had the privilege, but I did follow up on a lead that he and his brother were frequent visitors to the Council Oak Tavern. Maybe I asked too many questions and talked to the wrong people at the tavern. Maybe Janos got wind of it and took it the wrong way."

Aemon Bettis shook his head. "I'm not buying it, Mr. Hollis."

Right about then might have been a good time to bring up Olie Scharf and his meeting with Stakowski. My instincts, however, told me that I needed to talk to Arthur Lockwood about Scharf before any cops got wind of the increasingly mysterious shoe repair man. I also felt like I needed to take a crack at Scharf myself, before someone found a way to link him to the death of poor Janos. Besides, bringing up Olie Scharf with Detective Bettis would necessitate explaining why I was following Stakowski, rather than just chatting with him over a few beers, like a normal reporter. So, I lied.

"I was having trouble tracking Stakowski down, so when I was at the tavern, I might have insinuated that I had something on him, you know, of an incriminating nature. I made sure the people I talked to knew who I was and where to find me. Maybe that wasn't such a good idea."

Bettis stared at me with his brows deeply furrowed. "Is that it? Is that all you're going to give me?"

"Yep, that's it."

"If my investigation turns up something different

that doesn't match your story, you will be back here for another conversation with me, in handcuffs."

"I read you loud and clear, detective."

Bettis sent me to the secretarial pool where they kept me busy giving a written statement. When that was done, I grabbed my hat and made for the exit. Just as my foot hit the pavement outside, I felt the presence of a large man rushing up behind me. It was Theo Brown, who grabbed my elbow in a way that threatened to leave me with just a stump. He steered me down the block and into a doorway alcove. Brown pushed me up against the door and loomed over me.

"I don't like being a pawn in other men's games, Hollis," he hissed.

The man had a point. "You're absolutely right to be angry, Mr. Brown. I'm real sorry about what happened to you last night. I never imagined that you and Stakowski would ever cross paths."

Theo Brown's face was twisted up into a damn good imitation of a gargoyle come to life. "You got me angry enough to kill last night, Hollis. That takes quite a bit of doing, but that's where I am at right at this moment, seeing a lot of red in front of my eyes. Maybe I haven't shaken it off just yet and maybe I need to wring your goddamn neck!"

I quite literally cringed as he spoke. My hunch is my abject fear gave him just enough satisfaction to keep the old man from doing me in right then and there.

"I was a much younger man the last time someone

pointed a gun at me, Hollis. I was standing up to my knees in mud in Cuba. On that day, a man put two bullets in me and left me for dead in a flooded jungle lowland. I crawled for a day and a night before I was found by friendly forces. Somewhere on that crawl through that swamp, I lost my fear of death – and most everything else. But I am not going to take a bullet for you!" Theo Brown shook me like a rag doll, and I took it, because I more or less deserved it. Then he loosened his grip and his rage-filled face softened ever so slightly.

"You owe me the truth, young man," he said, slowly regaining his composure.

People talk about being owed things all the time and it's almost never true. Mostly, it's just a ploy to get something from someone when the other party is feeling guilty or under some kind of duress. I owed Brown an apology, but not the truth. That said, I knew that his files would be lost to me forever unless I could find a way to regain his confidence – or at least his curiosity. I took a chance, which was becoming a new – and increasingly common – habit for me.

"I'm not writing a story for the paper, as such. Someone hired me to look into the history of the park, and Stakowski's boss took offense."

"Who hired you?"

I sucked in a breath and pondered my options. Theo Brown was one of the most arrogant men I'd ever met, but he'd earned most of his swagger and Cornell McKim had a high opinion of him. I didn't have time to come up with a good lie, and withholding the truth from him would put me permanently on the outs with Brown. I was suddenly confronted with either making him an enemy or an accomplice. Trying to make an ally of him would invite unknown risks, but having him as an enemy was a sure-fire bad idea.

"Judge Arthur Lockwood, recently of Hartford."

Watching the change come over Theo Brown's face was pure magic. I had no idea what was going on behind those steely eyes, but the effect was priceless. The spectacle ended with him letting loose of me and stepping back a couple paces.

"So you're the mystery man that Lockwood was keeping in his back pocket." Brown nodded to himself. "I wish you luck, Hollis. You're going to need it."

"Wait a second," I said, straightening out my shirt. "You know about Lockwood's business here in New Eden?"

"Know about it? Hells bells, I helped recruit him! There was talk of me taking the job, but this little spot on the map is where I have lived and worked for most of my adult life. If things went off the rails and I was seen as being front and center in some kind of debacle, the consequences would be ruinous for me. Lockwood can just pick up the pieces and go back to Hartford – that is, if we don't all get hauled in on charges of treason."

"Treason, eh? That's a comforting thought," I mused. Brown stepped back onto the sidewalk, and I followed him into the daylight. "And you needed a local guy who was expendable, who could do the dirty work. Is that how the logic went?" I asked.

"In a nutshell, yes. Having a fellow like Mr. Stakowski wave a gun in my face was not part of the plan. If anyone took a bullet for the cause, it was supposed to be, well, you."

I wheezed in frustration, but not specifically because I was being offered up as a sacrificial lamb. "I keep being told that there is some sort of noble cause at play here. When I was a cop, people would sometimes tell me I was working for a cause – public safety, protecting the innocent, punishing the guilty – and most of the time I bought that logic. But you and your fellow co-conspirators seem to be a bit fuzzy about your cause, other than opposing mysterious boogie men. I hope you'll forgive me for being a skeptic."

"I welcome your skepticism. In fact, I encourage it. We don't need to preach to you about our cause, Hollis. If you do your job right, you will become a believer on your own. In the meantime, I hope the paycheck is incentive enough."

I nodded and smiled. "Yes, as a matter of fact, it is. I'll let you know if I ever feel a conversion coming on."

"I'll have the Children's Park client file delivered to you this afternoon, by the way."

"You still have it?"

"Yes, but remember, my sharing this file with you is breaking more than a couple lawyerly ethics rules – rules that I actually respect. So, don't get used to this, and treat the file like it's the only thing protecting you from the business end of my chrome-plated Colt. Agreed?"

"Agreed," I offered, solemnly.

"Good." Theo Brown relaxed a little and smiled slightly. "I was surprised that we still had it as well, actually. It's been an active client file for more than fifty years, which is unique, to say the least."

"So, you've met the mystery man?"

"All interactions have been in writing, once or twice every few years. No in-office visits and no phone calls."

"So, who's the client?"

"Adam P. Smith. Same contact person since the first correspondence back in 1870."

"An alias?"

"Very likely, but someone has been maintaining the correspondence for over half a century, and checks from Mr. Smith's account at the Merchants and Farmers Bank have been clearing just fine for that entire time."

I whistled at the news. "Thanks for the information, solicitor. For what it's worth, I'm glad that Janos Stakowski didn't do you in." I offered my hand to him. He glanced at it with his usual mock disapproval then broke into something resembling a warm smile.

"For what it's worth, Hollis, I hope you don't get done in by the next man with a gun, either," he said, shaking my hand.

CHAPTER 9

Brown and I parted ways just after 9 AM. An officer at the police station had mentioned that they were still looking for next-of-kin for Janos Stakowski, which made me think that Olie Scharf might still be in the dark about Janos being gunned down the night before. I wanted to have a chat with the shoe repairman before the news broke. But first, I wanted to check in with my boss, Arthur Lockwood.

I jogged down the block to a pay phone and called in to Lockwood's office, only to find that he would be out of the office that day, which struck me as particularly bad timing. I shook off my frustration and returned my thoughts to Olie Scharf.

Under a strict interpretation of the law, Scharf could be held responsible for Janos Stakowski's death, being that Olie gave Janos his marching orders, so I was about to confront a man looking at potentially serious jail time. I was trying to put together a game plan even as I pushed through the revolving front doors at Robertson's Department Store. That's when the strangest thing happened – my mother marched in right behind me.

"Henry!" she called out in cheerful surprise. "I'm so glad you're here. I need your help with something. Could you spare a moment?"

Like most sons, I was powerless before her. "Of course, just name it."

Dorothy Hollis is a plump, cheerful powerhouse, who is never without a floral hat perched on top of her shoulder-length salt and pepper hair. She held up a bag and, from it, she pulled a shoe. The heel of the shoe was hanging precariously from a single tiny nail. "The shoe repairman replaced this heel just last week and now look at it. I'd be grateful if you would accompany me when I confront him about this."

"Play the bad cop to your good cop?"

"Something like that, dear." She shoved the shoe back in the bag and stared at me expectantly.

"Of course I'll come with you. It would be good to dust off my police skills."

"Such a good son," she crooned, taking my arm.

We marched down the curving stairs to the basement level of the department store and up to Scharf's little shop window, which was open. Olie was sitting with his back to us, working on a shoe at his cobbler's bench. My mother rang the bell on the narrow ledge.

Olie Scharf swung around in his chair and greeted us amiably. From there, the conversation was a polite dance of gentle accusation by my mother and apologetic defensiveness by Scharf. I stood quietly to one side and never entered the conversation. He looked at me once, but my presence barely registered on his face or in his behavior. Everything was – normal. After Olie agreed to repair my mother's shoe at no cost, she thanked him, and they exchanged parting pleasantries as I took her arm once again. I mounted the stairs with her and gave her a peck on the cheek.

"Thank you, Henry. I hope that wasn't too much of a bother."

"Not at all. You had him on the ropes and he threw in the towel. Never stood a chance."

My mother blushed and squeezed my arm. "You're a good son. Have time for coffee?"

"Not just now, Mother. Maybe later. I came here to pick out a few shirts and then sprint to a meeting. Rain check?"

"Of course."

I gave her what passed for a hug in our family and sent her on her way. I loitered amongst racks of men's shirts until I saw her finally exit the building; then I made for the shoe repair shop. Olie was back at his cobbler's bench, now working on my mother's shoe. I knocked on the door frame.

He swung around and greeted me much the same as he did before, with only the mildest hint of confusion on his face. "The lady need anything else, sir?"

"No. Actually, I'm here with my own question."

"Yes?"

"It seems you did some work for a friend of mine, but he hasn't had a chance to pick his shoes up just yet. He asked me to stop by and check in on them."

"What's your friend's name?" he asked. My question didn't seem to throw him. He was calm and cool as a shoe-mending cucumber.

"The name is Janos Stakowski," I said flatly. I watched as my words landed with a dull thud on his ears. Nothing in Olie's demeanor changed. I could see his brain slowly chewing on the name, trying to recall it. He tilted his head slightly, as a dog does when confused, and then he turned to the little wooden box of cards on his bench that evidently held his job files.

"S-t-a-...." he slowly called back to me, clearly wanting me to finish the spelling, which I did. He fished in the card box for a while and finally turned back to face me looking slightly confused but innocent as a newborn babe. "I can't seem to find him in my files. Maybe he took his shoes somewhere else and got confused about where."

"Yeah, that must be it. The thing is..." I paused and pondered where to take things next.

"Yes?"

"Well, Janos is dead – shot dead, in fact, just last night." I said it with just enough force to make it more accusing than simply informative. That seemed to do the trick, but not how I suspected it would. Tears began to well up in Olie's eyes.

"What did your friend look like?" he said, reaching for his glasses with shaking hands.

"North of six feet but rail thin. Big mop of black hair on his head. In dire need of a new pair of pants. Any of that ring a bell with you?"

Olie Scharf nodded wordlessly, pulling a kerchief from a pocket and dabbing under his glasses.

"So, you remember him now."

"Why are you people doing this to me?" he asked in a whispered sob. His whole body began shaking with genuine grief.

"You have a soft spot in your heart for Janos?"

Olie took in several deep shuddering breaths and was eventually capable of talking once again. "I was terrified of him, and the silver-haired man."

"Silver-haired man? He and Janos work for you?"

"Work for me?" he said in a hoarse whisper. "I don't know them at all. I don't know what they want and I don't know what they've done to me." His face screwed up into something approaching horror. "Please make it stop!" His last words were on the verge of a scream, which caused him to recoil and cover his mouth.

"Looks like you're in a funny little predicament. How about you close up shop for a few minutes so that you and me can have a little chat." I tried to walk a fine line between sincere and menacing, giving him the option of seeing me as either a confessor or an existential threat – whatever got him to talk. I got the feeling he saw me as both.

Olie nodded in agreement while dabbing at his eyes. He pulled the bolt on the lower half of the door, allowing it to swing out. I entered and pulled both halves of the door shut. He shrank onto his little spinning stool at his bench while I made myself comfortable on a dented file cabinet and sat looming over him. "Who's the silver-haired man?"

"I don't know," Olie said, folding his kerchief. "He started showing up here about a month ago. That's when this all started."

"When what started?"

"I..." He slumped in his chair, eyes downcast. "I don't know."

"You don't know? That doesn't make any sense, Olie."

"You tell me, then!" he cried out, looking up at me with pleading eyes.

"I don't have anything to do with Stakowski or your Mr. Silver Hair. And don't forget that Stakowski's dead, maybe because of you. Now, I can be your friend or your enemy, but my next stop this morning will be police headquarters if you don't give me a damn good reason to think that this is all just a terrible misunderstanding." I said this in a savage growl, maybe overselling it. "So, I'm only going to ask you this once: what, exactly, do you know?"

Olie Scharf stared up at me with eyes like a damn basset hound. "The silver-haired man showed up at my shop one day and started asking me all kinds of questions – personal questions."

"Yeah? Like what?"

"It was just friendly chit-chat at first, then he started asking if I lived alone, if I had a lot of friends, where I spent my free time, when did I come in to work and leave again – the questions went on and on. I didn't want to tell him, but..." He suddenly hesitated.

"But what?"

"He scared me. He kept looking at me with these eyes. I've never seen anything like 'em before. They were like ice but they burned into my brain and I – I just couldn't stop. And then it happened." Olie started staring at his hands, splayed lifelessly on his lap, like he had entered into a trance. Seconds began to pass.

When I'd had enough, I grabbed Olie by the collar and pulled him up so he was standing on his toes. "*What* happened, dammit?"

"He said the name!"

I pushed him back onto his stool in mock exasperation. "What name?"

"That's the thing. I only ever hear part of it and then everything goes blank. It's like I fall instantly asleep and then I wake up later."

"You black out when they say a name? For how long?"

"Sometimes a few minutes, sometimes a few hours. When I come to, I'm usually just sitting here at my work bench, but sometimes I'm other places."

"You remember anything about the name?"

Sort of," he mused, straightening his shirt. "They say 'mister,' as in 'hello, Mr. Scharf.' But instead of saying Scharf, they say something that starts with 'Off...' and then everything goes black."

I whistled. "Jesus..."

"That mean anything to you?"

"Yeah..." I nodded distractedly. "I think I know the name."

"Please don't say it!" Olie pleaded.

There was no point in giving him any more grief. For some reason, I was buying Olie's story and he had given me almost everything I needed, for now. The only thing left was to get a peek at the very mysterious Mr. Offenbach. I patted Olie on the shoulder and gave him as warm a smile as I could muster. "I'll make you a deal. You let me spend the next few hours holed up in your shoe box of a storeroom back there, and I won't say the name unless you ask me to."

Olie doubled down on his confused look. "What's so interesting about my storeroom?"

"Nothing. But now that Janos is dead, I'd bet good money that someone will be giving you a visit in the next few hours. Janos had a brother, you know. I hope Martin Stakowski doesn't hold grudges."

CHAPTER 10

I grabbed a sandwich at the Oasis Cafe inside Robertson's Department Store and then took up residence on a step-stool in the storeroom at the back of the shoe repair shop. I left the door slightly ajar and propped up a small hand mirror on a shelf so that it gave me a view through the door while I sat in the dark. Olie Scharf was a wreck for the first hour, then fell into something resembling his comfortable daily routine. A few customers came and went, shoes got re-soled, a leather purse got mended. By two in the afternoon I was getting more than a little edgy. Finally, I heard the sound of someone taking the steps two at a time and skidding across the terrazzo floor. A very tall, thin man came into view in the mirror, almost crashing into the half-door that served as Olie Scharf's front counter. His face was flushed, and the man shook a crumpled hat at Olie. "You got my brother killed, goddamn you!"

Olie made a squeal not unlike a piglet and staggered back a step from the doorway of his shop. The best he could muster under the circumstances was to stammer, "I.. I..."

Martin Stakowski rolled his eyes up to the ceiling in unbridled rage and frustration. "Awe, shit. I gotta say the goddamn name, don't I?"

Olie elevated his end of the conversation enough to bleat out, "No! Please, no!"

Martin rummaged madly through his pockets while Olie jumped around in the close confines of his shop like a toad on a hotplate. I'm sure he wanted me to intervene, but I wanted to see this play out as far as I could let it before saving him from the grieving brother. Right about the time that it dawned on Olie to retreat my way, his visitor pulled a scrap of paper from his wallet and shouted, "Mr. Offenbach!"

A sudden calm came over Olie. His desperate hotfooting ceased, and, in the mirror, I could see his body straighten up. I couldn't see his face, but I could tell that he was looking around. Olie stepped toward his angry visitor, bracing his hands on the narrow counter. "You must be Martin. How can I help you, young man?"

Martin Stakowski stood dumbstruck, his anger lost for the moment. "My brother told me that if anything ever happened to him I should come see you."

"And I take it something's happened," Olie said calmly.

"You're goddamn right. He took a bullet in the forehead from that old shyster Theo Brown, that's what!"

"Did he, now?" Olie said, with a mildly curious but detached air. "My condolences. I wasn't expecting that."

"The old man shot him right there in his living room, like a damn rabid dog. Cops say it was self defense, so no charges. Goddamn bastards!"

"And now you're standing here, feeling angry but impotent," Olie observed.

"What the hell does that mean?"

"You want someone to pay for this, but you're not quite sure who or how."

"Yeah," Martin affirmed in a subdued voice, sounding very suspicious of where the conversation was going.

"So," Olie sighed, "you could try to exact revenge on the old man who shot your brother, but you would be the prime suspect for the police if he ever went missing or showed up dead. Or, you could lunge for *my* throat right now, but, upon full reflection, you would rightly suspect that I have friends in dark places who would take pleasure in your slow demise. The good news is that you have a third option: You could find solace for your wounded and grieving heart by accepting an additional payment of one thousand dollars, cash, from me and then continue your work. I would strongly encourage you to embrace that last option. Are we agreed?"

Martin was pacing in and out of the view my little

mirror afforded me. He was muttering and cursing. At last, he looked over at Olie Scharf and nodded. "Awe, hell," he said, mostly to himself, "I'll take the goddamn money."

"Smart lad."

Martin sulked for a bit then asked, "So now what?"

"Come back around 4 o'clock. I'll have an assignment for you by then – as well as your money."

"So, business as usual, huh?" Martin said bitterly. "You give me money, my brother gets chucked in the dirt, and things just keep going, like nothing ever happened?"

"As far as you and I are concerned, yes."

"You're a damn cold-blooded serpent is what you are."

"Wrong phylum," Olie replied, with a self-amused laugh. "Now, please try to stay out of trouble – and bars – until 4 o'clock."

Martin muttered a few more curses and headed for the stairs. Once his footsteps had receded into the distance, I heard Olie start tapping his fingers nervously on the workbench. After a few seconds, he rapped his knuckles on the bench and stood up. He flung the lower section of the split-door aside and exited the little shop without pausing to close the door behind him.

I decided I wasn't done with Olie just yet, so I waited a few heartbeats and then followed. I caught a glimpse of Olie at the top of the stairs, moving briskly through the department store. He made his way to the back of the main sales floor, under the shadow of the overhanging mezzanine, where he entered a phone booth. From about fifty feet away, I watched as he spent no more than a minute on the phone and then hung up, which was my cue to head back to the storeroom and keep quiet as hell.

Olie – or whoever this was – soon returned to the shop, but rather than getting to work on his little pile of distressed shoes, he hung up the "Closed" sign and shut the upper door. Through my hand mirror, I caught little glimpses of him moving about the confined space. To my surprise, he seemed to be doing a sort of slow calisthenics, stretching his arms, back, legs, and neck. Eventually, he settled onto the little stool and began taking slow, deep breaths, with his hands resting palms-up on his lap. He continued this for the next thirty minutes, until there came a knock on the door. Olie opened it and let in his visitor.

Mr. Silver Hair had arrived. Through the mirror, I could see that he was indeed blessed with a head full of silver-white hair. He must have started graying about the same time he started shaving, as he seemed to be not much older than me. He wore a light tan suit that seemed almost dark against his bone-white skin. The mirror did not afford me a good look at his face, but there was an intensity to him that made me almost jump off my step-stool perch. He was like a snow leopard in a bow tie, ready to pounce. Mr. Silver Hair handed an envelope to Olie. Then, they started talking. I would gladly relay the contents of their conversation, but I have absolutely no idea what they were saying. I heard them clearly enough but didn't recognize the language. In my day, I've heard people chit-chat in languages from just about every corner of every continent. I'm not claiming to know what the fine folks from Burma or the Congo are saying, but I can generally stick a pin in the continent at least. Not this time. They spoke fast, and the clipped words were made of sounds and intonations that were all new to me. I had a note pad at hand, and I wrote down a couple samples of what I heard, as best as I could, but the language and meaning were unknown to me. Neither man showed much emotion, and Mr. Silver Hair did most of the talking. He also seemed to be the one in charge and giving the orders. The two men kept things short and sweet. Within a couple minutes, they nodded to each other, and Mr. Silver Hair departed. It was beginning to look like my Mr. X and Mr. Silver Hair were either close buddies or one and the same.

Once he was alone again, this mysterious version of the man I knew as Olie Scharf set to fidgeting, with tapping fingers, a bouncing leg, and a particularly annoying ticking sound he made with his tongue. After a while, he began a new round of slow-motion calisthenics. He kept this up for the better part of a half hour, sounding ever more ill at ease. After that, he gave a sigh of frustration and sat back down on the stool. He then put his head down on the bench, cradled in his arms, and after a few minutes, the steady breathing of sleep began.

I have to admit that Olie's little nap threw me a bit. I wanted to stick around for Martin Stakowski's return at 4 PM, but I checked my watch and still had an hour to wait. I'd been cooped up in the storeroom since lunch and felt that I had been pressing my luck when it came to being discovered by Olie's alter-ego, or someone else. All things considered, now was a good time to leave. I chewed on the question for a few minutes, until I suddenly heard Olie stirring. He raised his head and gave his eyes a good rub, as if he were suffering a doozy of a hangover. Then, I heard him start to cry. He staggered to his feet and stood briefly in a daze. After steadying himself, he grabbed his handkerchief and turned toward the storeroom door.

"Mr. Hollis?" he called out weakly.

I pulled the door open and stood to greet him. "So, what the hell was all that?"

"I was really hoping you could tell me."

"That's one hell of an alter ego you've got. Do you remember anything from the last two hours?"

He shook his head wearily. "No, nothing. What happened?"

I gave him the general run-down on events and mentioned the anticipated return of Martin Stakowski, which didn't sit well with him. He wanted to call it a day and get the hell out of there, but I assured him that Martin was in no mood to play nice if Olie made the grieving Stakowski brother hunt him down. I finally calmed him down enough to put his backside on his little stool and at least pretend to work. I took up my perch in the storeroom and settled in for another wait.

The afternoon was turning into yet another eye opener for me, courtesy of my new job. In my day, I had witnessed carnival hypnotists make people bark like dogs and cluck like goddamn chickens, but Olie's alter ego, Mr. Offenbach, was a whole new level of mystery for me. The Offenbach version of Olie Scharf sounded confident to the point of arrogance, and he somehow stood taller. The voice was very different, but still recognizable as Olie's. Even more of a head scratcher was the fact that Offenbach clearly knew things that Olie did not. It was as if there were two file cabinets inside Olie Scharf's big, fleshy head; one for Olie and one for Offenbach.

Martin Stakowski showed up at four o'clock on the dot. He thumped the narrow counter impatiently and called out the name – Offenbach. Like a switch had being thrown, subtle things about Olie changed in an instant. He sat up straight and pulled his shoulders back; he tugged crisply at his shirtsleeves and tilted his head in a wry manner to greet his visitor. Martin pulled his hand away from the counter and withdrew a half-step.

"It's four o'clock. Where's my money?" Martin demanded.

Olie stood and held up a large envelope for Martin to see. "This is a hardship payment, for your unfortunate loss," he said, without much heart behind his words. "This does not need to be the end of our relationship, however. If you continue to do work for me, I will continue to compensate you, handsomely."

"Yeah, I got that," Martin nodded, his face still a mask of subdued rage.

Olie handed over the envelope. "I have a very simple task for you, but it will require some overtime. I want you to discreetly follow someone and report to me on where he goes, who he interacts with, and if anyone seems to be following him or taking undue interest in him."

"Great," Martin grumbled. "Who's the mark?"

"Me."

"You gotta be kidding me."

"Not in the slightest," an amused Olie/Offenbach said. "I am a complicated man, as you've no doubt discovered, and among my complexities is a dedication to keeping a low profile. I've done exactly that rather successfully for some time, but, of late, I worry that my anonymity may soon be compromised."

"Whatever, buddy. You're the boss."

"That's the spirit."

"So, when do I start tailing you?"

"Right now, as a matter of fact."

This presented a problem for me. I was stuck in a shoe-box of a storage room with two men just a few feet away who were on the lookout for someone acting suspicious – like me. If things hadn't been so serious, I would have laughed out loud. Offenbach shooed Martin upstairs to the main floor of the department store, asking him to mill about discreetly until he saw

Olie make his exit. After that, Offenbach closed the half-door, did some more of his stretches, and then laid his head down on the work bench. As before, the steady breathing of sleep soon began. A few minutes later, two women exited the beauty salon chatting loudly, and an operatic laugh stirred Olie into wakefulness.

The head snapped up, and Olie's whole body suddenly shivered. His shoulders assumed their regular slouch, and the whimpering started again.

"You're a popular fellow, Mr. Scharf," I said, forcefully enough to shake him out of his fear-drenched dazed state.

He spun around and stared at me with wide eyes as I shoved aside the storeroom door. "What happened?"

"Your other half put a tail on you – or himself – but mostly you."

"A tail? Why me?"

"Like I said, it seems you're popular." I pushed my way past Olie and opened the small box on the workbench containing note cards. I ruffled through them as I spoke. "Part of it is that the *other* Mr. O has a very reasonable suspicion that someone like me is snooping around, and part of it is something else – I'm not quite sure what, though." I pulled out a blank card from the cabinet and turned to face Olie. "That greasy-headed fellow, Martin Stakowski, is upstairs, waiting to follow you when you bug out of here for the day."

"What should I do?"

I scrawled my name and work phone number on

the card, along with my shoe size – 9 ½. "Make him earn his pay. Go do whatever it is you would normally do today – and don't act too much like a cat thrown onto a hot bed of coals. If you see him tailing you, which is likely, or start to feel panicky, just remember he thinks that you're his employer." I handed him the card. "File this away under 'H', for 'Hollis', and call me if anything unusual happens."

"Unusual? Like what?"

"Oh, you'll know it when you see it."

CHAPTER 11

I watched Olie Scharf plod up the steps to the main level of Robertson's Department Store like a man heading for the gallows and gave him and Martin Stakowski a good minute to clear out of the store before making my own way up. It had been one hell of a day and I was feeling a little shaky about a few things, including the state of my own sanity and what, exactly, to do next. It was time I had a chat with the honorable Judge Arthur Lockwood before making any more moves. With that in mind, my next stop was the very same phone booth that Olie Scharf – or whoever the hell that was – had visited earlier in the day.

Abner Dodds took my call. "Judge Lockwood is anxious to talk with you but something important has come up. He will contact you as soon as possible," Dodds assured me.

"Jesus! Something important came up?" I shouted into the phone. "You tell him that my day started with a policeman at my door. That was followed up by a trip to police headquarters and awkward questions about a dead body, and then I had a hum-dinger of a confrontation with one of your co-conspirators. Oh, and then things got *really* interesting!"

After a pause and some sputtering on the other end, I calmed myself down enough to give Dodds a more complete run-down of my day.

Once he'd taken my report, Abner Dodds said, flatly, "I'll let Judge Lockwood know. I assure you he has very important business to attend to."

"Yeah?"

"That's the best I can offer you right now, Mr. Hollis."

"That's just great. In the meantime I just cool my heels?"

"I would urge you to use your best judgment."

"I'll do that," I shouted into the phone.

I slammed the phone down and kicked the door of the phone booth open. As I stepped out, I was greeted by curious stares from the innocent shoppers passing by. I pulled my hat down low and made for the exit. Once outside, I took a few deep breaths and stood for a moment, waiting for inspiration to strike. It didn't. I shrugged and eventually found my feet beating a path out to West Humboldt Street and my tenement apartment.

I made it back to my place just as the last of the fading daylight drained out of the sky. I had picked up an egg sandwich on the way home and made a slow meal of it at what passed for my kitchen table. With that task done, I shut off the light and turned to head for my postage stamp of a bedroom but only made it as far as the wing-back chair in the darkened living room. I collapsed into it and stared absently into the deep shadows.

Somewhere between midnight and dawn, I woke up in that hand-me-down chair. My back hurt a little, and I resolved to summon the strength to stand up and stagger to my bed, an almost insurmountable distance of about fifteen feet. The first few tries were a failure, but just as success seemed at hand, I heard something. It was a very faint, metallic squeaking noise. The noise repeated itself a couple seconds later – barely there, but I heard it. The blood that had been pooling in my legs for half the night suddenly surged up to my foggy head. I was awake now.

The noise continued as I sat listening, rising slightly in volume over the next minute or so. I swung my head around and more or less zeroed in on a direction of the noise – toward the back of the building. I rose slowly from my chair and walked as quietly as I could across the room and into the kitchenette, to the back window. I braced my hands on the window frame and gazed out but saw nothing outside in the alleyway, which was almost pitch black. Right about then, the dull squeak stopped and was replaced by the barest hint of creaking wood above my head. That noise repeated a few times, and I followed its path as best I could, pacing a few feet back into my living room.

Then, a brief silence fell upon the darkness of my apartment. I stared up at the plaster ceiling above my head and cupped my ears, straining for any sound, and was rewarded by a faint scraping and ripping sound directly above me. That stopped and there was a forceful thump, and then another. After all of that, the creaking of wood resumed, and the noise retreated to the back of the building once again. I retraced my steps and took up a vigil at the window.

When the faint metallic squeaking resumed, I tried to get an angle on the fire escape ladder that I knew went down the side of the building, to the left of my kitchen window. I couldn't quite see it, but I did for a brief instant catch sight of movement – a black form descending through the darkness. Someone sure as hell was out there, climbing down that ladder.

I jammed my palms against the top of the window sash and pushed it up, then shoved my head out as far as I could. There, about ten feet below me, were two shining eyes staring up at me. An instant later, the eyes were gone, and I heard the loud clang of feet on the metal ladder. I swung one leg out onto the small iron balcony and then wedged the rest of my body through the open window, groping in the darkness for the ladder. Once I had two hands gripping firmly to the nearest rung, I sucked in a breath to steady my nerves and threw myself into the descent. I could feel the ladder shake and shudder with the movements of the fellow below me; then there was one large jolt and a moment later I heard the smack of shoes hitting the bricks below. I looked briefly down and saw a figure glance up again and dart west, down the alley. For a few more heartbeats, I worked my way frantically down the rungs, then launched into the air, knees bent. Another heartbeat later my shoes hit the bricks. I folded up into a deep crouch, absorbing most of the blow, but it still hurt like hell. I planted one hand on the pavers like a sprinter in the starting blocks and raced west, after my prowler. He was maybe five seconds ahead of me but still visible, running down the alley, and he was small, very small. I'm talking kid small. A second later he took a hard right turn between two tenement buildings, heading north, toward Humboldt Street. I pounded my feet down the alley as fast as I could and gained on him, then made the turn. I dodged a couple trash cans and squeezed down the narrow footpath, putting my hands on the walls for guidance in the almost pitch-blackness.

Suddenly, the world fell away below me, and I tumbled down three steps as the path between the buildings went under an overhang. I rolled with the fall as best as I could and climbed back onto my feet. I was in a tunnel of sorts, and there was light ahead of me, coming from Humboldt Street. I could see my that my quarry was just a few steps ahead of me, and I knew that I would overtake him soon enough in a sprint. But then the kid did something I didn't expect: he grabbed a wrought-iron gate and swung it shut just inches from my face. Before I could react, he had pulled some kind of tool from his back pocket and jammed it under the latch on his side of the gate. I gave an almighty yank on my side, but physics was dead-set against me and the gate didn't budge.

There we were for a few seconds, just staring at each other. The boy's face was deep in shadows, but I could make out enough to tell that he had dark skin and straight, dark hair. He also had twinkling eyes, and the longer I stared into them, the more I felt detached from the moment; a strange sort of peace came over me. Then, the boy spoke. "I suppose we were bound to meet sometime," he said in a hoarse whisper. "You're a brave man, Mr. Hollis, but you are surrounded by enemies. I'll try to help when I can, but my resources are limited, for the time being. I just hope we can keep you alive long enough to stem the tide of what's coming."

That voice. The kid's voice was all wrong. Sure, it was high pitched, but everything else was wise-old-man. "What the hell are you?" I hissed, shaking the gate.

"A friend. I've taken steps tonight to help keep you safe in your own apartment. It's not perfect, and it won't help you much past the hallway in your building, but it should allow you to avoid being killed in your sleep." The boy smiled to himself. "Now, I've got to go. Good luck, Mr. Hollis!" And with that, he turned and sprinted away.

"You're not a goddamn kid, are you?" I yelled after him. I shook the gate a few more times and cursed.

Killed in my sleep? What the hell kind of kid says that to someone?

I could have doubled back and found my way to Humboldt Street to continue chasing the kid, but I suddenly had trouble seeing the point. He was either on my side or he was out to do me harm. That was becoming the norm in my life. If he was my friend, then there was no problem, and if he was trouble, well, chasing down trouble seemed like a big waste of energy. So, all things considered, I just went back to bed.

CHAPTER 12

It was not long after first light the next morning when I found myself once again standing on the fire escape, gazing south at the alleyway and the backside of more tenements. The view was heavy on laundry lines and pigeons. I was surprised at how high up the little balcony was – or maybe it was just my strong aversion to heights. My building has a basement that's half out of the ground and then on top of that there are three full stories stacked above, making for a forty foot drop that got my blood pumping. I won't lie, it took the better part of a minute for me to work up the nerve to swing my body out onto the ladder and start the climb up to the roof. Ten feet of anxious climbing was rewarded with a view of my tenement's roof. It sloped gently back from the street and was covered in coal tar pitch and bird droppings. Three large and very distressed tin chimney stacks jutted out of the roof, each serving a boiler residing in the bowels of the building. It was also clear that people came up here from time to time. Some son-of-a-bitch had even dragged up a folding wooden beach chair, along with a small side table. People value their sun and their privacy, I guess.

I swung my leg over the top of the wall and tried to orient myself. I was directly above my kitchenette. A few paces north brought me to what I reasonably guessed was a spot above the center of my living room. I knelt down and gave the roof a close examination. If I hadn't been on the lookout for it, I would have completely missed the cut in the black pitch roof – more of a flap, in fact. I took out my pocket knife and gently lifted one edge. The pitch had some kind of backing beneath it. Both had been cut, and I could see the wood boards below. There, held in place with two bent nails, was... something. It was about the size and shape of a hamburger – if I had to describe it – but it was dull metallic gray and smooth. I touched it and it felt like stone. After a couple of minutes staring at the thing and pondering my options, I ended up simply giving a shrug, folding the flap of pitch roof back into place, and easing my way slowly back down the fire escape. Some people had a lucky rabbit's foot in their pocket; I had a dull gray rock nailed to my roof. I couldn't see the harm, other than maybe a leaky roof.

I made my way over to Jeanette's Diner for an early breakfast and cooled my heels there until just after 8 AM. Then, it was time to call Judge Lockwood's office. Abner Dodds took the call and said that the good judge wanted me to meet with him at 1 PM that day, but would not be available before then. I offered up some colorful language and let Dodds know that the deal wasn't to my liking, but he stuck to his guns on the subject and insisted that one o'clock would have to do.

I had a whole morning to wait, and I wasn't in a waiting mood. I paced up the street with nowhere in particular to go, when I found my thoughts drifting back to Olie Scharf. That potted plant of a man had a low-rent thug tailing him. The more I thought about it, the more I didn't like the odds of something stupid and violent happening. I was getting desperate to talk to Arthur Lockwood, but I also felt strangely responsible for the innocent side of Olie. By the time I had walked a hundred paces down the block, I knew I needed to check in on the shoe repairman.

Olie Scharf's shop didn't open until ten, and I knew that there was a good chance Martin Stakowski was already staked out near his apartment. I jogged back down the block to where I had parked the Ford coupe. I fished in one pocket for the keys and the other pocket for a scrap of paper that had Scharf's home address scribbled on it. Ten minutes later, I eased the coupe into a parking spot a block away from Scharf's address. I pulled my hat down low and walked up the block – not too fast, not too slow – keeping my eyes pointed straight ahead. Olie Scharf's apartment was in the last building on the block. Sure enough, there was Martin, scuffing his shoes on the pavement while he leaned up against a street light. I walked right past and turned at the corner, making for the alleyway. Scharf's building is a step up from mine, but nothing showy. From the alley, I noticed that each apartment had a small back porch with a set of wooden steps going up to a back door. Lucky for me, a number was nailed next to each. I checked them off – 2 – 3 – 4 – but Scharf was in apartment number 1. I took a few steps forward and looked down. Sure enough, at the bottom of some crumbling brick steps was a basement apartment, with a rusty and cockeyed #1 nailed to the doorframe. "Jesus!" I whispered. "The poor bastard spends every minute of his life in goddamn basements."

I started wondering why Martin Stakowski had looked so calm while staking out the front of the building when the place also had back exits, so I made a closer examination of the sunken entry. Sure enough, there was a long, heavy piece of lumber shoved under the outside doorknob. It was an amateur move, and not exactly subtle, but it meant that Olie would be obligated to head out the front of the building. It was also liable to send Olie into a certified panic.

I used the alley to circle back around to my car and settled in for what turned out to be a short wait. I could just make out Martin about three hundred feet up the street. When he moved, I would move. At just about 9:30, he did, but that's not what tipped me off. It was the sight of Olie sprinting down the front steps and making for the sidewalk at a flat-out run that really caught my eye.

But Olie Scharf wasn't built for speed, and he

began huffing and grabbing his hips after half a block. Martin Stakowski resisted the urge to run after him and set off at a stroll, staying about a half block behind his quarry. Martin's head was on a swivel, clearly on a lookout for God knows what – me, really, but he didn't know that. I jumped out of the Ford coupe and joined in the fun.

I crossed to the other side of the street and picked up the pace, so I was soon more or less even with Martin. Ahead, Olie kept glancing down at his shoes or up at the sky, which he did whenever the urge to look behind him would grow too great.

The older I get the more predictable other people get, which usually means that I keep having to lower my generally low expectations. I watched as the two men in front of me blazed a trail down the sidewalk, complete with flop-sweat and curious stares from passers by. They walked too fast, bumped too many shoulders, tripped over every crack in the sidewalk, and generally made a minor spectacle of themselves.

Things only got more amateur-hour when Olie arrived at an east-bound streetcar stop a couple blocks up, on LaSalle Street. He stood bouncing on the balls of his feet as he waited, his fists clenching and unclenching like he was about to sprint into a boxing ring. Martin took up a position about ten feet away from the small cluster of people waiting for the streetcar, rocking compulsively on his heels and fidgeting with his hat, which he proceeded to drop twice. I had no intention of joining them on the curb.

I saw no sign of the streetcar so I retreated a block west and hailed a cab. When the cabbie asked where to, I handed him a five-spot and told him to wait for the next east-bound streetcar and then follow it. When he asked why, I handed him another five-spot and told him I was a streetcar inspector. The cabbie offered up a bone-dry laugh.

After a few minutes of awkward silence in the cab, the streetcar rattled past and shuddered to a stop in front of the little sidewalk assemblage that Olie and Martin had joined. Olie got on first and made for the back of the streetcar, which put Martin in the awkward position of sitting up front and glancing nervously over his shoulder. Just as the streetcar driver unlocked his brake and the little wooden orange and black train car lurched forward on its rails, I could see Olie suddenly jump up from his seat and then sit back down again almost as fast. He was clearly having second thoughts about the situation. I ran some odds in my head and decided that I would need to get that idiot away from Martin as fast as possible.

The streetcar clattered east, past the long rows of tenement buildings that made up much of the Royal Gardens neighborhood. Next came the University Heights neighborhood and its bungalows and Sears kit homes. After maybe a half-dozen stops, I spied Olie Scharf leaping out the back door of the streetcar. Martin Stakowski darted out the front door a second later and hustled into the vestibule of a dress shop. I called to the cabbie to pull over. Olie stood flatfooted on the sidewalk and stared at the dress shop like a Bengal tiger might suddenly burst from its humble confines.

I hit the pavement a half-block west of Olie, in front of the State Theater. "Hey!" I shouted, and caught Olie's eye as he spun around at the sound of my voice. I then made for the ticket booth and handed over a quarter, then lingered in the almost-empty lobby just long enough to catch Olie's attention as he hotfooted up to the theater. I nodded to him and turned to climb the sweeping staircase that went up to the balcony seating. The concourse at the top of the stairs was open to the lobby below and people entering could look up and see four red velvet curtains covering the archways leading into the balcony seating. I slipped behind the first curtain and waited for my eyes to adjust to the darkness. Over my shoulder, a matinee screening of a western loudly entertained a handful of people sitting in the orchestra seating down below. The balcony was empty.

I pulled aside the edge of the velvet curtain just enough to get a view of the upper concourse and watched as Olie mounted the stairs. His eyes were big as half-dollars, and he was drenched in sweat. As he got close, I called out to him in a stage-whisper, instructing him to go in the second set of curtains and sit tight until I came to him. He made a gesture that was part nod and part gasp for breath, then moved on to curtain number two. I turned around and watched as his silhouette entered the balcony about twenty feet from me. He stumbled a bit in the dark but managed to park his backside in a seat without too much drama. I returned my attention to the upper concourse.

I could hear someone enter the lower seating area, then fast footsteps up the aisle. I skulked to the balcony railing and watched Martin Stakowski's dark form working his way past each row, lit by the flickering light of the silver screen. It didn't take too long for Martin to abandon his search downstairs and find his way up the sweeping staircase. I played it safe and simply stood on the right side of the curtained archway and watched for Martin's shadow to cross the thin slit of light at the bottom of the curtain.

During my college days I earned my varsity letters on the fencing team, of all things, but I also played a little football – poorly. The football coach would occasionally try to stoke the fires of my confidence by telling me that I had the reflexes of a jackrabbit, and urged me to take advantage of my speed rather than try the brute force approach to things. Prey animal comparisons aside, I took it as a compliment and saw some truth in it. If you make the first move – and do it fast – you can usually get an advantage over an opponent before his own reflexes or size advantage can kick in. So, with that in mind, I simply stuck my foot out under the curtain and down went Martin.

I grabbed him by the ankles and pulled him under the curtain and into the flickering darkness before he could even complain about the bruise on his forehead. In nearly the same instant, my knee came down on his throat, and I slapped him in the face twice, pretty hard, to knock some of the fight out of him. I noticed that his flat tweed cap had fallen out of his hand and I grabbed for it, shoving it over his eyes before his vision adjusted to the darkness. There was still a good chance that Martin didn't know what I looked like, and I preferred to keep it that way. I leaned in next to his left ear and whispered, "Tell your boss to leave Olie the hell alone. I'll be watching."

I looked over my shoulder, to the right, and spied Olie Scharf standing a short distance away, a silhouette in the dim silver light of the balcony. He was gripping two theater seats, staring at me with mouth open wide. "Beat it, Olie!" I called to him. Olie remained stone-still. "Now!" I hissed. He unstuck his hands from the chairs and bolted for the curtain, heading for the exit, I hoped.

My plan – if you could call it that – was to cut off Martin's air supply until he passed out, and then make myself scarce before the ushers caught wind of our little life-and-death wrestling match. It was all theoretical, really, having never choked a man into unconsciousness before. But I was improvising. And the thing about improvisation is that you have to accept a certain amount of risk, like, say, Martin's hand slipping free of my grip and then punching me in the kidney. Sometimes, lady luck is a harsh mistress.

The desperate blow Martin landed sent me reeling back on my heels. I doubled over in acute agony while Martin started coughing up a lung. Both of us were incapacitated for several seconds. Then he launched himself onto me, sending us both sprawling in the narrow aisle. I blocked his hands from clawing at my face only to have him grab ahold of my throat, which in retrospect seems only fair. His grip tightened, and I felt the sudden panic of losing access to life-giving air. I reached up for his neck, but he had the advantage now, with his longer arms, so I settled for punched wildly at the sides of his body. I could see the glint of primal savagery in his eyes and knew that my violent death was the only concept being entertained in his rage-soaked brain. My own brain was losing steam due to the loss of oxygen. I got in a few good licks to his ribs and gut, but he was way beyond feeling any of that. And that's when yet another very strange thing happened.

A hand cut in between Martin's extended arms and groped for his face. He yelled in frustration, but the sound was strangely muffled. In the dimly flickering silver light, I noticed that the mysterious hand held a rag of some sort and then watched in amazement as Martin's head was jerked violently back, followed by the rest of his body. My airway was suddenly freed up to resume its appointed task of breathing. It was then my turn to cough up a lung. Once I got that out of the way, I saw her silhouette.

The feminine curves were unmistakable, but the overall effect was pure strength and power. The dark figure I saw pinning Martin Stakowski to the carpeted floor with her knees and a forearm was the exact opposite of a damsel in distress. She was fast, and her movements were so – how to put it – artful and efficient, as if everything she did was choreographed down to the most minute detail yet completely natural to her. I saw Martin struggle fitfully then lay silent under her weight.

"He should be out for about ten minutes," she called to me, barely above a whisper. "Time to leave." With that she sprang up, grabbed a small leather satchel, and headed out the velvet curtain, all in one fluid motion. I was fresh out of ideas at that moment, so I followed her, but in contrast to her exit, I stood slowly and with some trouble, then staggered through the curtain.

It was only when we were out on the sidewalk that I finally got a good look at the woman who had saved my bacon. She glanced back at me quickly and nodded her head in a way that beckoned me to follow her up the street. I stood stock-still and stared at her dumbstruck until she nodded a bit more urgently.

"Sure, sure. Okay," I finally said with a rasping voice.

I got my feet moving under me and fell in line behind her. She turned right at the end of the block, and there, just around the corner and out of sight, was my favorite automobile in New Eden: Charles Victor's silver Stutz DV-32 sedan. Mohinder was standing at the rear passenger door, beckoning us to climb in. I smiled a big, dumb smile and made myself at home.

There, in the safe confines of the Stutz, I turned my

attention once again to my very new acquaintance. My mind was working overtime trying to figure her out. The woman sitting across from me in the car was about five-and-a-half feet tall and of a generally fit build. She had been wearing a woolen baseball cap until we entered the car, which she then pulled off to reveal a thick tussle of light brown hair that fell below the shoulders. The woman might have been anywhere between twenty-five and forty. She seemed both a kid and an old soul. She had a profound calmness to her, but her every movement and sinew made me think of a big cat, stalking through the primordial jungle.

"I hope you don't mind me helping out back there," the woman said as we pulled away from the curb, her voice startling me back into the moment.

I shook my head. "My goose was just about cooked up there, so I guess it's fair to say that I needed the help. So, thanks for that."

"It's my job," she offered.

That little turn of phrase grabbed my full attention. "Oh? And what job is that?"

"Same job as you, actually, but I spend most of my time in New York and Washington. Charles Victor asked me to come out here and keep a discrete eye on you while you were getting up to speed in your new position."

"New York and Washington, eh? I guess that makes sense. How long have you been working for them?"

"My team has been on the ground for about eight months."

I stared at her with wide eyes. "Team?"

"Well, yes. There are six of us, actually. We each bring our own unique set of talents to the job. There are many more people, really, if you count our informants and others who are sympathetic to our mission."

"I take it they didn't hire you to do paperwork."

She laughed warmly at that. "You'd be surprised how much paperwork this job can generate."

"Well, that's just great," I said in mock frustration. "I should've known that saving the world would involve a pile of damn paperwork."

"I'm Eleanor Stockton, by the way," she said, extending a hand.

CHAPTER 13

Any day that includes a ride in Charles Victor's Stutz sedan is a good day. I made small talk and generally enjoyed the ride as we headed back downtown. I was just about to start quizzing Eleanor Stockton a bit more on her work in New York when the Stutz crossed the Assinowa River and made an immediate right turn upon making it to the east bank. That didn't sit quite right with me, and I let my confusion show.

"We're heading to a meeting with Arthur Lockwood, but not at his downtown office," Eleanor said. "Circumstances on the ground have gotten a bit... well... we thought a change of venue was called for," she informed me cryptically.

My chatty mood dried up as we drove south on Assinowa Avenue, hugging the banks of the river. We drove past the Docklands barge terminal and then continued south, skirting around the imposing edifice of Union Station. Eventually, we drove past the massive brick-clad factory buildings of Red Arrow Motors, and then, just as the sprawling complex of the Victor Rail Works plant came into sight, we took another right, onto a small and very disused cobblestone access road. I had no idea where that little road went, other than west, toward the river. We snaked our way in between two looming red-brick warehouse buildings and back into the light of day, where the road abruptly ended. In front of us was what looked to be an old, seemingly abandoned factory building. For a few brief seconds, I couldn't quite figure where we were. To our left and right were tall gates made of simple chain link fencing, and behind them we could see the busy goings-on associated with the making of cars and trains.

My attention was soon drawn back to the derelict building in front of us. A gray-haired black man in overalls was slowly pushing open a large, rolling warehouse door near the north end of the building. Once that task was complete, he strolled slowly toward us across a cobblestone parking lot, and gestured for Mohinder to drive forward. As the man guided Mohinder slightly to the left and right, it suddenly dawned on me what I was looking at, and I stood up as high as I could in the back seat of the Stutz. Sure enough, I finally saw that there was a twenty-foot-wide man-made mill race running right in front of us and crossing it was a very rusted iron bridge, which was dangerously narrow and without guardrails. Under the old man's guidance, Mohinder cautiously lined up the wheels of the automobile with the metal-grate tracks that made up the driving surface and eased the Stutz across the mill race, which was currently filled with churning and roiling waters fed by spring rains upstream. I've got to admit, the kid in me got a kick out of it, not that I let it show. I think Mohinder allowed a smile to slip onto his stony face for almost a complete second.

The old building in front of us sat on a small island straddling the east bank of the Assinowa River. In all my years of living in New Eden, I had never actually been here, though I could generally place it on the map. If memory served me right, there were three man-made islands in a row, running along the mill race, but I had only ever been to the northern-most one – Shocknessey Island. I didn't even know if this little island had a name.

As our wheels touched the cobblestones, I could make out four figures standing in the shadows just inside the entrance to the building. One of them was clearly Arthur Lockwood. The old man in overalls was walking beside the car, slowly waving us into the building. Once we had fully entered the darkened confines, Mohinder brought the Stutz to a stop, and we heard the massive door being rolled slowly shut behind us. I climbed out of the Stutz and peered into the dusty haze that surrounded us. The cavernous space was completely empty, if you didn't count the pigeon droppings. The ceiling loomed some thirty feet above our heads. I could make out skylights, but they were covered over with scrap wood. Around the top of the walls was a continuous band of windows, now a patchwork of broken glass panes streaked with years of grime and soot.

"Welcome to what remains of the Victor Ordnance Works." Lockwood gestured grandly around him, his baritone voice echoing as he greeted us. Standing next to Arthur Lockwood was his assistant, Abner Dodds. Also present was none other than Charles Victor himself. Standing a bit apart from the others was a middle-aged woman that I didn't recognize. She was well dressed and paced deliberately about the space, eyeing every nook and cranny with keen interest.

Eleanor Stockton led the way as we greeted our hosts. Charles Victor seemed particularly pleased to see her. "Eleanor! Thanks for bringing our Henry back to us, safe and sound!"

I shook my head in mock disdain.

Charles frowned at me. "No offense intended, Henry. Eleanor is a bit of a legend in our little circle. Her exploits would make for a great story in one of your novels."

"No offense taken, Charlie," I assured him. "Eleanor can save my bumbling backside from certain death any time."

Arthur Lockwood interrupted our banter with a raised hand. "Henry, I want to assure you that Miss

Stockton's presence in New Eden is entirely due to the gravity of the current situation here and not a comment on your ability to do your job."

"I'll take all the help I can get, boss," I said, suddenly feeling the truth of my own words. Then I offered, "Hope you don't mind me being blunt, but, what the hell's going on?"

"Quite a bit, unfortunately. My colleagues are reporting an uptick in activity around the world. But what is most concerning and relevant to us is that the name New Eden has started coming up with sudden regularity, from the steppes of Mongolia to the streets of Paris. We've seen this kind of pattern before, in other places, and it's never good."

"Things are getting a little interesting around this town. I can vouch for that."

Arthur Lockwood nodded. "Yes, I've heard. Which is why we're here, in point of fact." Lockwood frowned for an instant. "But where are my manners?" He gestured to the old man. "This is Clarence Boyette. He works for Victor Industries and is the caretaker of this property, among others." Lockwood pointed in the direction of the woman poking about in the shadows. "This is my colleague, Mrs. Irene Wagner – my boss, in fact. She's come out here from the Wildflower Society office in New York to consult with me on certain matters."

Wagner looked my way, and I waved to her. "Pleasure to meet you, Mrs. Wagner. Glad to finally meet someone in charge."

Irene Wagner laughed at that. "Judge Lockwood has broad discretion with his work here, in New Eden. He is an old friend and I trust him to do a good job here, while I focus my efforts in New York. We're all colleagues, really, pursuing the same goals to the best of our abilities."

"You sure have a lot of colleagues in this little club of yours," I said, turning back to Judge Lockwood. "I met another one your *colleagues*, by the way. A fellow by the name of Theo Brown. He's quite a piece of work."

Lockwood laughed at that. "Yes, he is indeed. I've only met the man in person once, actually. I value Theo Brown's support for our cause, but I equally value the fact that he is aware of his own limitations. It just so happens that I'm in New Eden at his request. For that, the gentleman has my gratitude and respect."

"So, why are we standing around in an abandoned factory?" I asked, gazing at our dust-covered surroundings.

Arthur Lockwood nodded to himself before answering. "Yes, well, it's not quite as abandoned as you might think. I have something to show you." Lockwood began walking across the dim open space and motioned for us to follow. He continued talking as we headed for the distant southern wall of the building, some three hundred feet away. "As I mentioned, this old factory is owned by Victor Industries." Lockwood turned to Clarence Boyette. "Mr. Boyette, could you give Henry a bit of the history of this island?"

Clarence nodded and cleared his throat. "This here island was man-made. It was reclaimed from the river in the late 1870s as part of a big civic building project that built what folks now call the East Mill Race on the Assinowa River," he explained. That project, Clarence told us, built the island on which we stood, and the two other man-made islands up and down-stream from it. To the south – and upstream – lay City Island, which is where the remains of the city's first power plant can be found. It stopped operations in 1924. To the north lay Shocknessey Island, which is home to the state sanitarium. The middle island, he informed us, is ten acres, made of fill dirt and random debris that was dumped into a ring of thirty foot-deep pylons going down into the river bedrock. Nobody had ever gotten around to giving this island a name, so far as Clarence know. The Sanborn Fire Insurance maps from back when this place was built just call it Caisson Number Two.

"After the war, Mr. Victor – senior, that is – got a bad taste in his mouth about making guns for killing, so he shut the whole thing down." Clarence gave a wry smile. "It's kind'a funny, then, that the place got rented out by the U.S. Army and used as the city armory until round about 1930. That's when the Army reactivated Camp Savvage – you know, the old Civil War camp – out west of town. Last four years, this place has been left to the pigeons."

I nodded in appreciation to his tale. "That's a great history lesson, Mr. Boyette." I looked over at Lockwood. "Judge, I don't mean to be rude, but why am I here?"

Lockwood gave a wry smile. "I've added another responsibility to your job description."

"Oh, yeah? What?"

"Babysitter," he said with a twinkle in his eye.

We were standing near a door. Clarence stepped forward and unlocked it, pulling the door open for us. We entered a dim hallway, off of which I could make out several derelict and empty offices, with interior walls that had at one time evidently been partly comprised of large glass windows facing the hallway. At the far end of the hall was a boarded up doorway, which looked to be the rear exit of the building. But just before that exit, we came to another, rather unassuming-looking door. Once again, Clarence stepped forward and unlocked it, then handed Lockwood a flashlight. The judge pulled the door open and cast the beam of the flashlight around, revealing a rough-hewn and very narrow set of stone steps leading down into the darkness. Lockwood briefly steadied himself then began to descend the uneven stairway. We all followed cautiously. Some twenty steps down, the stairway came to a landing, then turned and continued further down.

I have been in the catacombs below Paris, where I got the chance to visit the bones of six million departed souls. I was once given an unauthorized tour of some ancient Egyptian Pharaoh's burial chamber along the banks of the Nile. I've been to more than a few places that people would say have "atmosphere."

Nothing – and I mean nothing – has set the hair on my neck standing on end like that particular descent into the earth under that island. "What the hell's that smell?" I asked as we continued down.

Clarence Boyette laughed from behind me. "That's quite a stink, ain't it? About four years ago, Mr. Charles Victor – the senior one – had me bring a civil engineer fellow down here to see what kind of shape this island was in. I put the same question to him. He said that when they filled in the caisson back in the day, they must'a used whatever they could get their hands on – the cheaper the better. He said the local dump was his bet, as that would account for the smell of rot that just won't quit. There's more to it than kitchen scraps though, if you ask me. It's like a wind blowing straight from the Devil's own outhouse."

I nodded at Clarence's observation and gingerly took the next ragged stair-step.

At the bottom of the third flight of stairs, we found ourselves in a low-vaulted brick chamber, standing on what looked to be a natural, uncut limestone slab. Bedrock. We cast our flashlight beams about and found that there were small pools of water covering part of the slab and a number of odd-looking instruments sitting off to one side. There were no other doors that I could make out. Lockwood and Victor walked over to a shipping crate that sat in the center of the chamber on a pair of wooden sawhorses. Irene Wagner took my arm and guided me over to join the others.

Judge Lockwood looked up at me with a gleam in his eye. "As I've said before, Henry, our little club is beset by many enemies, but we also have a number of friends and allies, as well. This," he said, patting the crate, "is a gift from one of our more enigmatic allies to – well – you."

"What?"

"It's true," Lockwood explained. "I was contacted two days ago by a friendly source of information that we have been calling the Sphinx. His message asked for me to meet with a go-between at a remote location. When we arrived, we were presented with this crate and a letter, instructing us to give the crate over to you."

"Specifically me, huh?"

Lockwood nodded.

"So, what's in it?" I asked, running my hand along the lid of the crate.

"Well," Lockwood said, drawing the word out hesitantly, "we are a bit fuzzy on that detail, other than we were told it would be of some assistance to you. The letter also said that it is not quite ready yet for use."

"Not ready? As in missing a few parts? As in some assembly required?"

"Well," Arthur Lockwood said, once again stretching the word out, "the note seems to indicate it would be more along the lines of water daily until blooms appear." With that, he and Irene grabbed the wooden lid and lifted it off. Clarence Boyette trained his flashlight on the crate's contents, which I can only describe as a greenish, dull-surfaced coffin with a small hole at the mid-point of its top. There was a tin funnel sitting upside-down next to the hole.

Unable to restrain myself, I ran my hand along the surface. It was very hard and cool and slightly textured. "This thing's made out of glass," I marveled, barely above a whisper. "What that hell is it?"

"We honestly don't know," Lockwood admitted. "The letter simply said to keep it in a dark, cool, and quiet place and add one gallon of distilled water to it every twelve hours. The process – whatever that may be – should take about one week."

"And my job is to come over here and climb down into this hole every twelve hours just to pour water into a funnel?"

"In a nutshell, yes. But you'll be here, anyway."

"Oh?"

"You'll be working out of this building from now on, actually," Lockwood explained. "It's become clear that you need greater security and privacy in your work. You will also need more help. Mr. Boyette will be on-site to supervise the renovations. Once those are complete, he will then stay on to maintain the facility and give technical assistance as needed."

Charles Victor chimed in. "Clarence can fix pretty much anything that you can roll or drag in the door, and he's a certified genius at turning junkyard scraps into just about anything you need."

I smiled at Clarence Boyette and extended a hand. "Looks like you and I are going to have the same crazy boss. I hope this isn't too much of a step down for you."

"Huh," Clarence grunted. "I like the change just fine. My hands don't get greasy enough for my liking these days. Besides, Mr. Victor promised to pay me extra just to keep you out of trouble."

CHAPTER 14

I finally got a chance to give Arthur Lockwood and his Wildflower gang an update on things over sandwiches from Finnian's Feast Cafe – my choice for lunch, but Judge Lockwood insisted we have the food brought up to his penthouse suite at the Essex Hotel.

Once we were all seated comfortably at a table on his balcony overlooking downtown New Eden, the debriefing began. The big news for them was the existence of Mr. Offenbach, a.k.a. Olie Scharf, and his enigmatic pale friend, Mr. Silver Hair.

Eleanor Stanton got particularly excited about Mr. Silver Hair. "I think I saw him. I didn't know enough to tail him, but, looking back, I think he drove by while your friend Martin Stakowski was staking out Olie Scharf's place."

"You were there?" I said, raising an eyebrow. "When did you start tailing me?"

"Very, very early this morning. How else do you

think I ended up at the movie theater in time to lend a hand?"

"Point taken. Can you remember what he was driving?"

"That's why he caught my eye. I nearly dropped my cover when I saw a man with silvery-white hair driving past in a racing-green convertible with the top down and the steering wheel on the right – English-style."

I smiled. "That's a start."

Lockwood turned the conversation back to an old topic. "You've covered a lot of ground since our last chat about the statue of the boy in the park. Any insights?"

"Judge, I have to admit, at first I didn't put much faith in the story you told me. But I guess you could say I'm feeling more open-minded these days." I put down my chicken salad sandwich and stared up at a flock of swallows arcing and twirling through the warm, blue sky above New Eden. "I could be wrong, but my money is on Mr. Silver Hair being your perpetrator. It's pretty obvious that he's the one who hired some muscle to scare me – and you – which didn't work out the way he'd planned. My bet is he had the same guys beat the hell out of that little statue with sledge hammers. The boys must have had a good laugh about that job."

"Why do you think your Mr. Silver Hair is threatened by the Oracle?" Lockwood asked.

I chuckled at that. "Yeah, he's feeling threatened by the Oracle, all right. But I don't know enough to make a guess as to why." I studied my lunch plate. "I'll say this, when a man like Mr. Silver Hair pays thugs to beat down a statue in a park, it tells me that he doesn't know how to get his pasty hands on the Oracle and he doesn't even really expect to, either. He's going after lower-hanging fruit – little bronze statues – oh, and you and me."

"Well, with that bit of the puzzle in place, I think we know what you need to do next," Judge Lockwood said, finishing off the last of his BLT.

"Yeah? What?"

"You need to find Mr. Silver Hair and, while you're at it, find the Oracle."

"Thanks for keeping my job easy, boss."

"You're welcome," Lockwood offered with a smile.

"While we're on the subject of mysterious characters, what can you tell me about this fellow you call the Sphinx?"

"Well..." The judge seemed ready brush me off on that topic, but fortunately Irene Wagner intervened.

"I think Henry should know, if it helps him understand things better," she said to Lockwood. Then she turned to me. "The truth of the matter is, I've never met the man. I've spoken with him on several occasions, however – in a most unusual way – but I digress. He has been in contact with the Wildflower Society for over two years. He is possibly based in the New York area, but it's hard to tell, exactly, as he has made contact with our affiliates in a number of cities throughout the world. The Sphinx, as we have come to call him, seems to represent a party or parties that are not... well... not residents of any nation or group on this Earth."

"So then, he represents what? Anarchists? The voice of God?"

"Anarchists? No. The voice of God? Well... that is another story."

"So, the Sphinx is some kind of preacher?" I said, trying to follow along.

"No, but he does seem to take his marching orders from what I can only describe as an individual or group that is beyond our current realm of comprehension, with insights and resources that stagger the mind of a mere mortal such as me," Wagner said, pointing up at the sky with her fork. "The Sphinx is somewhere out there – up there, if you will – but seemingly not of this world."

"You are all mad as hatters," I said, shaking my head. My lunch companions didn't seem to mind the insult and just shrugged at me without offering a defense. "So," I said, trying to get the conversation started again, "how does the Sphinx contact you?"

Irene Wagner leaned in a bit closer. "Our communication with the Sphinx predates the founding of the Wildflower Society, actually. The events that have conspired to bring us here today all began just about two years ago, in the spring of 1932, when a man by the name of Ambrose Halladay received a phone call at his Denver law office. The caller was a sheriff's deputy in Estes Park, Colorado. The Deputy informed him that a curious incident had recently taken place on the wooded foothills a few miles outside of town. Further, the event seemed to be linked to Mr. Halladay. The deputy went on to explain that some local residents had begun to complain several days earlier of a very loud noise emanating from deep in the woods. It was described as a siren or horn. Sheriff's deputies set out to investigate and soon traced the sound to its source: a steel box sitting on the ground in the middle of the woods. There was a single metallic switch on top of the box that someone summoned the courage to flip, thus ending the siren's blare. Also at that moment, the front panel of the box sprung open and revealed a compartment with a sealed letter inside, addressed to *Ambrose Halladay, Denver, Colorado*.

"Well, as you can imagine, Mr. Halladay was very surprised to hear about the incident and the letter. He swore complete ignorance of what he theorized was a prank, but asked that the deputy indulge him and forward the letter on to his Denver address.

"The letter soon arrived. It was hand-written, but had a precision to it that piqued Ambrose Halladay's curiosity. The contents of the letter were even more intriguing. The writer started by lauding Ambrose for his good work decades earlier on behalf of miners employed by the Copperhead Coal Corporation in Helena, Montana. The letter singled out his life-saving actions as peacemaker during the deadly standoff between miners and strike-breakers at the company's Wildflower Mine in 1912."

I whistled at the name of the coal mine. "Okay, now

I'm starting to get it. Not a coincidence in the name, I assume?"

"You assume correctly," she said with a nod. "The letter went on to state the writer's dire concerns for the state of the world and urged Ambrose Halladay to reach out to 'likeminded admirers of peace and human justice.' It even went so far as to offer a list of names of people that he should consider contacting. Now, that last bit of the letter struck Ambrose as a nod in a very particular direction: You see, after the Great War, he was appointed to the U.S. delegation attending the year-long Paris Peace Conference, which culminated in early 1920 with the founding of the League of Nations. The U.S. ultimately chose not to join, but Ambrose spent much of the next decade as legal counsel to the League on matters pertaining to labor. He resigned from his position in 1930, mostly out of frustration with the hardening of lines being drawn between nations and what he perceived as angry men sweeping aside the guiding principles of the League of Nations and their insistence on dividing the world into many competing camps and 'isms.' In the year before he left Geneva, Ambrose hosted a series of luncheons he called 'Humanity Tables.' These informal – and unofficial – events were intended to be brainstorming sessions on how to redirect the League of Nations. There was some initial enthusiasm, but events of the day and human nature eventually reduced the attendance at the luncheons to a small, dedicated core.

"Once back in Denver, Ambrose Halladay had

resumed his private practice and adopted a quieter life, but never abandoned his principles and dreams of a better world. From time to time, he had toyed with the idea of resurrecting the Humanity Table as an annual event but never seemed to find the motivation to make it happen. The mysterious letter changed everything.

"Ambrose reached out to his most trusted colleagues and began the process of making the event a reality. Paris was chosen as the location and an agenda was sketched out. He extended invitations to those who had been most enthusiastic during his time in Geneva, but he also invited some fresh faces, including those from the list provided in the letter.

"In the summer of 1932, the Humanity Table weekend was held at the Polish ambassador's residence in Paris. Ambrose had great hopes for the event. He prayed that it would be able to keep the embers of peace and human justice glowing on each of the continents.

"At the opening dinner of the assemblage, he told the audience of the letter and used it as proof that they were not alone in their cause. The event began building momentum, from that Friday night's speech on into the planning sessions of Saturday, and culminating with a boisterous and impassioned meeting on Sunday. The seeds of a plan had been planted and – in honor of Ambrose Halladay's good work – those in attendance dubbed it the 'Wildflower Plan.' The giddy optimism, however, was short-lived.

"On the following Monday morning, Ambrose and

two other attendees decided to have breakfast together at a small French brasserie near their hotel. On their way, they were intercepted by street thugs and beaten rather badly. No money or valuables were taken. As the poor men lay sprawled on the sidewalk, one of the thugs loomed over them. '*Non, non, non,*' he said, in French, of course, wagging his finger. '*Rentrer à la maison. Le monde n'a pas besoin de ton aide.*'"

I held up a hand as Irene Wagner spoke. "My French is a little bit rusty."

"My apologies, Mr. Hollis," she said with a slight smile. "It translates roughly to, 'Go home. The world doesn't need your help.'"

Mrs. Wagner returned to her story. "News of that incident quickly made the rounds of the Humanity Table attendees and it certainly got their attention. A few took the threat to heart and asked to be left out of any future communication or activities. Most, however, saw it for what it was: proof that their efforts were now needed more urgently than ever. Within weeks, a committed core took the framework of the Wildflower Plan and re-imagined it as something profoundly more proactive and engaged with the threats facing the world. Thus, the Wildflower Society was born."

"That's a heck of a story, Mrs. Wagner," I said. "Good to know how all this got started." I looked at her a bit sideways. "Say, were you a fly on the wall when all this happened?"

"Why, yes, Mr. Hollis, I was," she said. "I attended the Paris event with my husband, Bert Warner."

"Ah, I get it now." That tidbit gave me another piece of the whole crazy puzzle. The good Senator from New York was a big bear of a man and an occasional barroom brawler, but he walked every minute of his political life at the side of the doves. "But I thought he was a widower."

She nodded. "He was, for many years, but we were introduced to each other a few years back by my brother, Ambrose."

"Ambrose Halladay," I said flatly. She nodded and I stared around the table. "By god, you people move in tight circles."

"We are entering an era where trust of those around you is greatly valued – and increasingly rare," Arthur Lockwood said.

"So, I take it that Ambrose Halladay is the leader of this happy little band of well-meaning misfits?"

"He was," Wagner said in a guarded tone.

"Was?"

She nodded while casting her gaze at the floor. "There's a bit of an addendum to the story, you see."

"Yeah?" I said, waiting for the bad news.

She nodded and her face became very serious. "My brother traveled ceaselessly for the next half-year, after the events in Paris, attending to the many details involved in setting up and maintaining a clandestine organization. In January of 1933, he traveled to Moscow to meet with a contact about an emerging threat. I received a call in late January from the U.S. Embassy in Moscow, informing me that he had been found dead in a city park."

"Sorry to hear that," I offered.

"Thank you," she said, taking a short breath. "The authorities said that he had been killed in an accidental fall while taking in the vista from a bridge." A deep shadow came over Irene Wagner's face. "The embassy staff, however, reported that when they arrived to claim the body, the head was missing and the upper torso showed burn marks. The local authorities refused their request to take the remains and then the coroner's office staff took it upon themselves to bury Ambrose in a cemetery on the outskirts of the city. I have yet to locate the grave."

I raised an eyebrow at that news, and she lifted a hand to ward off my skepticism. "I know what you're thinking, Mr. Hollis, and I agree. The official story is nonsense, but there it is. I reject it, of course, but I must – we must – move on."

"I agree," I said solemnly, then gazed down at the table. "So," I said, after a few seconds, "the people we're up against are playing for keeps."

"Yes," said Mrs. Wagner. "And more blood has been spilled since."

"Good to know," I said, still staring at my lunch plate.

Eleanor Stanton must have seen where my thoughts were going. "Just so you know," she said, leaning in close over the remains of her lunch, "we may not be in the cold-blooded killer line of work as such, but I've already killed for this job – this cause. I hope you never have to do the same, but don't let anyone give you a sugarcoated sales pitch about your new position being anything other than a dirty, deadly business."

"Yeah, that's what I figured," I said. "I won't have a problem with that as long as I have a good handle on what side of right and wrong I'm standing on. If things get too blurry, I'll step away mighty quick."

"That's all we can ask, or should ask, really," Arthur Lockwood offered.

"So," I said, looking around the table. "No offense to Mrs. Wagner, but I'm feeling that one of my questions still needs answering. This Sphinx fellow – how did he contact you this last time?"

All eyes turned to Irene Wagner, who then nodded to Arthur Lockwood.

"Phone call, actually, just two days ago," he said. "It was my first communication with him, personally," Lockwood explained. "It's true about the monotone voice, by the way. Very odd. He introduced himself not by name but simply as the friend that had provided certain resources to the Wildflower Society, which he enumerated. He explained that current circumstances demanded he reach out to give what limited aid he could, specifically to you, Henry."

"I'm flattered."

"You are very important to him for some reason."

"If I find out why, I'll let you know," I said with a

dry laugh. "So, any chance we can get in touch with your Sphinx, you know, just in case?"

"Why, yes. But the invitation to communicate was for you, not anyone else."

"Yeah? So when were you going to tell me about that?"

The judge smiled. "I suppose I should tell you the whole story. As I said, I spoke with him on the phone a few days ago. He explained that he had something he wanted to give you – what you now know as the glass coffin. The fellow said that the safety of a hand-off could not be guaranteed if it happened in New Eden, so instead, he asked that the package be delivered to a private airstrip several miles outside of town. The airstrip in question happens to be owned by Victor Industries, as part of their aviation division. For added drama, our mystery friend insisted that the hand-over happen at precisely 1:15 AM. He was very insistent on the timing. He also asked that I bring a truck and one colleague, and that we wait at the main gate for him to arrive. And he suggested that I bring flashlights.

"I contacted Charles, of course, and he naturally volunteered to join me, as the hand-over would be happening at his property. He also brought the truck." Lockwood took a drink of his coffee before continuing. "Charles and I arrived just before 1 AM and waited just outside the front gates of the airfield. At precisely 1:15, the Sphinx walked out of the darkness and strolled casually up the road toward us. He was dressed in a simple white buttoned shirt and tan pants, and sported a Panama hat. He seemed very calm for a man making a clandestine delivery in the middle of the night. As he came closer, I could make out his face, which was surprisingly unremarkable – truly a random face in the crowd. I couldn't tell you much more than he was of rather fair complexion, medium build, and perhaps five feet, nine inches in height. He stopped a few feet away from us and stood silently, staring over our shoulders, into the darkened airfield. After the better part of a minute, I spoke up and thanked him for offering us assistance, but I also expressed my confusion for him arriving empty-handed. I asked him if the package was there, waiting for us. Curiously, he said it wasn't. He explained – in his slow monotone – that the package would be arriving soon, however. The man looked at me only briefly as he spoke, before returning his gaze to a point in the darkness, somewhere over our shoulders. We gazed back as well, but saw nothing.

"Once again, we entered into a brief interlude of silence. After perhaps two minutes, he spoke, with a hint of excitement in his voice. 'Now,' he said at last. 'It's arrived,' he declared in his deadpan way of speaking.

"I peered into the deep shadows around us but saw nothing, so I asked him where the package was. He pointed beyond us, into the darkness of the airfield and explained that we needed to go find it. And with that, we three walked into the darkness.

"I attempted to strike up a conversation with him as we strode through the gate, asking what we should call him. He replied that what name we use didn't matter. I explained that we had taken to calling him *the Sphinx*. He looked at me oddly for a moment, then nodded and said he was aware, but he made no effort to continue the conversation.

"'The Sphinx walked us along the southern fence and came to a stop about a hundred yards from the main gate. He then had us walk north from that point, spaced twenty paces apart. We walked the field for about ten minutes, across dark expanses of high grass and several paved runways until Charles called out in the darkness. We soon arrived at his side and followed the beam of his lamp to a spot in the grass, where we saw the same large crate that you've recently seen. It looked like it had been haphazardly dumped there.

"Charles and I were baffled at the presence of the crate and tried to gently grill our guide on why it was there, but he would only say that the answer would cause more confusion than clarity.

"Lifting large crates is a young man's game, so I left that task to Charles and the Sphinx. When they had finished, Charles and I climbed into the truck. I asked the Sphinx if he need a lift somewhere but he declined, saying it would be best if he left alone and on foot. Before departing, he handed us an envelope containing the instructions for the glass coffin.

"As Charles steered the truck slowly across the grass field toward the main gate, the Sphinx called out to us and said something that still puzzles me..."

"Yeah?" I asked the judge.

"He said that you, Henry, could contact him by

going to the mezzanine at Red's, then he disappeared into the darkness."

Judge Lockwood appeared to be done with his story, and I took few seconds to let the information percolate in my head. "The mezzanine at Red's?"

"That's what the fellow said. I assumed you would know what he meant."

"You sure that's what he said?"

The judge shrugged. "To the best of my recollection."

"Fair enough."

Then Eleanor Stanton said something strange. "Henry, there's a man watching us from a window on the building across the way."

She was sitting on the other side of the table from me, so she had a better angle on the situation. I refrained from swinging my big head around to get a better look. "Small guy?" I asked. "Greasy brown leather jacket?"

She nodded. "You know him?"

"His name's Wilmer. Last I knew he was working for a mobster named Di Parma. Wilmer must be freelancing now. Which is interesting, as it means that Mr. Silver Hair reached out to him directly."

"Is that good or bad?" Lockwood asked.

"Well, the bad news is that Wilmer is no amateur. He's a two-bit punk, but he's dangerous. The good news is that I know how to get him angry, and when guys like that get angry, they get stupid."

CHAPTER 15

By about dinner time, I was back at Olie Scharf's apartment building on the west side of town with a wad of cash in my hand. I skipped the front door, went around back, and gave a police knock, which is pretty good at motivating people to get off their ass and peek out from behind a curtain. When Olie's wide eyes peered at me from the kitchen window, I tipped my hat to him. Then I rattled his door to motivate him to get the damn thing open in a hurry. He obliged.

"Is he out there?" Olie asked pleadingly.

"Martin? Nah. He's somewhere licking his wounds and rethinking his job prospects right about now. He might not come nosing around again, but someone else will. Which is why you gotta get out of town."

"I can't leave! What about my shop?"

"How much do you clear a day in that hole in the ground, after expenses?"

Olie stared at me like I had just asked him to sing opera. Finally he said, "I don't know – maybe five dollars."

"Holy hell!" I sputtered. "You spend your whole life in that dungeon for five bucks a day? You're nine-tenths dead already." I shook my head. "It doesn't mater. The two hundred bucks in my pocket says you're skipping town today. You got a suitcase?"

He nodded. I grabbed him by the shoulder and steered him out of the kitchen. "You've got three minutes to pack."

"Where am I going?"

"Chicago. I've got a car parked a block away. I'm driving you up to the train station in Monticello."

"What? Why Monticello?"

"Because Mr. Silver Hair expects you to be on the run now. If he's half as smart as I think he is, he's got someone keeping an eye out for you at the train station here in New Eden. Hell, it might even be him, sitting with a coffee and a newspaper next to the ticket counter, waiting for your dumb mug to walk up."

"What happens when I get to Chicago?" Olie asked, shoving shirts into a dusty leather bag.

"You take a cab to the Prairie Hotel, on West Ontario Street. You check in under a fake name and wait for me to get in touch."

"How long will that be?"

"Christ!" I seethed at him. "As long as it takes! If you want to keep being turned into Mr. Silver Hair's personal puppet, then be my guest, stay here. If you want to get that thing you call your life back, then take the money and do what I say. If you've got a brain in your head, you'll nod right now and let me do my damn job."

On the forty-five-minute drive up to Monticello I put aside the tough-guy act and tried to give Olie a pep talk. Without giving away too much, I let him know that I was working with others who had his best interests at heart – more or less. I gave him the cash and a few restaurant suggestions, but told him to hold off on making new friends while he cooled his heels in Chicago. Olie sat silent and slack-jawed most of the way up. When we got to the station, I paid for the one-way ticket and a newspaper and then kept him company until the train arrived.

"This doesn't feel quite right, Mr. Hollis," he said as I walked him to the platform.

"It's the best I can offer under the circumstances," I replied. He didn't seem to take much comfort in that.

I watched him slouch his way through the train car and eventually take his seat. A minute later, the train jerked forward and began to roll north, to Chicago. I tipped my hat and gave a good long stare at the back of the train as it pulled away. I suddenly realized that Olie Scharf wasn't the only one who didn't feel quite right about the whole thing. Somehow, some way, this was going to get very messy.

CHAPTER 16

I arrived at the Redbud Grill just in time for happy hour. It's what passes for a high-class gin joint in New Eden. Cops in the NEPD usually refer to the Redbud as the Fifth Precinct – a tongue-in-cheek reference to the fact that there are four police precincts in town and that the Redbud Grill is the after-hours watering hole of choice for men in blue. It's also popular with newspaper men, criminal defense attorneys, and local politicians. A man by the name of Roy Gittings is fond of the place, too. He's a former police detective with the New Eden Police Department who also earned an honest-to-god PhD along the way, studying nights and weekends. The local cops call him Doc Giddings, or just Professor. Turned out he was a bit too rough around the edges for a quiet job in the halls of academia, so he stuck with the NEPD – that is, until he became a bit too rough around the edges for them, too. His drinking had always been a problem, but he was sent packing by the department when he added cocaine to his addiction menu.

We had both found ourselves adrift on the streets of New Eden at about the same time, in fact. Our paths crossed from time to time as we each tried to find our own way out of the dark places we had fallen into. Eventually, I turned to writing and he turned to private detective work. The man was born for the job. He can track down just about anyone or anything, like a bloodhound with access to a telephone and car keys. Gittings is still more or less a wreck, but he holds it together enough to keep his clients satisfied.

I found Roy Gittings perched on his usual stool at one corner of the massive rectangular bar that dominated the center of the Rosebud Grill. He was nursing a scotch and holding court with three men in rumpled suits. My best guess was that they were criminal defense attorneys. I got a beer and grabbed a ring-side seat, waiting for an opening in the conversation.

Gittings was in top form. "No, no! You guys got it all backwards. Your job isn't to defend your client. Your job is to make the prosecutor defend the *system*!" There were bemused looks all around. "Show the jury how full of crap the system is." And so the monologue went, until he caught sight of me. "Alright, boys, I think business is calling me." There were handshakes and backslaps for a minute; then we were left alone.

"Henry Hollis!" he said, a little too loudly. "Rumor has it that you landed a job as private security for the esteemed Charles Victor."

Desperate Days

I raised an eyebrow at that. "Well, you tell the rumor mill that they got it wrong."

Gittings shrugged. "Fair enough. Anything you want me to tell the rumor mill instead?"

"No, not a goddamn thing," I replied.

Roy Gittings is an amazing study in contrasts. He's one of the smartest men I have ever met, but he has a regular habit of making some just plain foolish choices in life. He's about as jaded as a man can get when it came to his fellow man, but I can vouch that there's a soft and sentimental core to his hard-shelled heart. He is also one of the biggest blowhards I have ever met, dispensing shot-glass wisdom and gossip to all who come within earshot – and yet he's better at keeping a secret than just about anyone this side of a parish priest.

"I'm looking for some people," I said, right out of the gate. With Gittings, I didn't need to beat around the bush or play it cute. I knew his hourly rate and he knew how to do his job.

"You got some names for me?"

I gave him a crooked smile. "Yes and no."

"So what do you have?"

I gave him a brief description of Mr. Silver Hair and the green convertible. He nodded, mostly to himself, as the gears began to turn in his head. "Not a lot to go on, but I'll see what I can do," he said finally. "And the other name?"

"Olam Eshtaw."

"What kind of a goddamn name is that?"

"My thoughts, exactly," I said.

Gittings frowned for a moment, then came back with something that surprised me. "I'll see what I can find, but my gut tells me I'm not the best guy to help you with that one."

"Oh?"

"I'm thinking..." he mused, tapping his chin, "that you might want to talk with a associate of mine over at New Eden University." He ruffled through his well-worn jacket and pulled out a notepad and a pencil. He scribbled something down and tore off a page. "Professor C.J. Guzman's the one you want to talk to. Always came through for me when I was trying to hunt down obscure ethnographic stuff – you know, back when I was neck-deep in my graduate studies."

"Oh, yeah? What did you study, anyway?"

"Sociology. I thought it would help make me a better police detective."

"And did it?"

"Made me a better drunk," he said, laughing at his own joke. "Guzman's an anthropologist, whose many talents include being a savant at all things cultural and linguistic. I think Dr. Guzman could help you more than I could – and academics are cheaper by the hour, too."

Once we had dispensed with business, I ordered myself some dinner – meatloaf and a baked potato – while Gittings regaled me and anyone within earshot with a treatise on the history and virtues of scotch. I stuck with my beer.

An hour later, I climbed off my barstool and left Roy Gittings to his vices and his bemused audience. It was time I made my way back to the Victor Ordnance Works building to water the plants.

I got there well after dark, and the man-made island seemed like the loneliest, most remote spot you could find in New Eden. There was a grand total of one electric light hanging on a bent pole in the parking lot, and that dim bulb mostly just served to send the rest of the island into even deeper shadows. It looked like a good place to dump a body.

When I crossed onto the island, the headlights of my Ford coupe helped me spot a weed-choked brick path skirting along the splintered wood pilings that formed the island's man-made boundary. I parked the car, but then decided a stroll around the oval-shaped island was in order. Watering a green coffin could wait a few minutes.

Caisson Number Two – as the maps call it – runs about four hundred feet from north to south and a little more than a hundred feet east to west. I could hear the water rushing through the mill race that flows between the island and the east bank of the Assinowa River, but could only see faint glimmering hints of movement below. Stepping carefully in the darkness, I followed the overgrown brick path around to the northernmost point of the island and stopped to take in the view.

I gazed up-town, to where the lights of the city set the night sky aglow and also served to outline the hulking mass of Shocknessey State Hospital, sitting maybe a hundred feet ahead of me. The hospital is the biggest in the city and has been built up over the past three decades so that it now covers almost every square inch of the island. If you are poor, crazy, a medical student, or just a strong affection for endless stretches of white tiled hallways and harsh lighting, that's where you go.

Things got a lot darker as I followed the path around to the west side of the island, where I looked out over the broad expanse of the Assinowa River. I could just make out the low mound of the old levee on the western bank of the river, almost two-hundred feet away. The new flood wall loomed a short distance beyond the levee. There was a dull glow coming from the strip of land hidden by the levee and penned in by the new concrete wall. That glow was generated by the campfires of Trenchville, the city's unofficial home for the homeless.

There wasn't much room between the west wall of the Victor Ordnance Works building and the water's edge, so I took it slow as I walked toward the south end of the island. Floating downstream to oblivion wasn't part of my evening plans. When I got to the southern-most point, I stood in a small stand of dogwood tress and looked out at the defunct city power plant, which at this time of night was not much more than a black rectangle kept company by a crumbling smokestack. Something about that place gave me the shivers. This was a hell of an address that Judge Lockwood and his

Wildflower Society friends had set me up in. I finished my circuit of the island and went inside.

It turned out that Clarence Boyette had already brought several large steel drums to the island, each containing 30 gallons of distilled water. Lugging the drums down the narrow stairs to the green glass coffin in the sub-basement didn't sound like much fun, so I was glad to discover that one drum had been tapped with a spigot and that a tin bucket hung from it. I made the journey down into the bowels of Caisson Number Two, clutching the filled bucket and a flashlight. The glass coffin was waiting for me, just like we'd left it.

I found a good spot to put the flashlight, then grabbed the tin funnel and fit the end into the hole on the top of the box. "Drink up," I mumbled as I carefully tipped the bucket of water. A minute later, I grabbed the flashlight and was about to head for the stairs when I noticed that the air in the low-vaulted chamber had changed. When I had first gotten there, it was damp and cold – the ambient temperature of the earth. Now, just a couple minutes later, the cavern was still damp but it seemed warmer, a lot warmer. I looked back at the green glass coffin and saw a few beads of condensation gathering on it. I put my hand out and touched the surface. Sure enough, the thing was radiating heat. Whatever that contraption was designed to do, it was doing it.

I got back topside and hung up the tin bucket on the spigot. I was standing on the old factory floor, which stretched away from me for hundreds of feet into utter darkness, save for where I swung my flashlight's beam. Clarence Boyette had assured me that the place would have electricity and lights in the next few days, but for now, it was just me and my flashlight standing in the void. It was time to go home.

I stepped outside and looked over to the Ford coupe waiting under that one lone lamp post. I swear to heaven above that the car looked like it was cringing with fear. The sight shook me up for a second or two, and I peered into the darkness around me. I started thinking about all the dire warnings that Judge Lockwood had sent my way. And that got me thinking about the strange kid who had climbed up on the roof of my tenement building, and the fact that Offenbach and Mr. Silver Hair were sending thugs like Martin Stakowski and Wilmer after me. It was getting pretty clear that I had a target on my back, and I was starting to take offense.

I squeezed my fists tight, trying to get ahold of myself. I forced myself to laugh, but the joke was on me at that moment, as that's when I saw movement on the other side of the mill race, about a hundred feet up the narrow street that led away from the island and between the towering factory buildings that loomed over the riverbank. Whatever I saw moving in those deep-of-the-night shadows was bigger than any alleycat or stray mutt. It moved fast and it had eyes. Beyond that, I didn't have a clue. The sight made my skin crawl, and I couldn't drag my eyes away from the patch of darkness ahead of me.

I squeezed my fists tight again. "Dammit. Dammit. Get a grip."

I palmed my car key and tried to pace myself as I walked across the cobblestone parking lot to the coupe, my eyes leveled on the spot in the distance where I had seen movement. I pulled the door open and swung into the driver's seat, switching my gaze to the side mirror. The engine kicked to life, and I eased the car into reverse, then swung the Ford around to face the little iron bridge, casting my headlights down the brick road. I squinted into the light and saw... nothing. I shook my head at how spooked I was. If there was a boogey-man in the darkness, it was most likely Wilmer, who was hopefully smart enough not to put a bullet in my windshield. Just to be on the safe side, I leaned over a little and pulled my snub-nosed Colt .38 from under the seat and laid it next to me.

I took my foot off the brake and gunned the Ford across the bridge, taking it a lot faster than was smart, but I lucked out for once and hit the far bank in one piece, surging into the tight passage between the buildings. I had one hand on the wheel and one on the Colt as I fishtailed down the street. My eyes darted back and forth, from the dogleg in the road ahead to the brick walls that were tight up against me. Right before the dogleg there was a recessed side entry on the right and I expected my headlights to show me somebody standing there, but it was empty. In the fraction of a second I had to spare, I gazed up the wall, to a window ledge about fifteen feet above the door. And there it was.

It wasn't Wilmer and it sure as hell wasn't a pigeon. The light was bad and I was moving like my ass was on fire, but I saw it. Even hunched on the ledge, I could tell it was big. Not a stitch of clothes on, just matted fur that hung like fringe. I remember two other things from that split-second – the hands and the eyes. The thing had hands that were just too damn big. They hung heavy at its sides like frying pans. The eyes caught the flash of my headlights and glowed, big and bright. This thing was made for the dark. I got my own eyes back on the road just in time to watch my fender give the wall a love-tap, but I got the wheel back under control and kept moving at top speed.

I finally let out a breath about two blocks later, as I headed uptown at a more reasonable clip. That thing was watching me, waiting for me. But what the hell was it? I hung a left onto the Humboldt Street bridge and took it slow until I got to my building. Every shadow on the way home looked different now. The thing that went bump in the night was real – and it was looking for me.

I gave my apartment a once-over like I'd never done before. Yeah, I was spooked, but more than that, I felt suddenly naked and vulnerable and out of my depth. I spent the next hour pacing my little apartment trying to come up with a reasonable next move. At just about midnight, I resolved that in the morning I would motor over to Judge Lockwood's office and tender my resignation. Everything was just too... nuts. I would get out while the getting was good. With that, I gave myself permission to get some shut-eye.

No rest for the wicked, they say. Right on cue, about two hours after hitting the pillow, I woke up to a noise. I laid there, perfectly still, listening. I heard a dull thud, and the bed shook slightly like a heavy object had been placed on the floor. Next, my living room floor began to creek as heavy feet shuffled slowly across it. That got me fishing in my night stand for my snub-nose .38. I grabbed the revolver and pulled it under the covers, resting it on my chest.

My bedroom door was already standing open a few inches, and I watched in the darkness as the door swung fully aside. There, outlined in the dim light trickling in from the living room windows, was the thing. I could make out the dangling fringe of its fur as it stood for a moment in the doorframe. It ducked its head as it took a step into my room. The goddamn thing was north of seven feet tall and as wide as a phone booth. The massive head swung slowly left and right, the glowing eyes eventually landing squarely on me, gazing into my face. That was more than enough for me; I set the revolver upright on my chest and fired. Nothing. I had pulled the trigger, I heard the hammer fall, but nothing. No loud noise, no misfire, no muzzle flash. A goddamn dud. I spun the cylinder and pulled the trigger again, but no luck.

My visitor picked up on my sudden movement and was at my bedside in a heartbeat. His – or, its – hands were around my throat and over my face before I could struggle out of my bedsheets to defend myself. I could feel the astounding strength of the beast pushing down on me, but then... the pushing stopped. The thing was still trying to throttle the life out of me, but it was as if it had suddenly been robbed of its strength. It snarled in rage and leaned in on me, and I could feel his great weight pushing down. But even as it leaned in, its hands became shaky and the beast lost its grip on my neck, enough for me to slip sideways off the bed and out of its grasp. Once I was standing on my own two feet, I desperately tried to pistol whip the thing in the head. Now, I am no Hercules, but I know my own strength, and I gave it my all. There should have been some blood at a minimum. Maybe this thing could take my best shot and keep on coming at me, but this was not my best shot. I suddenly went weak as the pistol arced through the air. I hit that furry, snarling head with all the might and muscle of a sleepy toddler. I could barely keep from dropping the gun. In shock and horror, I threw myself up against the bedroom wall and waited for the inevitable attack. When it came, it was giant, furious fists and fur, flailing at my face and torso – but the effect was a lot more like a circus clown with a set of fringe-covered pillows. Again, the beast roared in rage and frustration at his apparent impotence. It was a comic stalemate.

The confrontation continued for about another minute, with the thing bellowing and chasing me around my apartment and me ducking and occasionally slugging. No harm was done, other than a kitchen chair being knocked over. I made it to a wall switch and put some light on the subject. My very angry visitor was straight out of some dime novel's description of a hell-beast. In proper light, it looked to be a cross between a grizzly bear, a wolf, a gorilla, and maybe a couple bouncers I'd met at a speakeasy in Chicago, all shoved into the worst floor-length fur coat ever made. Oh, and it stank. It looked every bit the part of the creature from your worst nightmares, only it was now shading its eyes and panting and fuming with frustration as it stood next to my comfy chair. Just about this time, I realized that my apartment door stood open – or rather, had been lifted off its hinges and was now leaning up against the wall next to the doorway. I pointed at the door and screamed, "Get out!" over and over again.

Eventually, the thing and I came to a sort of unspoken agreement, which went something along the lines of, "Get the hell out of my apartment right now and maybe you can try to kill me later." And just like that, it was gone.

Quitting my new job didn't seem like a real option anymore.

CHAPTER 17

Judge Arthur Lockwood and Eleanor Stanton arrived at my tenement apartment at eight the next morning. I'd called Lockwood's office from Jeanette's Diner an hour earlier.

"Good morning, Henry," Lockwood said as he stepped in, offering up a handshake.

"So, this is where you live? It's very... efficient."

"It's a tiny dump," I corrected him. "But I call it home. And, I have to admit, I'm liking it more than ever right about now."

"I don't mean to pry," Lockwood said cautiously, "but, where's your front door?"

"I'll get to that in a minute," I said, pointing a thumb in the direction of my uprooted door leaning against my living room wall.

"I take it that's part of why you called and insisted we meet you here this morning. Care to share with us the details?"

"Absolutely. But first, you need to take a seat at the kitchen table."

Bemused, they went into my little kitchen and sat down at my excuse for a table. They were both curious about the two items on the table: a large knife and a jar of pickles.

"I'll get to that in a minute," I told them, then described my experience the night before at the Victor Ordnance Works building and the thing that paid a visit to my apartment. I stopped before I described the actual fight, if you can call it that.

"So," said Eleanor, "a giant, nightmarish hell-beast came to your apartment last night?"

"Yes."

"And what did this thing do?" Eleanor asked, leaning forward across the table.

"It tried to kill me in my bed."

The judge looked me up and down. "You seem to be doing remarkably well for a dead man," he observed. "We know you're resourceful. So, is there some trick we should know about?"

"Yeah, there is, in point of fact. That's why we're sitting at this table." I turned to Eleanor. "Pick it up," I said, pointing to the knife, "and stab me with it."

Eleanor Stanton raised an eyebrow and gave a nervous laugh. "That's not a good idea."

"Oh, I'm sure you've done years of training with French sword masters and Japanese samurai warriors, and the like. I'll make it easy for you – just stab me in the arm," I said, rolling up my sleeve.

She cast a wary eye at Judge Lockwood and then looked back to me. "You're serious?"

"Dead serious," I replied, putting my bared forearm on the table in front of her. "And don't hold back."

She picked up the knife and gave it a once over. She judged it legit and gave me one more chance to back out. "You sure?"

"Do it!"

With that, she swung the knife up and down again like she was chopping off the head of a snake. I winced as my instincts kicked in, but at the last second, her hand began to shake violently and her grip loosened and the knife skittered sideways onto the floor. She pulled her hand back and cradled it like it had been bitten.

"What the hell was that?" she blurted.

"I have no earthly idea, but I'm pretty sure it has everything to do with the visit I got from that kid a few nights ago, and whatever that thing is he put on my roof," I said, pointing up.

Lockwood gazed at me in wonderment. "I've never heard of such a device. Have you, Eleanor?"

She shook her head.

"But there's a catch," I said.

"Oh?"

I pointed to the pickle jar. "Open it."

Eleanor flexed her hand and reached for the jar. She worked at twisting open the lid until her hand started shaking again. Frustrated, she shoved it away and began rubbing her wrist. Lockwood gave it a go next, with similar results. "My hand – it felt paralyzed," he observed in muted wonderment.

"Put too much energy into anything around here – feat of strength, kinetic velocity, whatever – and you get shut down," I explained. "I guess it's better than me being stabbed to death in my sleep."

"Yes, it is."

"Your honor," I said the judge. "Before that thing came here to kill me last night, I had made up my mind to tender my resignation, but..."

Lockwood interrupted me. "But now you understand that there is no hiding from this."

"Yeah, that pretty much sums it up."

Lockwood gave me a sympathetic smile, raised an eyebrow, and laughed. "Well, if that's the case, isn't there a mysterious glass box that you should be adding water to right about now?"

"I suppose there is, boss. I'll get right on that."

CHAPTER 18

It was a very different experience going to the island that morning, and I went about my little errand without sweating bullets and making a general fool of myself. The light of day has a way of changing things. I found Clarence Boyette there, along with a half-dozen workmen. They were tackling the daunting task of making the building and the island usable again. I asked Boyette to throw some extra lighting onto the outside of the building, which he said was already in the plans. Once I had my watering can hung up, I headed for my next appointment, at New Eden University.

Agar Hall looms over the main plaza of the campus like a red-brick version of a gothic cathedral, stained glass and all. It's home to the social sciences at the university. The main entrance to the building leads onto a grand, round foyer off of which are several ornate doors leading to large lecture halls. On either side of the front entrance sweeping staircases climb the periphery of the circular space, their steps disappearing into archways high above. Once upstairs, things get more intimate. It's a rabbit warren of narrow hallways, bad lighting, and cramped, often-windowless offices. Men in sweater vests shuffled by me, avoiding eye contact as they went about their studious tasks. I may have spent my college years at the university, but I was lost up in the catacombs of academia. I wandered aimlessly until I eventually came to a secretarial pool, where I was given directions to the office of Professor C.J. Guzman. I found the office, right next to the entrance to a small library that I had no idea existed on the campus: the Rodes Library of Rare Books. Guzman's office door was open, so I gave a courtesy knock on the doorframe. The office was bigger than I expected and at first I didn't see anyone.

"Enter!" a rather theatrical woman's voice called out, source unseen.

I stepped fully into the office and took it in. It was a madhouse of exotic and strange objects overflowing from bookshelves and tables. Every surface was pile high with leather-bound tomes, clay pots in various stages of repair, ancient-looking tools, the occasional animal bone, and a hundred other things that I didn't recognize at first glance. The walls were adorned with tribal masks and headdresses, iron-tipped spears, hunting bows, knives of almost every imaginable design, wood carvings, paintings on bark, et cetera. It was as if the pages of *National Geographic* had come to life, except for the fine layer of dust on everything around me.

The office was very large – more like a laboratory or archive – with tall windows on one side that flooded the space with light. A woman stepped out from behind a bookshelf at the far end of the room. She wore a heavily stained tan lab coat and her long silver hair was held out of her eyes by a checkered bandana. I pegged her to be nearing sixty, but she had a youthful spring in her step and the smile of a kid in a candy shop. She absently fiddled with the skull of a small animal as she strode over to greet me.

"Can I help you?"

"I hope so," I said. "I'm looking for Professor Guzman."

She gave me a sly smile. "You found him!"

"Oh? Good to meet you," I said, blushing a little as I extended my hand. "A fellow by the name of Roy Gittings sent me your way."

"Ah," she said, knowingly. "You must the Hollis fellow that Roy told me to keep an eye out for."

I nodded.

"So, what can I do for you?"

"Well," I said to her, "I'm looking for someone, but I'm at a dead end. The name's pretty unusual and our mutual friend, Roy, said that you might be able to give me a little background and point me in the right direction."

"I'm not exactly a walking phone book, but I suppose I could give it a whirl. What's the name?"

"Olam Eshtaw," I said, pulling out photographs of the statue of the little boy. I extended them to her.

She took the photos and studied them, mumbling the name. Then she noted, "It's all in capital letters."

"What?"

"On the statue. The words on the plaque are engraved in all capital letters. Are you sure it's a name?" Her eyes flashed between me and the photos.

"Alright," I said slowly, "if it's not a name, what does it say?"

"It's that second word – Eshtaw – that's got the gears in my head churning." She put down the photographs and beckoned me to follow her as she marched excitedly out of her office. We made a quick right turn and headed down the hall to the next door on the right: the Rodes Library of Rare Books. Professor Guzman swung open the framed glass doors dramatically and swept dramatically into the foyer of the library. She nodded absently to the librarian as she made a bee line for the next set of double-doors, these being a good ten feet tall and made of solid oak. "Have you been in here before?" she asked over her shoulder, grinning.

"I didn't even know it existed until a few minutes ago."

"Let me introduce you," – she paused for dramatic effect – "to my favorite place on campus." With that, Professor Guzman threw the double-doors wide open. I followed her into the space beyond and gazed in wonder. The room was only about thirty feet by twenty feet, but the ceiling was maybe forty feet up and crowned with a skylight of stained glass. Below that, the space was entirely wrapped by three levels of balconies overlooking the main reading area. The place was a woodworker's dream – or nightmare, depending on the pay rate. Tall rolling ladders with brass wheels at each end leaned against the bookshelves, secured in brass rails that circled the place. The room was a slightly dusty, faintly musty, and leather-bound jewel box of wood, glass, and brass.

"Holy cow..." I mumbled after taking in the sheer grace and beauty of the place. The next thing I noticed was the smell of old books.

Guzman put a finger to her lips and nodded in the direction of two people seated at tables. They glanced up briefly as we walked past, making our way to the far end of the room. There, we came to a surprisingly short door – I'm talking five and a half feet high, max – adorned with a carved relief of a lion's head and completely surrounded by bookcases, even above. The professor rummaged briefly through her large key ring, unlocked the door, and pushed it open. Beyond the little door was a narrow set of stairs going down about ten steps. She led on. Guzman was a half-foot shorter than me so she descended the stairs easily, but I had to duck down and turn around to navigate the stairway backwards, grasping a well-worn handrail while staring at my feet. At the bottom, I was relieved to find that the ceiling allowed me to stand to my full height but with only about an inch of clearance. The hallway was a stark contrast to the refined, woody opulence above. It had simple white plastered walls and extended for maybe fifteen feet. There was one small but sturdy-looking metal door on either side of the hallway. Ahead was an open archway, leading into a larger space beyond.

As we passed the metal doors, Professor Guzman pointed to them and said, "Fireproof doors. The real gems of our collection are in these rooms."

We went for the archway and entered what I can best describe as an antechamber, without windows or ornamentation of any kind. The room contained two simple wooden desks, each equipped with a hooded reading lamp, a magnifying glass, and a pair of white cotton gloves. "Supervised reading room," she informed me.

On the far wall was an unassuming wooden door, painted a very institutional sage green. Guzman took me through that door and again we descended a flight of stairs. At the bottom was a landing and yet another door. "Almost there," Professor Guzman mumbled, fiddling with her key ring.

Once past that door, I stopped dead in my tracks. I whistled and shook my head in wonder.

"We are directly under the student quadrangle," Guzman said, pointing up. We were standing in what was more of a warehouse than a room. The dimensions were a bit hard to make out with all the metal shelves and wooden crates that surrounded us. I could see the far wall, maybe two hundred feet ahead. The ceiling was about twenty-five feet above us. "This is the university's new central storage facility. It was installed less than two years ago during the refurbishment of the central heating plant system that runs across campus. The digging already needed to be done so the powers-that-be decided to put the land under the quad to some useful purpose, rather than build a new warehouse on land that could be better used by future generations – for classrooms and the like."

"Sounds reasonable," I said. "How did they get all this stuff down here?"

"There are two electric lift stations down here – giant elevators that rise up thirty feet to small utility buildings just off the quadrangle."

"So, how did the powers-that-be pay for this?"

"Anonymous donor," she said with a raised eyebrow.

"This sure is a funny thing to throw a pile of charity money at," I said. "So, why are we down here again?"

She walked over to the first long line of bookshelves ahead of us. "It will take years – decades – to fill this place up. In the meantime, these shelves have been set aside for my personal use," she said, beaming.

Professor Guzman rummaged the shelves for a minute or two and grabbed several large tomes, which she handed to me. She then led me about half way down the long aisle until we arrived at a makeshift work area, where card tables and folding chairs had been set up. We each took a seat, and Guzman began flipping through the pages of the first book. At length she tapped her finger on one of the pages and spun it around for me to see.

"Almost all languages belong to language 'families,'" she explained. "Each of the languages within a family shares common traits – root-words and grammatical structure – that they received from a parent 'proto-language,' which existed sometime in the past. There are often core words that express basic or very important objects or concepts that are found in most or all of the sibling languages in a language family. This book lists core words from many language families. This particular chart, here," she said, underlining a word with her finger, "lists twenty core words from a specific sub-group of language families – spelled phonetically in the Roman alphabet, of course. What do you see here?"

I looked where she was pointing and saw a word: Eshto. "Yeah, I see it. Eshto. What's it mean?"

Guzman's eyes sparkled with excitement. She looked back at the page and ran one finger up the column of words. "That word is associated with one of the twenty core words listed in this chart, which is is..." her finger arrived at the top of the column, "'child or children!'" She looked gleefully at me. "I think that's what your second word, 'eshtaw,' means."

"Yeah? Child or children? In what language?"

She ran her other finger across to the left side of the page. "M.O.," she mumbled. "Hmmm... there's an annotation number..." She dropped her finger down to the bottom of the page and gave a satisfied nod. "Meso-Ohioan."

"An Indian language?"

Professor Guzman nodded. "A native American language family, to be more precise, but yes." She closed the book and pulled the other tome in front of her. "That was the easy part. I had a hunch on the word *eshtaw* and that has paid off. Now, I need this other book – and a little luck – to help us solve the riddle of *olam*." She flipped the book open and began reading.

A good fifteen minutes passed, and I started to get restless sitting at the card table, so I took the opportunity to stretch my legs and stroll the long aisles of the underground warehouse. Only a fraction of it was filled, but large areas of the space seemed to have been set aside for various future uses. There were color-coded painted lines on the floor outlining areas for various departments and offices within the university, although most of the space inside remained empty. One area marked "Groundskeeping" in green lettering contained long rows of gleaming new park benches, clearly ready for installation. Another large area outlined on the floor in red paint and marked "School of Law" housed piles of boxes neatly labeled as various volumes of the Indiana State Code, all presumably waiting for the next crop of incoming law students. I walked over to another section of the floor that caught my eye. It was roped off with warning signs stating "Do Not Enter." The stanchions stood guard just inside of a blue outline marked "Department of Physics" and just outside of a set of heavy curtains made of canvas tent material hanging from the ceiling, obscuring from view the contents within.

"I think I found it!" I heard Professor Guzman call out from a few aisles over.

I trotted back to the work area where she sat amidst the card tables. "What's the scoop?" I said, looking over her shoulder.

"Look: *olama, ulam, olume, eolem*," she said, excitedly, running her finger slowly along a line of words in the text. "They are all words from the Meso-Ohioan language family, and they all clearly match the pattern of *olam*."

"Yeah? And?"

"They all have the same meaning – 'taken or stolen.' It is my professional opinion that your word has the same or similar meaning."

"So... *olam eshtaw* is not a name. And those two words etched into the statue mean..."

"They mean 'stolen child – or children,'" she said triumphantly.

"Well, I'll be damned," I whispered. "And I'll lay good odds that you're right. That little statue in the park is of a miserable looking kid, so it makes sense. These dusty old books come in handy sometimes after all."

"But why would someone etch those two words onto a statue placed in a park in New Eden?" the professor asked.

"I don't know, but somebody's paying me good wages to find out."

As Professor Guzman walked me out of the warehouse, I pointed a thumb in the direction of the cordoned off area designated for the Department of Physics. "What's behind the curtain over there?"

"One of the physicists told me that they were building an atomic pile, whatever that is," she said with a shrug.

CHAPTER 19

Mid-day found me back up on Dalton's Bluff, pacing the weed-choked grass of Children's Park. It was the first genuinely hot day of the spring and that got me rolling up my shirt sleeves as I strolled about, trying to make sense of why someone would put a statue here in honor of *olam eshtaw*– stolen children. I went from one end of the park to the other staring intently at the ground, at the benches, at the trees around me, and finally out at the city below. No revelations came to me. Nothing jumped out and helped me unravel the mystery. I was feeling a bit frustrated, and standing there with my hands on my hips wasn't going to cut it. Finding out what happened to that statue – and why – was my assignment. So, I needed to get a new perspective. I turned away from the bluff and looked to the north. Across the street from the park was a low rise of ground covered with a mix of stunted bushes and mature trees. The ground there rose only about fifteen feet above the level of the street, but I wondered if that spot would give me the change in perspective I needed.

I mounted the short, steep slope, pushing my way through a thicket of thorny bushes. Once I reached the top, I turned around and gazed back out at the park. The extra height did add a bit of drama to the place. The city to the south shimmered in the warm afternoon haze, and the Assinowa River, to the west, was a silver ribbon cutting through the landscape. But nothing about the park itself became more clear to me. I walked fifty feet in either direction, trying to get some insight, but no insights came to me – that is, until I tripped and fell.

I pulled myself back up onto my feet and rubbed my knee, staring down in search of what had tripped me. I spied a rusted and bent piece of metal protruding from the undergrowth. In mild frustration, I kicked at the bramble around the piece of metal and felt my shoe make contact with something that wouldn't budge. That made me curious, so I pushed aside the old leaves and low bushes with my foot and discovered the top of a milled piece of limestone with a very rusted metal spike protruding from it. That got my attention and I paced a few feet to the east, kicking at the side of the limestone. It kept going, and so did I. With a few breaks, I found that a straight line of cut limestone extended for a good two hundred feet, east to west. It seemed obvious even to my untrained eye that this was the foundation for a building, now long gone and reclaimed by mother nature. I found a corner of the foundation stones and followed it into the trees. That line of limestone extended for well over a hundred feet to the north. Whatever had been built here, it was big.

This was as good a lead as anything I had currently going, and my gut told me that I should run with it as far as I could. I got back in the car and headed for the New Eden Public Library, downtown. When I got there, I made my way down to the basement, where they have a long line of cabinets with wide, roll-out map trays containing Sanborn Fire Insurance maps. These maps were compiled by the Sanborn company for use by insurance companies and local insurance agents who wanted to keep track of what people were building on city lots and what they were using those structures for. The maps detail building dimensions, construction materials, window and door locations, water-source locations, structure uses, etc. After that, the insurance companies would put aside the maps and move on to actuarial tables and risk assessment – pretty dry stuff, until you have a fire or get hit by a tornado.

I've actually done some freelance work over the last couple of years with Sanborn, as an inspector. I would drive around the Midwest, to small towns and big cities, collecting data for their building census updates, which is done in a never-ending cycle that gets around to every plot of land and every built structure in the United States just about every two years. They have thousands of guys like me, picking up work now and then, as needed. A lot of us are cops or ex-cops – people who didn't wilt at the first sign of resistance. Things usually went well enough, as folks who had insurance policies on their property – meaning most people – were required by their policies to comply, but there was the occasional old coot with a shotgun.

The maps are assigned grid numbers and are drawn at a scale of 50 feet to the inch. It takes a lot of maps to cover every property in a city the size of New Eden. Standing at the map cases, I found the grid guide and then made my way to the corresponding drawer. The map on top of the pile was the latest edition available – the 1932 edition. I shuffled through the stack below, grabbed the oldest edition at the bottom, and placed it on top of the cabinet.

I ran my hand over the map until I found my bearings. There, plain as day, was Children's Park. Immediately to the north was... nothing. There were no buildings shown on the map and no description of what the land was being used for. It was simply a blank spot on the map. I checked the date on the map legend – 1880. I knew that the Sanborn maps for New Eden normally went back to 1872, so I pulled the drawer back open and looked at the date on each of the maps inside. It looked to be a full set going back to 1880, but no sign of the four maps I expected to find from before then and no sign of the building I had expected to find. People misplace things now and then, so I repeated my search in each of the drawers above, below, and to either side. Nothing. That got me wondering.

I went over to the librarian's desk with the 1880 map in my hand. "Excuse me, ma'am. I'm looking for the 1872 edition of this map, but I can't seem to find it."

She took the map from me and studied it. "Have you looked through the stack of maps in the drawer?"

"Yes."

She furrowed her brow and rose from her chair. "I'll take a look." I followed her as she walked through the periodicals section back to the line of map cabinets. "These should only be put away by library staff," the librarian said, pointing to a hand-printed sign. "But people sometimes take it upon themselves to put them back."

"That's what I was thinking," I said. "Maybe someone checked it out."

"No," she said firmly. "These maps cannot be checked out. They stay here."

"Got it. Say, maybe a colleague of mine from back at my office came in to look at them. Did someone come in here recently looking for these particular maps?"

"I really wouldn't know. People come in here almost every day looking at the maps. Some need my help and I try to help them, but most folks don't. If they don't ask for my help then I usually just leave them to it."

"I see," I said, scratching my chin. "Any chance you

remember a fellow about my age but with white hair coming in?"

That's when something clicked in her bookish head. The librarian straightened up and pushed her glasses back up the bridge of her nose. The look on her face was midway between vague fear and muted disgust. "He work with you?"

"He's the competition, actually. Works for another insurance agency."

"Right," she said with surprising distaste. "I think he was here, maybe two weeks ago. Asked for directions to the maps, but didn't need me for help after that. He a friend of yours?"

"No. Like I said, he's my competition."

"Well, your competition gave me a serious case of the jitters. The way he looked at me – the way he moved. It was like a snake in a tan suit."

"He gets a lot of that," I said. "Say, did he have a briefcase with him?"

"Hmmm... yeah, maybe."

The circle was getting smaller and a few of the dots were starting to connect. Mr. Silver Hair had been to the map room at the public library, and from the looks of things, he pocketed some maps. Why would he want to hide the existence of a building that got knocked to the ground more than fifty years ago? Why had it become so important all of a sudden? Then I remembered something that made me smile.

I grabbed my hat and walked a few blocks over to the New Eden Gazette building, then headed down to their archives room. *The Gazette* has more than just newspapers in their archives; at the back of the room they also have a long line of cabinets with wide, roll-out map trays containing Sanborn Fire Insurance maps – the same damn maps they have at the public library. It isn't cheap for *The Gazette* to maintain updated Sanborn maps, but the maps give the reporters and editors insight into the history of every single building in the city. The collection has a sixty-year record of every church, bank, livery stable, whiskey bar, candy shop, hair salon, and fraternal club in town. And since much of the editorial work at the paper happened after five PM, the public library collection was not much help. So, years back, the paper footed the bill for the entire collection.

The *Gazette*'s Sanborn maps – and their newspaper archives – are generally off limits to the public, so I was betting Mr. Silver Hair had no idea that the *Gazette*'s collection even existed. I had been to the newspaper archives dozens of times on official *Gazette* business, and I had seen the rows of map cabinets. I know the lady at the front desk by name. So, I walked in, tipped my hat to her and got waved into the room with a smile.

Five minutes later, I was standing at one of the cabinets hunched over a map. My index finger was resting just under the outline of a building on the 1872 edition. The label on the map said "Pelley Home for Boys." All I could think was: who the hell was Pelley and why did that name sound so familiar?

CHAPTER 20

For the second day in a row, I showed up at the Rosebud Grill just in time for happy hour. Roy Gittings was tucked into a booth with what looked to be a business client. I caught his eye, and he held up a finger, asking for a moment of patience, so I headed to the bar and grabbed some peanuts. Less than a minute later, Gittings stood up and shook hands with his client, who I suddenly recognized as none other than the mayor of New Eden. Gittings nodded to me as the mayor headed for the door.

I walked over to Gittings and gave him a slap on the shoulder. "Taking a meeting with you can't be good for the mayor's re-election prospects."

Gittings laughed. "Probably not. If you haven't noticed, things are going kind of sideways in this town right now."

"I've noticed," I said, sliding into the booth. "By the way, thanks for the tip on meeting with Professor

Guzman. She's got me pointed in the right direction, I think."

"Yeah? Glad to hear it."

"Any progress on finding my silver-haired friend in the green convertible?"

Roy Gittings shook his head. "Not luck yet. Got another hint to throw my way?"

"Well... maybe." I pulled a notebook out of my vest pocket and slid it in front of him. "Does this mean anything to you?"

Gittings rested his finger on the page and squinted at what I'd scribbled there. "Pelley Home for Boys?" he read aloud.

"Yep."

"It doesn't mean a damn thing to me, but..."

"But the name is familiar," I offered, completing his thought.

"Yeah," he said, then stood up from the booth. "Be right back."

Gittings went to the bar and exchanged a few words with the bartender. He was soon back at the booth with a phone book in hand. He thumbed through its first few pages, which turned out to be a series of gridded city maps. "Look here," he muttered, pointing to a map. Above his finger was what looked to be a small park just to the north of downtown, near the bluff that loomed over that part of town. "Pelley Square," it said in fine print. Gittings then flipped to the street index and ran his finger down the list of street names. "Pelley Court," he read aloud. It turned out that Pelley Court was the circular road that ran around Shocknessey State Hospital on the man-made island, just to the north of the old Victor Ordnance Works island.

"So, some guy named Pelley was one of the founding fathers of New Eden?" I mused.

He nodded. "Yeah, possibly. I can't say I know anything about him, though, which is a surprise. How is this related to your silver-haired man in a convertible?"

"My mysterious Mr. Silver Hair was trying to hide the fact that there was once a building up on Dalton's Bluff called the 'Pelley Home for Boys.' Funny thing is, the building's been scraped clean off the map – and the earth – for more than fifty years now."

"That's a head-scratcher," Gittings said, pondering the issue. Then he wagged a finger in the air. "Tell you what, how about we roll the dice and see what comes up when we open this here phone book to the 'P' section?"

He turned the book so we could both have a decent view and began flipping pages. When he got to 'P', he ran his finger down the column of names. "Pegowski... Pekar... Peltier... Peyne...." he read. "No luck on 'Pelley' – which, I gotta say – surprises me."

"Yeah?"

"I mean, if he was a founding father here in New Eden, there should be a couple great-grandkids in the phone book – maybe a distant cousin or a nephew at least."

"Maybe the family fell on hard times and none of them can afford a phone."

Maybe," said Gittings. "I've still got your retainer money burning a hole in my pocket – mind if I do a little research on my own and get back to you tomorrow?"

"I was hoping you'd say that. In the meantime, I've got one more lead to follow up on before I call it a night."

CHAPTER 21

It was just after 6 PM when I walked up the long, wooden ramp at the entrance to the New Eden Home for the Elderly and Infirmed. The place is up on Dalton's Bluff, situated on about five acres of prime real estate at a bend in Bluff View Road, about half a mile west of Children's Park. The facility looks more like a country club than a retirement home. The bulk of the grounds is dominated by at least a half-dozen manicured gardens awash with spring blooms and containing either a large stone replica of some famous statue in Italy or an ornate fountain shooting water from the mouths of whimsical stone animals. Paved walking paths cut across the property and connect the various garden plots. There is also an intricately carved limestone wall that runs along the bluff edge, where the residents can stroll and take in the view. The street-side of the building is wrapped in a massive teak-wood veranda that could rival any promenade on the grandest ocean liners, right down to the bone-white lounging chairs and smartly dressed staff hoisting trays stacked high with refreshments. As I stepped inside, I made a note to save up for my golden years.

I found my way to the reception desk in the rotunda and asked for Mr. Archibald Flood. A nice lady in a starched white hat directed me to the main dining room, where I was met by another nice lady in another starched white hat who escorted me to Archie's table. She leaned over and let him know he had company, which brought a big, mostly toothless smile to his wrinkled face. That smile didn't last long when Archie got a good look at me.

Archie Flood has some of the bushiest brows that I have ever seen. They are more like dancing gray ferrets than anything a man could reasonably grow on his face. I was tempted to laugh, but Archie looked anything but amused. His dancing ferrets rose high into his wispy hair-line and stayed there, unmoving, as his eyes went wide and his jaw went slack. He went so far as to put his shaking, wrinkled hands up, as if fending off an attack. This introduction was getting off to a very bad start. "Archie Flood?" I asked.

Archie mouthed a couple of silent words, which I think were something along the lines of, "Mother of god." He nodded slightly in what I took to be confirmation of my question. I raised my hands slightly, showing my lack of deadly weapons, and slowly put my backside into a chair at his table. "Sorry if I surprised you. I don't want to cause you any grief, Mr. Flood. I'm just here to ask a couple questions."

Archie nodded again without uttering a word and lowered his hands to the table, on either side of his Cobb salad. Just then, a nice waitress in a starched white hat appeared at my side and politely shoved a menu into my hands. "Welcome to the Vista Dining Room, Sir. Here is the cash menu for visitors," she said.

I handed it right back to her without opening it. "The Cobb salad looks great – and a coffee."

As the waitress walked crisply away, Archie leaned in close, his eyes still wide but his ferrets were now riding low, partly obscuring his view. "You a ghost?"

"What?"

"Why you haunting me after all this time? I saw you dead and buried, what? – a good forty years ago?"

I leaned in a little, my hands still up where he could see them. "Mr. Flood, you've clearly mistaken me for someone else. I'm a few months shy of my 38th birthday, and, as best as I can tell, I haven't given up the ghost just yet."

Archie shook his head, rejecting my assertions. "They must'a dug you up is what they did," he said in hushed awe. "They dug you up and put a spell on you. I know we did you wrong, but I'm an old man now, and I feel nothing but bad about how things went for you, 'specially after all the good things you did for us folks up on the Bluff."

"Mr. Flood, My name is—"

Archie interrupted me. "Mister Adam P. Smith," he

said reverently. "We never forgot you, ashamed though, as we were. Ghost or rambling dead, you were a good man, sir, and I'm mighty sorry for how things went."

"I don't mean to be rude, but you gotta' stop talking nonsense." That name – Adam P. Smith – that name was awfully familiar to me. Part of my brain started working on that name.

Archie raised a hand, almost pleadingly. "We used to put flowers on your grave every year, on your birthday," he said. "And, nowadays, I always give that picture of you in the rotunda a quick nod when I walk by. I swear it on my mother's grave."

"Picture?"

"Yep. Good one, too, if I'm any judge. I always like that you look cheerful and like a man who's got things to do."

"Show me," I said. Things were going sideways in a hurry, as usual.

Archie Flood rose and walked with me out of the dining room. He waved me down the hall, toward the entry rotunda. We passed through the archway into the grand, domed space and made a quick right turn, just beyond the hall door. There, hanging in a heavy, gilded frame, was a photograph of me – not one single doubt about it – smiling, well dressed, with a shovel in my hands. "Holy hell," I muttered.

The plaque under the photograph said, "The honorable Adam P. Smith, Board President, Eden Home, Ltd., 7th of April, 1893. Groundbreaking."

I walked back to the dining room in a daze,

following in the wake of the thin, shambling little man that had just sent my mind reeling into near-madness. "Adam P. Smith," I muttered, then snapped my fingers. "The legal file, with the old bank account... The honorable Adam P. Smith footed the bill for Children's Park back in 1872 – and then this place in 1893?"

"Park?" Archie asked.

I looked into Archie's clouded brown eyes. "You've lived up here on the Bluff for most of your life, right?"

"Yes, sir."

"You remember a place called the Pelley Home for Boys?"

"Remember it? I worked there for the best part of two years. So, yes, sir, I remember it."

"Could you walk me over and show me around?"

"Nothing to see but wild roses and beer bottles."

"Humor me."

"Suits me fine. Was gonna take a walk after dinner anyways – soon as I finish my Cobb salad, that is."

Archie Flood and I made short work of our Cobb salads and then headed for the veranda, where Archie pulled me aside to take in the view.

"You did a real good thing, building this fine place up on the Bluff, sir," the old man said, beaming. "Even better was you making special allowance for the old folks from up here, on the Bluff. I most likely would have died years back, in a dark, smelly old rooming house out on the west side."

"Special allowance?"

Archie nodded. "You made a list of every soul living

up here on Dalton's Bluff and handed it over to the folks you put in charge of the Home. You said, 'Any one of these good people make it to seventy years on this Earth and they get free bed and bread 'til they croak!' Now that's what I call neighborliness."

"How many of you folks from the Bluff are living here now?" I asked.

"We've been whittled down to about ten nowadays," he said. "There was a time when half of the three hundred residents were Bluff people."

"What about the rest of the residents?"

"Rich folk, paying the full fare. I hear they fork over close to a hundred bucks a month for three squares a day on fancy china and a feather bed to drop dead in," Archie said cheerfully, stepping off the veranda.

"Sounds like I was a nicer guy, forty years back," I said, playing along with whatever the hell this was.

"And better dressed, too!" Archie exclaimed, shooting me a mischievous smile.

We walked east along Bluff View Road, with Archie setting a decent pace. He might have been as old as the pharaohs, but that crusty old coot could still move when he felt the inclination. I asked him a few questions about life up on the Bluff and got a rundown on the colorful history of the place and the people. The Bluff was in fact three separate neighborhoods, broadly speaking. There was the three-mile stretch on the north side of town heading north to south along the river. That bit was called Buena Vista Heights and was home to a few grand homes and a half-dozen unfinished neighborhood developments that the Great Depression had ground to a premature halt. Once the Bluff reached the Home, it turned east – inland from the river – for the better part of a mile, and that bit had been called Dalton's Bluff for more than half a century. It was home to about two thousand working families living in shotgun shacks and scratching out meager lives on dirt-patch homesteads. Generations of these simple folk had spent their days and nights laboring in the riverside factories that had made New Eden thrive. Finally, the bluff turned south, creating something of a bowl around the main city center, below. This section was called Olympus Heights, and hosted some of the grandest homes in New Eden. Archie took delight in telling me tales about each of the neighborhoods.

After about a half-mile of walking, we reached the edge of Children's Park. Archie showed me a spot on the former site of the Pelley Home for Boys where a set of limestone steps were obscured by tall weeds but could still be used to mount the short rise to the main property. I offered him a hand up as we mounted the steps. "I come up here, sometimes, to pay my respects."

"Pay your respects?"

"On account of all the dead boys," he said, reluctantly.

"Dead? This was an orphanage, right?"

"Yes, sir. But the Indian boys – they scooped 'em up and brought them all here and then they just kept dying."

I put my hand on his shoulder and gently turned him to face me. "Indian boys?"

"Yep. Younger folks these days don't know it, but back a hundred years ago, this whole area was thick with them Assinowa Indians, right about the time the white settlers came along. Funny thing about the Assinowa tribe – they got along real good with the white folks and nobody ever gave 'em much thought until around 1860, when somebody started a rumor that the tribe was gonna scalp us all in our sleep, as opposed to showing up for their day-shift at the flower mill or the wagon factory. It was a whole bunch of nothing, but people still got scared. Then, that same somebody convinced some government folks in Washington D.C. that the Assinowa were about to go on the warpath. Those government folks hopped to it and set up an Indian detention camp on the west side of the river and put the whole thing inside a fence and under armed guard. Two years later, the whole tribe was packed up and sent to Oklahoma and plunked down on a reservation out there."

"What about the boys?"

"Well, when the camp opened, Mr. Pelley opened up his Home for Boys – Indian boys, that is. He made a stink about the Indian boys needing to be civilized and said he could set 'em on the straight and narrow, even though those boys had been attending the local white schools for decades by then. That man, Pelley, he got the government to round up every last one of them

Indian boys in the detention camp and plop them in his Home."

"And then what?"

"Then what? Well, nothin', for maybe five years. Them boys were schooled and made to iron their white shirts and to put a proper crease in their britches and polish their leather shoes. Rumor had it, Pelley was looking for one boy in particular. Then, somewhere along the way, Mr. Pelley got to thinking that the boy he wanted to get his pasty white hands on wasn't one of the boys in the Home. That's when boys started getting sick and dying. I was there, near the end, working as a janitor. I saw boys walk into the infirmary on two feet and then come out on a stretcher. The Home always had a patch of ground out back of the main building where they had chucked a few boys who'd been taken by the pox, or whatnot, but now, that little burial plot got real crowded. I'd say a hundred or more got put in the dirt in under two years.

"All murdered?"

"Nobody said it out loud, back then, but that's what folks working at the home started thinking."

"So, the workers stopped the killings?"

"No, sir, I'm ashamed to say. Truth is, you stopped the killings."

Me?" I exclaimed.

Archie nodded. "Way I hear it, you got a high-priced lawyer to gin up a lien claim on the property. The Pelley Home for Boys was front page news for a few weeks. No more boys died after that. A year later, the Home was shut down and you were standing on the font steps swinging a set of keys and waving in the demolition crew. But..." Archie shook his head.

"But, what?"

"The rest of the boys were put on the orphan train before Pelley closed the doors."

"Orphan train?"

"That's what they did, back then," Archie explained. "Something like two hundred boys from the school got taken down to the train station and put on a special train. It chugged out of town and spent a month heading south and then west, stopping at every station and cattle crossing along the way. The local farmers got a chance to look over the boys and adopt 'em on the spot – once they handed over an adoption fee. Them boys got put to work in corn fields, dairy barns, and cotton fields all across this nation. Way I hear it, the last of the boys made it all the way to Colorado. True story."

"I'll be damned," I muttered. "What happened to all the bodies?"

"The bodies of the dead boys, you mean?" Archie asked. He pointed to a spot some distance away. "That's where they got put, but you moved 'em. I don't know where to."

I walked Archie Flood back to the Home and thanked him for the tour. It was just about sunset as I began my drive down the Bluff, and I planned on stopping by the Victor Ordnance Works to water the coffin. My thoughts were about as far from the driver's seat of that car as they could possibly be, but I still saw him – the kid. I noticed him standing at the street corner about a block from the Home, just as plain as can be, watching as my car passed by. He had long dark hair and nut-brown skin, with a large black hat pressed against his chest.

I hit the brakes and threw the car into reverse. The boy stepped away from the corner and broke into a jog, heading north up the side street. I got the car into first gear again, punched the gas, and followed him up the hard-packed dirt street for about a block. After another block, he stopped and looked back at me, then waved his big hat and jumped a fence. For some reason, I had to follow him. I pulled on the parking brake and jumped out of the car. Peering over the fence, I could see clear to the other end of the block, some five hundred feet away. Each backyard had a small vegetable garden, clothes lines, and an outhouse. Some had chickens pecking away at the dirt. Several women were standing at the knee-high picket fences that separated the yards, chatting away, with gaunt children and bone-thin dogs running and playing around them. The long-haired boy was jogging away from me, bounding over fences, in the midst of all those hardscrabble, hungry, indomitable lives. Nobody seemed to mind his intrusion. He turned, three yards in, and smiled back at me. Following him any further didn't feel right, somehow.

CHAPTER 22

I got up good and early the next morning and made my way to the Victor Ordnance Works, to water the coffin. When I got there, I found the place already humming with activity. There were at least twenty workmen running around dragging wires, swinging hammers, setting up ladders, and generally looking very busy. Clarence Boyette was in the middle of the empty factory space, guiding a team of men in setting up a steel rolling gantry that had an impressively large block and tackle set dangling from it. Irene Wagner stood stoically at his side. I waved to them and headed down to the coffin with a tin bucket in hand. When I'd finished my appointed task, I came back up and strolled over to where Clarence was working.

"You've got this place buzzing, Clarence!" I called out above the din.

"Month of hard work ahead, best as I can figure."

Irene Wagner nodded. "I would have estimated two

months, but Mr. Boyette seems to have quite the dedicated workforce."

When I got up closer, I noticed that Clarence was standing over a rusted metal ring as thick as my arm, which was bolted to the heavy wooden floorboards. "What is it?" I asked.

Clarence pointed to a spot on the floor a few paces away in response to my question. There, I noticed that the direction in which the wood floorboards ran was briefly interrupted by two heavy beams running at ninety degrees from the rest of the flooring. I followed the beams and realized that I was standing on the largest trap door that I had ever set eyes on. It must have been twenty feet on a side. At the far end were six massive hinges, each likely weighing as much as me.

"Christ! What did they keep down there? Elephants?"

"Artillery," he said flatly.

"What?"

"This here factory used to make field artillery for the army and big guns for the navy. They would test each one they made down in that hole."

"You mean, they would live-fire cannons down there?"

"It's a fact. Mr. Charles Victor says he has other plans for the space now, though."

"Like what? Storage?"

Clarence Boyette pulled a set of blueprints out from under his arm and unrolled them for me to see. He jabbed his finger at the center of the plans for the main floor, which showed a square marked simply as "Large Electric Lifting Station."

"Big elevator. Got it," I said.

Clarence flipped to the next blueprint sheet, which showed the space below. That level was nearly two hundred feet by about seventy-five feet. The blueprints showed three distinct areas. At the south end of the blueprint was a cluster of rooms marked "Flammable Storage." To the north of that were two large rooms marked "Secure Storage." Finally, the north end of the drawing showed three other rooms, each marked "Hardened Detention."

"What the hell is *hardened detention*?" I asked.

"I was hoping you'd tell me, Mr. Henry."

Irene Wagner cracked a thin smile. "Oh, I think you'll find a use for them," she said.

My conversation with Clarence Boyette and Irene Wagner was cut short by a voice calling out my name. I turned to see a young man in a Western Union outfit standing at the threshold of the rolling warehouse doors, now wide open to bring in the daylight. The young man stared around awkwardly as he held an envelope in the air.

I marched across the factory floor toward the young man. "That'd be me, son." After fishing in my pocket for a tip, I grabbed the envelope and thumbed it open.

The message read, "Your man has gone missing. Call ASAP. --Wallis."

"Shit." I crumpled up the note and pitched it as far

as I could. "Clarence!" I called out across the cavernous space. "Do we have a telephone line in here yet?"

"Nah. Phone company says we can expect it tomorrow."

"Shit." I set out of there at a jog and headed for the car. Where was the nearest pay phone? Five minutes later, I was taking three steps at a time heading into New Eden's Union Station. Off to one side of the main waiting area was a long line of phone booths. I ran over, digging in my pocket for change. A minute after that I was on the phone with Bert Wallis, who was working a shift at the front desk of the Prairie Hotel, in Chicago. I knew Bert from my days as a detective with the CPD. He was a mentor, and he retired about the same time I left the department. Since then, he'd been picking up extra money and extra pounds while sitting on a padded stool at the hotel.

"So, what happened?"

"Your guy had a visitor at about 6 PM last night," Bert said.

"Dammit. Who was it?"

"An older woman. I pegged her to be his mother. She was upset, blubbering all over the lobby like he'd robbed a bank or something. They went up to his room for a couple hours and then she left. I checked in on him just after that, listening for signs of life. He was in there – sounded like he was crying, I think. But when I came back to work this morning, he was gone. The overnight guy said he left with another man around 2 AM."

"You get a description of the guy he left with?"

"Yeah," Bert said. "A tall, skinny guy, with slicked-back dark hair. Ring a bell for you?"

"Yeah, it rings a bell. Thanks for the heads-up, Bert." I slammed the phone down and sucker-punched the wood-paneled wall of the phone booth. "Goddamn Martin Stakowski."

Mr. Silver Hair was smart, I had to give him that. I fully expected him to find out pretty quick that Olie Scharf had made a run for it. I even put good odds on him having me pegged as the guy who made that happen. But Mr. Silver Hair's little bit of genius was realizing that Olie was a momma's-boy, who would sure-as-shit place a phone call to old lady Scharf after poor little Olie spent a day crying in his hotel room. Then, dear old mom would head for the train station, looking to comfort her grieving, wayward boy.

I should have figured something was up the night before, when I didn't catch a whiff of either Wilmer or Martin nosing around outside my place. With Olie on the run, I'd expected them to keep an eagle-eye on me. Turns out I wasn't nearly as interesting or as smart as I thought. I guess they call that a learning moment.

My best bet now was that Olie Scharf/Offenbach and Martin Stakowski had made plans to return to New Eden on the first available train heading south out of Chicago. If memory served, there was an early-bird train heading south out of the Chicago's Randolph Street Station. I stood under the arrivals board and stared up. The 601 train on the Hoosier

Central Line was first on the board, arriving at 9:18 AM. I glanced down at my watch and shook my head in wonderment: 9:05. Olie was being delivered right to me – in less than fifteen minutes. Problem was, the Offenbach version of Olie would most likely be the one stepping off the train. He wouldn't exactly run over and give a hug to his old pal, Henry. So, what to do then?

I jogged back to my Ford and pulled it around so I could get a good view of the cab stand in front of the train station. There was a growing line of cabs outside the main doors, dropping off fares and waiting to pick up new customers from the morning arrivals. I had barely settled in for my vigil when a cab pulled up and out climbed none other than Mr. Silver Hair. He handed some cash to the cabbie and climbed the steps into Union Station.

Like clockwork, I soon saw a long plume of steam rise above the buildings immediately to the west of the train station, as a passenger train chugged its way across the rail bridge that spanned the Assinowa River and entered Union Station. I kept a vigil on the front steps for a few more minutes and was rewarded with the appearance of Olie Scharf, Martin Stakowski, and Mr. Silver Hair, as they descended the font steps of the station and walked over to the cab stand. Olie looked cheerful and confident, which tipped me off that I was watching Mr. Offenbach. Martin was scanning his surroundings and scowling as they arrived at the cab at the front of the line: cab 219, of the Checker Cab Company. Olie and Mr. Silver Hair climbed into the back, and Martin climbed into the front, next to the driver. A few seconds later, they were on their way.

I tailed the cab for a few minutes, as it headed north on Assinowa Avenue toward downtown. The cab took a right on Elizabeth Street and then turned north again a few blocks later. I nodded to myself as I hit the brake and made a U-turn, heading for a slightly different destination. Truth be told, tailing someone to the bitter end of their journey is a risky proposition. The three passengers in this particular cab were likely on high alert for someone like me. Once they got to their destination – wherever that was – I had no guarantee that I would not stick out like a sore thumb or maybe even get put on a wild goose chase. But I had another option.

There are about a half-dozen cab companies in New Eden, but things here don't work like they do in New York or Chicago. The cabbies here swing by the hot spots for fares when they can – the train station, the county courthouse, the downtown hotels, maybe one of the department stores – but most of the time, they check in with their dispatchers for new fares by using any one of five taxi call boxes scattered around town. The boxes are different from police or fire call boxes and are specifically for the shared use of the cab companies, who all pitched in to have them installed. They are an unassuming army green and have no markings on them whatsoever. They're locked, but all the cabbies in town have a copy of the key. A cabbie would take a fare to, say, the north side of town, and then swing by the nearest taxi call box and place a call to his company's dispatcher to get the address of his next paying customer.

I knew the layout of the city and I knew where the call boxes were. Once a cabbie crossed north of Elizabeth Street but stayed east of the river, the logical place for him to go after dropping off his fare was the "near-north" call box. That box was on the 900-block of North Packinghouse Road, a block east of the river and the Atlas Steel factory. The call box also happened to be just steps from the Port-o-Call Restaurant, which was open all hours and was popular for its breaded tenderloin special that it served up to shift workers from the rail factory and to cabbies hungry after a night in the driver's seat.

There was a line of taxi cabs ten-deep along the curb when I got there. A couple cabbies were standing in line at the call box, but most were in the Port-o-Call. I parked across the street and waited for Checker Cab number 219 to arrive. Sitting on stakeouts in my musty Ford coup had become my life. Beats heavy lifting, I guess.

The cab showed up about five minutes after I arrived. The driver climbed out of his cab and bypassed the call box, heading for the Port-o-Call. I hopped out of my coupe and made my way across the street. By the time I got to the restaurant, the cabbie had already taken up a spot at the counter and was having a coffee poured for him. As I slid onto the stool next to him, I took a sideways glance at my new friend and saw him fish a twenty dollar bill out from a fistful of twenties and push the bill across the counter to the waitress. "Keep the coffee coming," he said.

I ordered a coffee and leaned over to grab the sugar from in front of the cabbie. As I did, I juggled the container a bit and let it tip over and spill a little sugar on the cabbie's cap,which he had placed on the counter. He looked over at me, more startled than annoyed. "Sorry, brother," I offered.

"No problem," he said, returning his gaze to his cup. The guy looked tired.

"Long day in the cab?" I asked.

The cabbie turned to look my way again, but his eyes weren't exactly focused on me. "No. Couple hours is all," he said, sounding distracted.

That was interesting. He had a fistful of twenties after only a couple hours in the cab. The way I figured it, most days he would be lucky to clear twenty bucks above and beyond expenses in a twelve-hour shift. He would have to pay the Checker Cab Company about twenty bucks just for the cab rental for the day, and gas was on him, too. That fistful of twenties looked to be tip money from a big-spending fare. Big tips happen sometimes, but those twenties were clearly not bringing that man any joy.

I had planned on trying to bribe the cabbie into spilling the beans on his last fare, but it looked like cash wouldn't be the answer to what ailed him. I decided to take a different angle. "Say, buddy, you look like you've seen a ghost."

The cabbie turned to me with wide eyes and a stunned grimace on his face. "How the hell..."

"Let me guess," I said, lowering my voice to keep things a bit more private. "You just picked up a fare – three guys – at Union Station. They gave you an address, uptown. You drove them where they wanted to go, and the white-haired man paid the fare. Am I right so far?"

The cabbie responded by wagging his head slightly.

"But right about the time you were arriving at the address they gave you, Mr. Silver Hair started talking to you, and the more he talked, the more you got fuzzy in the head."

That got the cabbie nodding at me again.

"You were getting scared, too, but you just couldn't turn away. There was something about that guy... the way he talked to you and the way he looked at you. It got ahold of you and it wouldn't let go until he was good and ready to let go." I pointed to the cab driver's wallet, which was still gripped tightly in his right hand on the counter. "Then, he handed you a big wad of cash and told you to forget everything about the three men you'd just driven around and the address you were dropping them off at. Sound about right?"

The cabbie looked genuinely frightened. "Look, I was just doing my job. I'm not nosey and I'm not looking for trouble."

"Well, you just let a whole car-load of trouble take a ride in your cab."

"You a cop?" he asked.

"Worse," I replied.

"Whatever *worse* is, I don't need any of it," he said, in a hoarse whisper.

It was time to play my ace card, which I had picked up a couple days earlier. I took out my wallet and pulled a business card from the billfold. I placed it in front of the cabbie. "Rosen's Dry Cleaning," it read in bold letters across the top. Below that, in smaller print, it said, "Lou Rosen, Proprietor." I flipped the card over and showed the cabbie the brief hand-written note on the back: "Do what the man says. -Lou."

The cab driver buried his face in his hands while I returned the card to my wallet. "What do you want?" he mumbled.

"The address, for starters," I said. I pulled out my notepad and a pencil and pushed them across the counter to the cabbie. I put a twenty on top just to be a nice guy. He scribbled down an address – 1202 North Park Court, which was the cul-de-sac that ran around Pelley Square. I shook my head in wonder. "Small world," I mumbled.

"One other thing," I said. "The three men – they talk about anything in particular on the cab ride?"

The cabbie shrugged. "I didn't listen much, but the two in the back were chatting it up in some foreign lingo. Didn't make any sense to me, but they kept saying the same name enough times that it stuck in my head."

"Yeah? What name was that?"

"Hollis."

I smiled. "If you ever cross paths with that Hollis fellow, steer clear of him. He's trouble."

The cabbie shook his head. "Not him – her. They were talking about somebody named Evelyn Hollis."

CHAPTER 23

My wife, Evelyn, went missing more than three and a half years ago, along with our baby daughter, Charlotte. My wife penned a note, saying that she was sorry for leaving but she just had to go. Yes, it was her handwriting, but the way things were between us, her leaving like that just didn't add up. Sure, we'd had our tough days here and there, but we were both all-in on the marriage and in love. What we had was the real deal, and her running out on me just didn't make sense. It was flat out impossible.

I left the Chicago Police Department to dedicate my waking moments to finding them. What I found was – nothing. I went over our house like it was the scene of the Lindbergh baby kidnapping and the Lincoln assassination wrapped together, looking for any hint of foul play. I found nothing. I traveled from Portland, Maine, to Portland, Oregon, and every point in between. Nothing. I called in every favor and greased every palm. Nothing. I hired private detectives from twenty states and a dozen countries around the globe. Nothing. The only things that stopped me looking was that I ran out of places to look – and money. Let me be crystal clear, I spent over a decade in law enforcement and never had a case like this. There was no motive, no threat, no blood, no body, no trail, no nothing. That cabbie mentioned my wife and I about dropped to the floor of the Port-o-Call.

I left the restaurant in a daze and got in my car. A few minutes later, I found myself parked on the south end of North Park Court, looking north across the manicured park around which the street made a cobblestone loop. On the far end, a hulking limestone house dominated the quiet and stately cul-de-sac. Mr. Silver Hair was over there, chumming it up with Olie Scharf/Mr. Offenbach and chatting about my wife. I felt a great need to pound their heads together until answers spilled out of them, but I was also suddenly very... what's the word I'm looking for?... scared, I guess. There were too many coincidences – too many things that came across like one giant practical joke on me, planned out years in advance. Pounding heads together would have to wait until I had another chat with my boss. Maybe he could talk me down off the edge.

I made it to Arthur Lockwood's office a little before lunch. Abner Dodds was sitting at the desk of Judge Lockwood's office manager, Amelia Knobloch, and looking very out of place. He spotted me as I came through the outer door and waved me over.

"Miss Knobloch's gonna be mad at you for sitting in her chair, Abner."

Dodds responded to my teasing with a prize-winning pained grimace. "A man came by looking for you this morning," he said.

"Yeah? What'd he want?"

"I don't know, but he left something for you," Dodds said, rifling through the top drawer of the desk. He gave me a folded note. "Also, Judge Lockwood wants to talk with you."

"Good. That's why I'm here."

"I'll tell him."

While I waited, I opened the note and gave it a read.

"*Your silver-haired friend goes by the name William D. Pelley. He lives in a flashy mansion on the north end of Pelley Square. Small world, huh? One more thing: The original owner of the property also went by the name William D. Pelley – back when it was first platted in 1843. No record of a change of ownership since then. -Roy*"

I got called into Lockwood's office a couple minutes later. The judge was sitting on the edge of his mammoth desk, fiddling with an envelope in his hands. I held up the note from Roy Gittings as I came closer. "Looks like all the kids are passing notes in school today."

Judge Lockwood looked up and gave a sour smile, holding up his letter. "Yes. Yes it does."

I handed my note to the judge. "This is the guy who smashed your little statue."

"Thank you," he said, more like a man receiving a sympathy card at a funeral than a man receiving the answer to the question that he'd paid good money to get answered. Lockwood set the note aside without looking at it.

"There's something else that we need to talk about," I said to him.

"Yes," Lockwood said, sounding very distant and distracted.

"Remember that bit of my history about my wife and daughter having gone missing without a trace?" I asked. The judge nodded in acknowledgement. "Well, I've been looking for them for three and a half years without a whisper of a lead, and now I have a New Eden cabbie telling me that my wife, Eve, was a hot topic in the back of his cab this morning," I explained, watching his face as I spoke. "Say, is this conversation a little boring for you?"

Lockwood smiled weakly. "I'm sorry for being distracted, Henry. I am in fact surprised to hear that and I'm also glad for your good news."

"Good news? You've got low standards for calling something *good news*."

"Yes, well, on this day of all days, I do." With that, he handed me the envelope that I had seen in his hand when I walked in. "Give me your thoughts."

I opened the envelope and pulled out a single folded sheet of paper. As I unfolded the letter, a small card fell out. I picked up the card and saw it was an Indiana driver's license – with the name Amelia Knobloch typed across the top. I glanced up at the judge. "That's not good."

"No, it's not." His words came as a low rumble. He nodded, encouraging me to read the letter, and I obliged.

It was hand-written, with precise lettering and impressively straight lines.

"Lockwood,

We have taken your colleague, Amelia Knobloch. She is safe, for now, but time is of the essence and our patience is very short. Failure to meet our terms will result in her swift and violent death. Those terms are simple: We will release her to you in exchange for your man, Henry Hollis. We have no desire to harm him, either, but that is entirely in his hands. The exchange will happen on the Ridge Walk Trail at Pierre Marquette State Park. Mr Hollis must walk north on the trail from its southern terminus, alone. Our agents and Miss Knobloch will meet him at a point of our choosing. He must begin his walk on the trail at precisely 5 PM tonight. Any deviation or interference will result in the immediate death of Miss Knobloch."

I looked up at Arthur Lockwood's ashen face. There was an anguished battle going on behind his gray eyes. When he spoke, his voice cracked with the strain of the moment. "I have known Amelia Knobloch for more than twenty years," he said, "but I want you to know that I value your life every bit as much as I value hers. I am very aware that this situation goes well beyond your job description."

"Don't waste your breath. I'll go," I said, slumping into a padded chair in front of his desk. "I've got a few questions for them, too."

"Eleanor Stanton, returned to New York yesterday, but she will be returning to New Eden within the hour. She will no doubt be very helpful in this situation. We still have several hours to strategize..."

"You don't have to give me a pep talk, Judge. Look," I said, standing again, "I'm heading over to Irwin's Deli to get some corned beef for lunch. I'm not sure when I'll get another chance to have a decent meal. You and Eleanor are welcome to join me."

"The corned beef is on me," the judge offered.

"You're damn right."

CHAPTER 24

I didn't talk much during my lunch at Irwin's Deli. Eleanor Stanton arrived late but then she endeavored to fill in most of the silence with details on how she might be able to help. She had a few tricks up her sleeve, but mostly she was there to make me feel not quite so alone in this impossible situation.

"My bet is they won't let Knobloch go until you're trussed up like a Christmas goose," she said.

"Yeah," I mumbled.

"They'll have her waiting some distance from where they will take you into... um... custody." Her voice was muted, matter-of-fact. "I can stay about one hundred feet behind you as you walk up the trail and still have a high degree of confidence in going unseen."

"That's great," I said absently, poking a fork at a cold potato pancake. "Why would they be talking about my wife?" I added to nobody in particular.

"Not a clue," Eleanor said.

I shifted my gaze in Lockwood's direction.

"I have no earthly idea either," he said.

I wagged an angry finger at Lockwood. "You people keep talking about planet Earth like it's just *one* of the options for where a gent can hang his hat – no matter what the topic."

"Yes, I guess we do."

"You people don't know what the hell you're talking about," I said, grinding my teeth.

"I suppose you're right about that, too," Lockwood admitted.

I sent a crooked smile at him. "I need some advice I can actually use. What, *exactly*, did the Sphinx say about how I can get in touch with him?"

"He said that you could speak with him at the mezzanine at Red's, any time," Lockwood said.

"Well, I'm gonna hold him to it." I pushed back from the table and threw my napkin down.

Ten minutes later, I was standing in front of a local pool hall called Crazy 8s. In the early '20s, the place had been called Red's Pool Hall. Not much has changed with the place in about twenty-five years, except for a change in name and ownership in 1924 – that's when the original owner, James "Red" Garrity, was sent up the river for selling bootleg liquor. You can't tell from the outside, but Red's Pool Hall has a secret second story, or mezzanine, which had originally been put in as a makeshift storage loft when the property had been a furniture store back in the 1890s. The mezzanine had a brief career as a speakeasy from about 1920 until '24, when the excise cops busted the place and carted Red off to jail. I had never been up there myself, but I'd heard some pretty sordid tales about the good times to be had up at what people back then called "Red's Roost."

I walked into Crazy 8s and made a slow circuit of the wide-open space that was the main pool hall. It was the middle of the afternoon on a weekday, but the place was packed. There must have been thirty pool tables in there, a game in full swing at each one. A long bar stretched across the back of the room and was serving up beer and whiskey to the patrons at breakneck speed, which struck me as pretty ironic, considering the history of the place. God bless the 21st Amendment.

After finishing one complete go-around of the place, I figured I had my bearings. I'd heard stories about Red's Roost being accessed by way of a set of stairs tucked into a broom closet. I hadn't yet seen anything that looked like a closet, so I was hoping that there was more to the place than I had seen so far. There were a total of three ways out of the main billiard room. The first was back the way I'd come in. The second was a swinging set of doors behind the bar. The third way out was a wide archway just to the right of the bar. I headed for the archway.

Once I got there, I found myself standing in a dimly lit hallway. There was another archway about twenty feet beyond me, through which I could make out a smaller billiard room with three or four tables being put to use by a slightly higher-class clientele. Besides the archway, there were three other doors: one marked Gents, one marked Ladies, and one very humble-looking closet door. I walked casually toward the door marked Gents and then veered off course and tried the doorknob on the closet, which creaked open after I gave it a sharp tug. A second later, I was inside, groping for a light switch, which I found after a few tries.

Sure enough, I was surrounded by brooms, mops, buckets, stacks of toilet paper, and the like. At the back of the closet was what at first looked to be shelving, but after a little investigating, it became clear that there was in fact a very, very steep and age-worn set of stairs running up from the back of the closet. I pushed a few mops and buckets to the side and started to tentatively mount the stairs, ducking under a naked lightbulb that hug on a long chord. When I got close to the ceiling, I could make out a trap-door above me. I put my shoulder into it, and it gave way in a rush of billowing dust. The trap-door swung just past vertical then came to a stop, safely leaning against something behind me on the mezzanine. I coughed and wiped my eyes as I climbed the last couple of stairs.

That's when the smell hit me. Sure, there was the stale, musty air of a long-abandoned space, but there was another odor, too, unique and powerful. It hit me like smelling salts, but the scent was almost sweet. My eyes popped open and my lungs drew in a breath, like a silent gasp that I couldn't stop. My heart started beating a mile a minute, and I felt a peculiar sense of excited anticipation. The dark space smelled like... like... a world of trouble and temptation and danger and tantalizing mystery, all floating in a pool of rosewater.

I got my breathing under control and stepped fully onto the floor, peering around. There were no sources of light up there other than the dim lightbulb in the closet below. That light was just enough to give me the general gist of my surroundings. It was obvious that I was standing in the ruined remains of a speakeasy. The excise officers had clearly gone to work on the place with sledgehammers, leaving behind a rum-soaked tomb strewn with broken bottles and shattered tables. What struck me next was how low the ceiling was. It might have been a couple inches past six feet, max. After I planted both feet on the floor, I got a sense of just how makeshift this place was. The floor groaned under my weight, and I could feel the slope of the floor change as I walked. The place was a goddamn death trap. What some people will do for a stiff drink...

I tiptoed to the remains of the bar. "Hello?" I called out in a husky whisper. I leaned over the battered bar. "Hello?" Nobody was there, which didn't surprise me. I did a slow turn, squinting into the dark and cluttered corners. Nothing about this made sense. No one had been up here in years – maybe even a decade. There was no way some guy was standing around up here waiting for me to drop by and chat.

Imagine my surprise when, after about thirty seconds, I heard a cough and then a tentative voice calling out from somewhere in front of me. "Hello? Yes?"

There were a couple of tables tipped over about ten feet from the bar. I walked gingerly across the undulating floor and peaked behind each, but didn't find anyone. "It's Hollis – Henry Hollis," I called out, squinting once again into the darkness.

"It sounds like you've found Red's Roost, then," the voice said, now sounding somewhat louder, and distinctly closer.

"*Sounds like*? Where the hell are you?"

"I'm at home, actually. I'm speaking to you via a two-way wireless system, of sorts."

"So, you set up one end of a wireless system in your living room and then you picked this tumble-down hell-hole as the spot to put the other end of it?"

"Very sorry about that. I didn't have any other options at the time," the monotone voice said. "I hope to find a better option soon."

As he spoke, I carefully picked my way through the debris, zeroing in on the source of the voice. As best I could tell, it was coming from a point about three feet off the ground, just to the left of one of the upturned tables. I lifted up a mostly-intact chair and took a seat. "Your voice is coming out of thin air – no speaker in sight."

"When I said wireless, I very much meant it."

"Great. Everybody's got a shiny toy to show off around here. Do you know what I've gone through this past week?"

"Some of it. My... I am only one man and I have very limited resources in your area. I'll try to help in any way I can."

"Why?" I asked. "Why help?"

"Well, it's become clear to me that our goals very much overlap."

"We overlap?" I parroted back to the disembodied voice. "What happens if we stop overlapping?"

"I sympathize with you, Mr. Hollis. You've taken quite a few of leaps-of-faith recently and the rewards for such faith might seem... elusive... right now. I know it's not easy to have faith when you don't have all the information that you rightly feel you need and when your opponents seem to have the upper hand at every turn. There's a reason you're in the middle of all this, Henry – more than just getting a paycheck from the Wildflower Society. Please know that you have a critical role to play. You're not a foot soldier, you're a spark in the darkness."

I had no idea what he was talking about – still don't. "Enough with the preaching. What do you know about my wife?"

"Your wife? Absolutely nothing, but..."

"But what?"

"We're not the only players in this game. I've seen evidence of more allies in your area, and some of them seem to have a keen interest in you as well, but I simply don't know what they know. It's very possible that they have some information that will shed light on the fate of your wife."

"Fine. When I get a chance, I'll pound everybody's heads together and see what falls out, but right now, I've got another problem."

"Yes?"

I told the Sphinx about Mr. Silver Hair, aka William Pelley, his stooges, the Angry Fur Coat hellbeast, and the kidnapping of Miss Knobloch. I also told him about the kid who had climbed onto my roof and was keeping tabs on me. That really got his attention.

"The boy is not what he seems," he said.

"I figured. What is he then?"

"This is the first I've heard of him, but from what you've described, he is a very special person – and much more brave than me."

"So, he's one of these allies you were talking about?"

"Yes, he would seem to be an ally – at least as far as keeping you alive is concerned."

"I'll keep that in mind if I live to see tomorrow." It was time to get the conversation back on track. "I'm here for advice about tonight. You got any?"

There was a long pause, during which I assumed that the Sphinx was pondering my options while adjusting the pillows on his sofa. "Two things come to mind," he finally said.

"Glad to hear it."

"First, do not allow Mr. Pelley to catch your gaze with his eyes. I know what he is and what he is trying to do to you."

"So, what the hell is he and what the hell is he trying to do then?"

"He's in many ways like the boy you encountered. And I would guess, from what you've told me, that they are from the same place – but from different factions. They are both what I would describe as emissaries, or ambassadors, if you will. They have both sacrificed a great deal to be here, but I suspect that their goals – and the goals of their respective factions – are rather different."

"Are you an ambassador from yet another faction in their little turf war?"

"No, I can't claim to be an ambassador – more a lone-wolf, really – and I'm from an entirely different... patch of turf. It's true that there is a turf war going on, as you put it, but it's very much bigger than just those two or their factions. And there is a war breaking out, bigger and more terrible than any before. The first battles of that war are now being fought in many places around your... around the world, and I confess that I am one of the combatants. New Eden is unlucky enough to be another battlefield in that war."

"I get it. I get it. So, what's Mr. Silver Hair trying to do when he gets into staring contests with people?"

"If Mr. Pelley captures your gaze long enough, he can enslave you – worse, really. He can turn you into an enslaved vessel for his compatriots to control and exploit."

"Like Olie Scharf."

"Yes, like Olie Scharf."

I nudged a broken bottle with my shoe, sending it rolling a couple of feet through the heavy carpet of dust on the floor. "I gotta ask – where are you right now?"

"As I said, in my home."

"Where, exactly? New York? Paris?"

There was a pause, then he said warily, "A bit farther."

"Stop being so goddamn coy with me. Everybody around me is playing cute word-games and I'm sick of it," I said, raising my voice. "Tell me the truth, are you *and* your couch *and* your whole damn house sitting on the same planet as my couch and my house?"

Again, a pause. Finally – "No."

"You're a goddamn space alien."

"I confess it's true," he said awkwardly. "Does that fact change our circumstances?"

His answer threw me, but then, so did his question. I bunched up my fists and planted them on my knees, rocking a little in the chair. As best I could tell, the world hadn't suddenly changed, for better or worse. "No. No, I suppose it doesn't." Then I let out the mother of all sighs. "So, what's the second bit of advice for tonight?"

"The beast that you described. You said he sat in wait for you and then he followed you to your home."

"Yeah."

"My hunch is that he's another victim in this drama and that he is under the control of someone else – a compatriot of Mr. Pelley."

"Yeah? And?"

"And, it means that if you can isolate him from Pelley and his people, and then if you can render him unconscious, he will likely awaken free of his enslavement."

"Knock him out and he'll become my new pal?"

"Well, at least he would no longer see you as his primary focus of aggression."

"Great. I'll see what I can do. Any other advice?"

"Yes. Try to think of Mr. Pelley and his associates as figures from Greek mythology."

"Yeah? And how does that help me?" I asked.

"They are powerful, but flawed, and they often plant the seeds of their own destruction."

CHAPTER 25

I pulled my Ford coupe into a small gravel parking lot and tossed a map of Pierre Marquette State Park onto the passenger seat. My hope was that anybody watching from the shadows would think I arrived alone – which was mostly true. The wristwatch I had wedged into a crack in the dashboard showed it was 4:50 PM. I got out and went around to the back of the car and tucked the key inside the fender, for someone in Lockwood's office to grab later, hopefully. I was unarmed and dressed for a hike in the woods. It just so happened that the day had been warm for spring and it looked to be a good evening for a walk in the woods.

I did a slow survey of my surroundings and saw no sign of Eleanor Stanton, but I held onto the cold comfort that she was out there, somewhere nearby, as she swore that she would be. Just to the north of where I had parked was a trail-head. I made my way over there and began my hike, feeling like a condemned man taking the final walk to the gallows. The first few minutes were the worst on my nerves, seeing as I was waiting to be abducted; then the drama of the situation slowly receded into the background of my thoughts and I simply fell into the rhythm of walking.

I'm generally a city guy, so I'm always surprised by how much noise forests can make. You've got woodpeckers and frogs, crickets and cicadas, trees and wind, all adding to the mix. There's a rhythm to the sounds of nature, much like there's a rhythm to the noise of the city. I got more used to the sounds as I walked. The trail led across a series of low, wooded crests and into shaded valleys, filled with silver maple, the occasional sycamore, and close to the trail there were small clusters of redbuds.

I actually started enjoying my walk and a solid half hour passed before the forest suddenly went quiet. Then, I heard other noises. I looked to my left – west – and squinted at the dense, shadowy undergrowth. A low, distant thumping sound was soon joined by the rustling of tree limbs and then finally the grunting and panting of an animal on the move. After a couple more seconds, I saw the brown, fringe-covered beast that I'd gotten to know up close and personal in my apartment now bursting free from the undergrowth about fifteen yards away. The trail at that point was tight up against a long thicket of thorny bushes on my right. I could run up or down the path, but not away from the freight train of fur coming at me from the woods. I stared desperately around me but soon just gave up and covered my face and got into a crouch.

The Brown Beast hit me like a sledge hammer wrapped in a musty mink stole. I was plucked off my feet and tucked under an enormous arm in less than a heartbeat. The panting creature reversed course and barreled back into the forest, holding me more or less like a football. Branches and bushes raked across my head and shoulders as he pounded his way through the dense growth of trees. He was moving at almost a sprint and kept it up for a solid ten minutes. I was beginning to doubt that all my internal organs would survive the trip. There was also little hope that Eleanor had been able to keep up – not at that pace. Now I know how Fay Wray must have felt on her first date with her new boyfriend, Kong.

When we finally came to a stop, I was thrown unceremoniously onto the ground in a sun-dappled clearing, where I stayed for a couple minutes, trying to breathe and taking stock of my various injuries. There were four men standing around me, all sporting guns and smiles.

"Welcome, Mr. Hollis," William Pelley said, standing over me as I coughed up a lung.

"You're an ass," I said between groans.

Then it was Wilmer's turn to give me a warm hello. "Get up on your feet, funny man," he said, just before he landed a kick to my ribs.

I rolled onto my back and wrapped my arms around my midsection. I wanted to give Wilmer a smart comeback, but that would have to wait. "Shit," was all I could muster.

Mr. Silver Hair nodded to Martin Stakowski, who walked around behind me and hooked his hands under my armpits. Martin hauled me onto my feet and grabbed my wrists. I didn't fight him. It was Olie Scharf who had the honor of tying the rope around my wrists.

I looked Olie in the eyes as he pulled the rope tight. "I gotta say, Olie, I'm thinking of taking my shoe repair needs to one of your competitors."

"That's very funny, Mr. Hollis," Olie said. "Wilmer, here, mentioned you had a sense of humor. He can't wait to show you how much he appreciates your wit." He handed the long end of the rope to Martin. "Take him to the truck."

Martin gave a sharp tug on the rope that nearly put me on my face, but a kick to my backside from Wilmer straightened me up pretty quick. Just beyond the forest clearing was what looked to be a logging road. A farm produce truck was parked there on the dirt road, with high wood-plank walls and a tarp pulled over the top. Wilmer pulled the wooden tailgate of the truck up on its pegs and set it aside while Martin gave me the bum's rush into the back. I landed in a pile of corn husks, where it was dim and dusty under the tarp.

After some hushed discussion, Wilmer climbed up into the back of the truck and sat down next to me, his knee pressing into my ribs. "Stay down," he snarled. Wilmer pulled a red, checkered bandana from his back pocket and leaned in close, over my face. "The gents said you can't see where we're going. I said to them that they should let me punch the hell out of you until everything goes black, but they don't want me to break anything on you just yet." He pushed the bandana over my eyes and began working at tying a knot at the back of my head. "So, you get a blindfold."

I bounced around in the back of that truck for maybe fifteen minutes, with Wilmer and Martin taking turns holding me down and generally treating me like an unloved sack of potatoes. When the ride finally came to a merciful stop, I was hauled up on my feet and then dropped to the ground from the back of the truck. Someone – probably Wilmer – tugged the rope binding my wrists hard enough to send me face-first into the dirt. A second savage tug on the rope got me up and moving.

"Easy boys. Don't break the merchandise," I said, staggering along behind them.

About a minute later, a downward yank on the rope put me on my backside on the bare dirt. I could tell through the bandana that the light had changed; it seemed darker. "Sit tight," I heard Martin Stakowski say. Soon after that, I heard the sound of large, uncooperative doors closing, and then a hand pulled the bandana loose. I squinted at my surroundings. It was a barn, complete with honest-to-god live farm animals, and I was next to a horse stall, sitting in the main open space surrounded by other stalls and pens. I looked down at my wrists, which were already starting to bleed a bit, then watched as Martin tied the other end of the rope to a post at one corner of a horse stall – the horse didn't seem to mind. Across the way, I noticed Amelia Knobloch sitting on a pile of straw and looking none-too-pleased. Pelley and Scharf entered the barn from a door somewhere behind me.

"Time to send Miss Knobloch home," I said as the four men congregated in front of me.

"Tut, tut, Mr. Hollis," Pelley said. "We enjoy her company far too much to send her back to her dull desk job just yet. I think she likes being here, back on the farm." That got a round of laughs from the boys.

"I've met the lady," I said. "She's not that fun – farm or no farm." I felt I had to take a shot at getting them to set her loose, not that it was going to do any good. "And besides, you've got me to entertain you now. Just stick to your deal and everybody will be happy."

"Deals change. Times change. Who knows what the future will bring for you and Miss Knobloch?" Pelley said. Then he turned to Olie Scharf and spoke to him in some kind of man-from-another-world lingo. Whatever he said, it got Olie/Offenbach heading for the exit with his marching orders.

I sat and watched while Pelley gave surprisingly mundane instructions to Martin and Wilmer, about feeding horses and tending to pigs.

"You give the regular help the day off?" I said, trying to be funny.

"Yes, actually, I did," he said, sounding very matter-of-fact. "I didn't want to be distracted from giving my full attention to my special guests."

"I'm honored."

Olie Scharf came back a few minutes later, carrying what looked to be a tiny aluminum suitcase. He was followed in by the furry, fringed beast, now walking amiably – very un-beast-like – at Olie's side. The Brown Beast and Olie strolled over to William Pelley and chatted briefly in hushed tones, while Olie set the box on top of a wooden barrel and opened it. The two men and the beast stared at the box's contents for a few seconds, then Pelley gave Olie a nod. Out of the little suitcase, Olie lifted what was clearly a syringe. He and the beast turned toward me and walked over. Olie's syringe had my full attention. As best I could tell, the syringe was empty, which got me thinking that they were about to take some of my blood.

Olie said something to the Brown Beast that I didn't understand, but I assumed went something along the lines of, *hold the bastard down and don't let him move a muscle*, because that's what happened next.

"If you want to know my blood type, you can just ask," I offered, as the beast loomed over me.

"We're not interested in your blood type," Olie said, distractedly staring at the syringe.

It was just about then that the Brown Beast smothered me with his arms. I had more chance of breaking a half-dozen of my own bones than breaking free of his grip. He made the strong man at the circus look like a swaddled infant. I was his play-thing for as long as he deemed fit to throttled me. In light of that fact, I barely noticed the needle going into my arm. A few seconds later it was all over, and Olie and the beast stood up and retreated back to where their silver-haired friend waited. Olie returned the syringe to the aluminum suitcase and closed it up. The three aliens from another planet had another quick chat and then Olie and the Brown Beast departed.

"That didn't hurt very much, now did it?" Pelley asked, rising from his perch on a hay bale.

"Your nurse doesn't have much of a bed-side manner."

"I'm trying not to get my hopes up, but with a bit of luck, that little blood draw will be all I need from you," he said, walking slowly over to the smaller barn door. "And then we can all go home."

"Is that it? You take my blood and we call it a night?" I asked.

"Oh, I've been waiting a very long time for this night – much longer than you would believe. If I find what I'm looking for, I'll soon be celebrating a very long-delayed homecoming, and I will have you to thank. But, for the next few hours, I suggest you get some rest. I'll be sure to wake you when I have the results." And with that, Mr. Silver Hair made his exit, leaving Martin behind as watchdog.

I settled in on my pile of hay and started up a conversation with Amelia Knobloch, who was sitting tied up about ten feet away. I've got to admit, she surprised me with her strength of character.

"I'm sorry about all this," I said.

"Sorry for what, young man?" she said, in a tone

that was equal parts condescending and calming – a neat trick that I doubt many others could pull off. "I made my choices and I will live and die by them." The lady had guts. She gave me a steely-eyed gaze. "Mr. Hollis, I have no intention of giving an inch of ground to these animals, and I fully expect you to show what stuff you are made of, as well." She was certainly no damsel in distress.

We kept the chitchat going for a while longer. Martin Stakowski tried to shut us up a few times, but Amelia made mince-meat of his half-hearted attempts with her pitch-fork of a tongue and her long-practiced school-marm demeanor. He couldn't quite bring himself to lay a hand on her, so Amelia won that battle. I worried that when it came Wilmer's turn to babysit us, things would go differently.

Eventually, close to midnight, the talking stopped and the silence slowly gave way to fitful sleep. That didn't last long. I don't think I've ever been more disoriented in my entire life than when Martin Stakowski woke me later that night. He poked at me a few times with the end of a rake and then yelled my name. I blinked and looked up into the dim light of two lonely bulbs hanging high in the barn's rafters. William Pelley loomed in the shadows nearby, and he didn't look happy. Olie and the Brown Beast stood on either side of him.

"I was right about one thing, Mr. Hollis," Pelley said dryly. "We've met before."

"My blood told you that?"

"Yes, but I am disappointed to say that the *other* test on your blood came back negative." He frowned and said, wistfully, "I can't say I'm too surprised."

"Sorry to disappoint you. What's next?"

"Plan B," he said.

I sat up and rubbed my face. "And if plan B doesn't work, you have a plan C?"

"Yes, but I very much doubt that you'll like it."

"Let's give plan B a shot then," I said, trying to sound helpful.

Pelley and his entourage walked over to me, and Mr. Silver Hair took a seat on a large, upturned bucket. He stared down at me with the eyes of a predator, ready to pounce on its prey. I made a point of avoiding his gaze. "Where are your wife and daughter, Mr. Hollis?" he asked.

"Is this your plan B?" I said, somewhere between angry and stunned.

"Answer the question and we can both go home."

"I've spent most of the last four years looking for them," I explained, my voice close to rage. "I didn't find a damn thing. Not one clue."

"I'm more disappointed to hear that than you might imagine," he said, offering up his own version of suppressed rage.

"If plan C is beating the hell out of me, it won't help."

Pelley shook off his angry face and stood up, trying to smile. "I don't doubt your bravery, Mr. Hollis, but plan C has a rather different flavor to it. You see, it just so happens that I have a unique resource available to me, one that will render your tough-man act an utterly needless bit of theater." He turned to Martin. "Go fetch Wilmer and his little friend."

I half-expected to see Wilmer come in with a pit bull on a chain, but what he dragged in made me gasp. Turned out I was wrong about the Brown Beast. That smelly bastard was not the main attraction in my worst nightmares. The little thing that came stumbling in on the end of a chain, however, was.

Wilmer came in first, followed by the chain. He gave it a yank and into the barn skittered a thing that would have given Dracula the cold sweats in his coffin. It was equal parts vampire bat and... well... did you ever see that German silent flick, *Nosferatu*? Yeah, kind of like that guy, but this little charmer was naked and a lot shorter, sporting greenish-gray skin and bat wings. I barely noticed when the Brown Beast came shuffling in after Wilmer and the hellish man-bat creature.

Amelia Knobloch – who took the furry, fringed beast in stride – let out a shriek.

"Christ on a bike," I wheezed. "What the hell is that?"

"He's a distant relative of mine, actually, from the homeland," Pelley said. "His kind is from a different branch of our evolutionary tree, mind you. Not as tall or handsome as my kind, but they have their uses. Back where I'm from, these little fellows are kept as household slaves."

Without giving too much away, I can confirm that

the Hell Bat did indeed look to be male. He also seemed to be very put off by being paraded around naked. He bared his long, gray fangs and hissed savagely as Wilmer yanked him into the center of the barn. But for me, the icing on that cake-of-terror was the death-stare he gave Pelley. If that damned thing – and I do mean damned – ever looked at me the way he looked at Pelley, my heart would seize up and jump clean out of my chest. The only two things keeping me from letting out a sustained scream were the chains on his tiny wrists and his almost comical stature. The thing was on the downhill side of four feet, if you don't count his bat-ears that stuck up nearly another foot.

Pelley took the chain leash from Wilmer and pulled Hell Bat in for an up-close and personal chat – in alien speak. Hell Bat hissed and shrieked his responses, but Pelley was unmoved by the show. I got the feeling that this was old territory for the two of them. Finally, Hell Bat clearly gave in, performing a bat-winged shrug and then the most terrifying-yet-amusing eye-roll that I have ever seen. William Pelley turned his attention to me.

"I would like to introduce you to Plan C, Mr. Hollis," he said, motioning for Martin Stakowski to head my way. "Martin, please restrain our guest."

Martin came over and took hold of the rope. "Restrain him how?"

Pelley sighed, slightly exasperated. "Just... just keep his head facing our little friend – and make sure his eyes stay open."

That was my cue to squeeze my eyes shut, tight. I soon heard Pelley sigh again. "Martin, please take that rake over there and beat Mr. Hollis with it until we have his full attention."

The first couple of blows to my back were tentative and easy enough to take. But there was soon a brief commotion behind me. "Gimme that damn rake," I heard Wilmer shout. That was bad news.

The next couple of blows were sharp jabs to the kidneys from behind. That got me doubled over and gasping in pain. A third blow to my ribs was quickly followed by a jab to the back of my head, at which point I rolled onto my back, waving my bound hands in front of my face. "Stop, dammit! Stop!" I yelled.

"Are we going to have any more problems, Mr. Hollis?" Pelley asked.

"No," I mumbled. "Dammit."

Martin lifted me back up into more or less a sitting position and turned me to face Hell Bat. The little beast stood about ten feet from me, with his thin, chained arms dangling in front of him in forlorn resignation.

"Don't worry, Mr. Hollis. This won't hurt a bit," Pelley said. "Head up, now, Mr. Hollis. That's a good fellow."

The Hell Bat came closer as I lifted my gaze and waited for the end of life as I had known it. I could've taken the beating for another few minutes, but I knew that Wilmer would have eventually done some permanent damage, and I would be back in the same place, just with more blood-loss and fewer teeth. I wondered in that brief moment if I would ever be allowed to reclaim my own body or if I would forever be an unconscious passenger along for the ride. Hell Bat's all-black eyes narrowed, and the greenish-gray skin on his forehead became wrinkled. The slits that made up most of his dramatically upturned nose widened briefly as he took in a deep breath. Finally, he clenched his jaw, leaving two fangs protruding downward from his long, thin-lipped mouth. Then it hit me – I could feel the little winged nightmare reaching inside my head, rooting around. I can't say it hurt, exactly, but there was an anger and a viciousness to it that made me gasp. It was kind of like your dentist telling you to open your mouth and then watching as he reached for a crowbar. Hell Bat yanked and pulled and pried into every corner of my thoughts and memories. Somewhere in the middle of having my brain ransacked, I suddenly remembered – this had happened to me once before. That short, dark figure standing in the shadows with the big hat had done the same thing to me, a few nights before. That experience had been far less traumatic, but the technique was basically the same. From there, my mind made a small leap to the boy who had climbed onto my roof, and how he had been sporting that same big hat when I spied him on that dirt street up on Dalton's Bluff. I almost smiled, even as the last bits of my memories were tossed around like books torn from a shelf. In that moment, the pieces of the puzzle snapped together. That dark-haired little boy was none other than the Oracle of Dalton's Bluff, and somehow, in some way, he was also from the same damn planet as the four-foot tall vampire bat now scouring my memories. It seemed a shame that I would only know that for a few seconds more.

But I was wrong. Hell Bat let out a pained gasp after what seemed like an hour, but in reality was somewhere short of a minute. I saw him stagger a bit, even as I slumped to the floor. Martin let me drop. From my prone position, I watched as William Pelley interrogated the wheezing gargoyle. The upshot of the conversation was clearly not to Mr. Silver Hair's liking. Hell Bat defended his efforts with snarled alien words, fang-baring hisses, and some bile-filled spitting. He was rewarded with a vicious smack across the face that sent him back the better part of ten feet and down on his naked bat-ass in a pile of feed hay. It looked like I got the better part of the bargain, as my brains seemed to still be more or less intact. Now all I needed to do was avoid Pelley's zombie-making gaze.

"So, you believe me now?" I asked with my face in the dust.

"Yes," Pelley said, straining to regain his composure. "I must admit that I'm deeply disappointed, but..." He paused to take in a deep breath and slowly let it out. "At least I know where *not* to look for answers. And that brings me a step closer to finding your wife."

"You've got a beef with me, not with her," I said. "She doesn't know a damn thing."

"That's where you're wrong, Mr. Hollis. It turns out that you are, in fact, the one who doesn't know a damn thing. It's clear now that your wife is the only one who has the information I need – the information that will help me get home."

"That's not possible."

"I would have said the same, a few months ago. But new evidence suggests otherwise. Your wife is not who she seems, Mr. Hollis. In fact, she just might be the most important person in the world – in many worlds, really."

"You're talking about my wife?"

"Yes, Mr. Hollis, I'm talking about your wife. I will find her, mind you, sooner or later. In the meantime, I'll just have to be satisfied with taking out my frustrations on you." His words were interrupted as he was struck by a mighty yawn. "That is, after a few hours of sleep." Pelley looked over at Wilmer. "Take that thing back to the house," he said, waving in the direction of the crumpled figure of Hell Bat.

Wilmer was soon followed out of the barn by William Pelley and Olie Scharf, which left me in the charming company of Martin Stakowski and the shaggy beast.

A long moment of brooding silence fell on the barn. The Brown Beast began to pace the dirt floor of the barn, seeming restless. Then, we all watched as it loped casually over to an empty horse stall and picked up four sets of chains that looked like they should be hoisting a ship's anchor. The big beast calmly slapped the leg-irons on himself and then waited patiently as Martin locked the wrist manacles. Martin hung the keys up on a nail some twenty feet from the horse stall. After that, the beast made a bed out of straw and simply curled up to go to sleep.

Several more minutes passed in silence, until the snoring began. I saw that as an opening I needed to take advantage of. "Martin, he's going to kill us in the morning, you know," I said to our jailor, trying to gauge how deep in he was with all this. I looked over at Amelia Knobloch to see how this was all playing out for her. She was clearly surprised by what I'd just said, but the icy glare she soon sent his way left no doubt how things would play out for Martin on his own judgement day at the Pearly Gates.

Martin turned his gaze away. "That's none of my business," he said, shuffling his feet.

"He's a goddamn alien, Martin. He keeps gargoyles for pets and he makes slaves out of shoe repairmen."

"Shut up," Martin shouted, without much conviction.

I nervously glanced over at the slumbering beast. The snores continued. "You think this is going to end well for you?" I said in as loud a stage-whisper as I could muster. "I'm telling you, it won't. The good news is, you can stop this madness right now. All you have to do is untie this rope and..."

My sales pitch was interrupted by the sound of the barn's side door swinging violently open. Wilmer marched through and gazed menacingly at us all, then pointed a finger at me. "Shut your trap, funny man." He grabbed a wooden bucket from the floor and chucked it at Martin. "Hey, idiot, you're done chumming it up with these two. The boss says for you to go up to the house and get a few hours sleep."

Martin stood stark still for a brief moment, staring wide-eyed at Wilmer, then hung his head and made his way to the side door, closing it behind him. The beast in the stall grunted a few times but soon returned to snoring.

Wilmer strolled past a horse stall and grabbed up a particularly nasty looking three-pronged hay fork that had been leaning against the stall door. He continued walking slowly toward me, making stabbing motions in my direction. "Boss says I get to make you bleed when he comes back down," he said, putting the words into rhythm with his stabs, like hitman poetry. When he was close enough, he started making short jabs at my face, coming up just shy by an inch or two each time. I got a good look at the flakes of rust on the two-foot long tines. Wilmer cracked a smile that was a portrait of cruel and murderous urges. The guy was born to kill.

I figured it was time to take some big risks. I wanted to get him in close to me, where I could maybe loop the ropes that bound my wrists around his scrawny neck. "Yeah, I'm pretty funny, but you're a damn joke," I said, sweating bullets. "I remember kids like you on the school playground. You shake your little fists and throw your baby tantrums, but it doesn't impress anybody. You can act as tough as you want, but everybody knows you're a coward inside."

I've never seen a man get so red in the face. He looked like a ripe, red apple, but with teeth and bulging eyes. For better or worse, my plan was working. He was set to pounce and I started praying to heaven above that I could survive the first stab with that hay fork and then maybe, just maybe, get my hands around his throat. But that's not how things worked out.

Right in the middle of his back swing with the hay fork, Wilmer's whole body suddenly made a ninety degree turn, sideways and into the air. Turns out that Amelia Knobloch had spent the previous few hours slowly working on the knot in the rope binding her dainty wrists. Long nails and patience are powerful weapons. She could see that Wilmer was about to go in for the kill, and, while I was staring up at those deadly, rusty tines, she jumped into action. There was a pile of rough-cut lumber a few feet from where they had trussed her up and she had apparently grabbed onto a long timber on top and put all of her weight and strength into swinging it like a baseball bat. The timber never made it more than a few inches off the floor as it arced through the dirt, but that was enough to take Wilmer's feet out from under him. He hit the dirt floor hard and wound up flat on his back. Miss Knobloch pounced like a cat with its fur on fire. Her target was Wilmer's right hand, which had a loose grip on the hay fork. She put her bony knee into his wrist, grabbed the handle of the hay fork, and sent it skittering my way through the dirt and hay. Wilmer let out a wild scream.

I was just as surprised as Wilmer, but I had enough of my wits about me to grab the wooden handle of the hay fork between my two bound hands and heaving myself to my feet. Wilmer rolled away from me onto his side by then and got a foot under him, but it looked like he was just within range. I launched my full body at him and swung the hay fork out ahead of me. The three metal tines hit the side of his chest and plunged in about an inch deep, strait through that greasy brown leather jacket. Not a killing blow, but he was a stuck pig. I pulled down on the handle and that forced him to roll onto his back. His screams told me that we only had a few seconds to get ourselves free.

I looked over at Miss Knobloch. "My wrists!" I shouted desperately.

She raced to my side, even as I pushed the tines a bit deeper into Wilmer's side. While she worked on getting my hands free, I gave Wilmer a warning. "Don't move, little man. I can end you right now if I have to."

Wilmer shot me a look that was everything I had hoped for. It was two slices of fear wrapped around a big, juicy serving of anguished pain. I smiled, taking a little too much joy from watching him eat that sandwich. A few seconds later, the rope fell from my wrists, and I dove on Wilmer. The hay fork was still dug deep into his side and my weight on his chest probably didn't make life any easier for him, but it couldn't be helped. I called for Miss Knoblock to bring some rope and returned my attention to Wilmer.

"Put your hands out above your head," I instructed. He wheezed and tried to talk, but I got his attention back when I brought my knee up and gave the hay fork a bit of a shove. His leather jacket was getting slick with blood. Soon enough, his now-shaking hands were fluttering above his head. Miss Knobloch returned with rope and I got Wilmer on his side. Miss Knoblock had the honor of binding his wrists behind his back. Once that was done, I dragged him to the same beam that I had been tied to, secured him to it, and finally pulled the hay fork from his chest.

That's when the howling began. I looked over at the horse stall where the Angry Fur Coat had been sleeping and saw him standing up and wagging his head back and forth, howling plaintively. He shook his chains and seemed to be a completely different creature from the one that had bedded down a few minutes earlier. That got me thinking. Could Wilmer turn him back into the raging beast that tried to kill me in my bed? I couldn't chance it, so I pulled a kerchief from my back pocket and turned to Wilmer with the hay fork still in my other hand.

"Open your damn mouth," I said to him. Wilmer complied when I rested the tines on his stomach. I handed the kerchief to Miss Knobloch who gave me a questioning look. "Trust me on this."

Once we had Wilmer properly bound and gagged, we made for the exit. It was maybe four in the morning by then and we found ourselves in the dark on a gravel driveway, with a classic American farmhouse looming in the moonlight across from us. I turned to Miss Knobloch and pointed down the driveway, into the darkness. "Run like hell, that way," I said. She nodded and lit out of there, into the darkest hour of the night.

I should have left, too, but my blood was up and I needed to do something more than take a jog on a gravel road to make me feel better about things. I hoisted the hay fork off of my shoulder and swung it into a ready position in front of me, testing the weight of my new weapon of choice. The house was dark except for one porch light next to the front door. I made my way up the front steps and took brief peek in a window. All quiet, for now. I stepped back to the front door and tried the knob. Locked. But on either side of the door were narrow glass panels adorned with flowered curtains. I looked at the wooden handle of the hay fork and smiled. Maybe this wasn't the smartest move, but I was feeling the need to break something, anyway. The butt of the handle worked like a charm on the window. I ran the wood handle up and down to clear the glass shards, then reached in and fumbled with the lock. A few seconds later, I was in the house.

I could already hear movement, upstairs. The rooms to my left and right were shrouded in darkness, but I made a bet that they were empty. Ahead of me was a hallway, back to the kitchen – as best as I could tell – and also a stairway in front of me, heading up to the second floor. I didn't want to be caught downhill from whoever was on the move upstairs, so I made a dash up the stairway. I hit the first landing and made the turn, only to see a dark figure at the top of the stairs. A moment later, the warm, incandescent glow from the light above the stairs flooded the scene. I briefly shaded my eyes then squinted up to see that it was William Pelley, in a robe and slippers.

Pelley calmly raised a revolver and pointed it at me. "Is that a pitch-fork, Mr. Hollis?" he said, almost casually. "It looks quite dangerous." He made a halfhearted attempt at taming his ruffled white hair as he stared down impassively at me. "Is Wilmer alright?" he asked.

I shook my head.

"Shame. Bit of a loose cannon, but it's nice to have a cannon, sometimes," he said. "And Miss Knobloch?"

"Gone," I said, lowering the pitch-fork

"That's bad news – for both of us. Well, at least you'll die quickly now." He looked over his shoulder. "Martin!"

I heard footsteps in the hallway. Martin Stakowski stepped into view a few seconds later. He had clearly just pulled his pants on and was still working an arm into a shirt. The other arm was noteworthy for the .38 revolver it was sporting.

"Take Mr. Hollis outside and put a bullet in his head," Pelley said, a bit too casually for my liking. "Come to think of it, walk him into the woods a few hundred feet and do it, then fetch a shovel and bury him."

Martin's bleary eyes cleared up real quick when he

heard the order from his boss. I had no illusions about Martin being a Boy Scout, but I had a hunch that "killer" was not yet on his résumé. He wavered and swayed slightly as he looked at me and then back at Pelley. "Yeah?" he said, struggling to grasp what was happening.

Pelley let out a frustrated sigh. "Just get him outside and I'll take care of the rest." With that, Martin's feet unstuck from the floor. He began heading down the stairs, toward me. Martin stopped a few feet from me, gun firmly between both hands. "Drop the pitch-fork," he ordered.

I complied, slowly lowering it to the floor.

"Turn around," he barked. "Get moving."

Martin was a head higher but he seemed to have shrunk a bit in the last hour or so. He was also shaking like a leaf. This was all clearly more than he'd bargained for.

Martin waved the gun at the stairs. "Down."

I took the stairs nice and slow, walking sideways as best I could, keeping constant eye contact with Martin. Pelley and the Tin Man followed. I got to the bottom of the stairs and slowly walked the ten feet or so to the front door.

Years ago, a rum runner that I had busted gave me a bit of advice about unarmed fighting in confined spaces. "Run away from a knife and toward a gun," he said. "Why?" I asked. He responded, "Shooting a moving target is harder than most people think, and guns get obsolete pretty quick when two guys are slugging it out."

"Open the door," Martin said, which was my cue to turn and run straight at him with my hands reaching out for his face.

Martin never even got off a shot. I was on him in less than a second. He tipped back onto the stairs and then rolled with me onto the floor, part-way into what might have been the living room. Our fists were flying in a desperate fight to what I assumed would be the death. I heard footsteps coming down the stairs but didn't have the luxury of taking in the scene of Pelley playing audience to our mortal struggle. Martin had a height advantage, but he lost that as soon as we went face-to-face on the carpet. It was also soon clear that he was weaker than me and untrained. I blocked the worst of his jabs and scored a few stingers on his chin and ribs. It didn't take long for us both to get a feeling for how this would end. Martin began to scream in a panic. I almost felt bad for the poor guy as I rolled him onto his back and wrapped both hands around his throat. That moment of reflection was interrupted by two sets of headlights swinging their beams into the windows of the farmhouse.

"Damn you, Hollis. You've worn out your welcome," I heard Pelley say, over my shoulder. I swung my head around just in time to see Mr. Silver Hair lift the hay fork and prepare for a coup de gras strike to my back. I flung myself aside just in time to take a glancing blow and then watched in horror as the two-foot-long tines plunged their full depth into Martin's chest. And just like that, the Stakowski brothers were no more.

Pelley yanked on the handle of the hay fork a couple of times but it wasn't budging. He abandoned the effort, opting instead to spin on his heel and hightail it out the back way, through the kitchen. I was left sprawled on my back, bleeding, with a very dead body for company.

CHAPTER 26

The front door nearly popped off its hinges when someone put their foot into it. I was up on one knee about the time the flashlights caught me in their beams. Four dark-clad figures swarmed into the house, one of whom knelt quickly at my side. I recognized the shape and the fluid movements as belonging to Eleanor Stanton. It looked like she'd brought help.

"I'm fine. Get after Pelley," I said, pointing toward the back of the house. Eleanor nodded and dashed away. I pulled myself up on my feet and took a step toward the front door, when two more men walked in. One of them used his brains and flipped the light switch. There, in the light, stood Charles Victor and his bodyguard Mohinder.

"You're too late for the party," I said.

"Who's the stiff?" Charles asked, tapping the handle of the hay fork and making it sway slightly.

"It's a long story," I said. "How the hell did you find this place?"

"The way you talked up your friend, Roy Gittings, we decided to call him for a little help." Charles said, staring down at Martin.

"How'd he find me?"

"Paperwork. Turned out Roy already had a list of properties owned by William Pelley. We assumed Pelley would need to take you somewhere he felt safe to beat the hell out of you. This place was number three on our list."

"Paperwork is Roy's secret weapon," I said.

"As good as a pitch-fork, most times," Charles said, admiring the hay fork.

Just then, a voice rang out from upstairs. "Found a live one!"

The two of them jogged up the stairs ahead of me and followed the commotion to a back bedroom. I climbed a bit more slowly, finally feeling the pain from the jab to the ribs. I found them in a small room with Olie Scharf, who was handcuffed to a bed. He was sobbing and guarding his face from a man in a black balaclava pointing a semiautomatic pistol at him.

"I'm Hollis," I said to the masked man as I entered the room. He nodded, but kept his eyes and gun trained on Olie. "This man's a victim – not a threat," I said. "You from the New York field office?"

"Yes, sir," the agent replied, with the crisp cadence of a military man.

We made a quick search of the room and found a key for the handcuffs in a desk drawer. Dawn was just breaking outside, and about the time we got Olie off the bed, we spotted Eleanor Stanton out a window. She was making her way across the back yard toward the kitchen door. We all headed for the kitchen, where we found Eleanor pulling a black woolen mask off of her head. She didn't exactly look happy.

"Found a small barn across the field behind the house," she said, catching her breath. "There was a gravel drive leading away from it. Looked to me like that driveway went south, to the county road. My guess is that Pelley had a car parked there. Dust was still hanging in the air."

"We'll find him," I said. "We have to. He's a cold-blooded killer from another planet." I jerked a thumb over my shoulder. "Which reminds me, I have something to show you folks in the barn."

Out on the gravel driveway, Eleanor opened the back door of one of the cars and offered up a seat for Olie Scharf. "Wait here, sir," she instructed. Olie nodded and slid onto the bench seat, where he found himself sitting next to Miss Amelia Knobloch. "We picked her up on the road, a few minutes ago," Eleanor explained.

When we got to the barn door, I held up my hand. "So, remember when I told you about the furry, fringed beast from my worst nightmares that attacked me in my bed? Well, let me introduce you to him," I said, pulling the large barn door open.

"Look at that..." Eleanor muttered in awe at the sight of the shaggy beast as we walked in. Charles Victor whistled. Mohinder grunted. The beast was howling and stamping his massive feet and thrashing his chains around like – well – a chained animal. Wilmer was on the ground not too far away, trussed up and bleeding, but alive. "Whose the guy?" Eleanor asked.

"Name's Wilmer. I told you about him."

She nodded. "Looks like you were right about how to handle him."

"Yeah, but now what do we do with him? And the beast, too."

"Right," she said, scratching her chin. "It's a tricky thing – and a surprisingly common problem for us. We can't hand Wilmer over to the local authorities for fear of exposing our work here, and we don't want to hold him captive for the rest of his life, so..."

"So... you're saying we kill him?"

"No, we're not in the murder business, Henry. Maybe a few casualties along the way in self-defense. But murder? No. That's not what we do."

"Agreed. So what *do* we do?"

"We let him go," Eleanor said with surprising calm.

"What?"

"Think about it. He's neck-deep in criminal activities, all while working in the service of a sinister alien from another planet, bent on the destruction of humanity."

"Destruction of humanity?"

Eleanor shrugged. "I don't know. Maybe. It doesn't matter. He can't tell his side of the story to anyone and then not expect to be locked up."

I nodded in appreciation. "Yeah, I see what you mean."

"The odds are good that he'll cause trouble again someday as a thug-for-hire, but, then again, there's always somebody willing to cause trouble on behalf of the people pulling the strings in this world – or any world, for that matter."

"I guess so. And what about the beast?"

"Yeah, well, that's even more tricky. He's not human, so I suppose we could put him out of his misery, but it looks like he's every bit as much of a victim in this situation as your man Olie Scharf," Eleanor said slowly, pondering the situation. "Letting him loose to roam the countryside doesn't sound like a good idea, either..." she added, her voice trailing off. Then she snapped her fingers and smiled. "I think I might have a solution – a temporary one, anyway." She patted Charles Victor on the shoulder. "Charlie and I were chatting last night, to pass the time, and he told me about something that Clarence Boyette is working on, over at your ordnance works building, on the island."

"The FOHQ," Charles Victor offered up.

"FOHQ?" I said.

"Yes, as in: Field Operations Headquarters," he explained. "That's what I was thinking we could call the building."

"That's one of the worst acronyms I've ever heard," I mused. "When I get a chance, I'll work on a better name for the place."

"Yes," Charles said cheerfully. "Please feel free to call it whatever you want."

Eleanor added her two cents to the topic. "We ended up calling our field office in New York 'the Temple', on account of the building being the former home of a fraternal order."

"Nice. Catchy."

"Yeah. Anyway," Eleanor continued, "Clarence is putting in some oversized detention units in the basement of your place. We're planning on getting some installed in New York."

"Oh, yeah. Those detention cells were a head-scratcher for me when I first heard about them." I looked over at Charles. "Maybe this is the kind of situation you had in mind."

He nodded and smiled. "Seemed like the best use for that old firing range under the building."

"By the way, anyone putting water in the green coffin?" I asked.

Charles nodded. "Clarence has taken care of that."

Just then, a blood curdling scream erupted from the farmhouse.

I grabbed Eleanor Stanton's shoulder. "Shit. I completely forgot about Hell Bat in all the commotion. I should'a warned them."

"Hell Bat?"

"That's my pet name for him," I said. "I think maybe we're gonna need a couple detention cells."

Down in the farmhouse root cellar, we found a field agent pressed up against a wall, shining a flashlight into what looked to be an extremely large, overbuilt dog cage. There, in the beam of the flashlight, was Hell Bat, now sitting on a canvas cot.

"Oh, my god!" Eleanor gasped. Mohinder said something in Punjabi that didn't need much translation.

Hell Bat was shielding his eyes from the flashlight with a thin, winged arm. He had a small blanket bundled around him at the waist, and looked slightly dazed and uncomfortable, but was – surprisingly – not spitting rage and venom. Then he spoke. "Please get that light out of my face," he said, plain as day. His voice was rasping and full of gravel. There was a hint of an accent, but it was otherwise completely recognizable as American English.

"It can..." Eleanor began to say.

"Talk, yes," the little gargoyle said. "I've been doing it since before your grandparents were born, if you want the details."

Hell Bat scooted across the cot and turned on a bedside lamp. The trembling field agent lowered his flashlight. I took note of the stack of books and magazines on a small desk beside the cot. There was a radio, as well. The entire scene now looked more like a small dormitory room than an animal's cage.

"This is where you live?" I asked.

"This is not living. But, yes, this is were I'm held captive, when I'm not being dragged out naked and forced to rip memories out of some poor human's head."

"What's your name?" Eleanor asked.

"Humans can't pronounce my name. Pelley called me the Pet, when he referred to me in the presence of humans. I never warmed to that one, so, for simplicity's sake, how does the name *Maurice* sound to you."

"Maurice?" I said, feeling out the name, then nodding. "Sounds good enough. You read that name in a book?"

"Why, yes, Mr. Hollis, I did," Maurice said, sounding slightly demonic and patronizing.

"How do you know my name?" I asked.

"I just spent some quality time with your every thought, rooting around inside your head, remember?"

"Yeah. Can't say I enjoyed that too much."

"Neither did I."

"Has Pelley been taking care of you down here?"

"No, he has very well-paid servants that have been doing the honors of feeding me and taking away my shit bucket. Pelley spends most of his time at his house in town. The servants takes care of the farmhouse and the animals – and me."

"We'll look them up and talk to them, when this is all over," I assured the creature.

"Great. That's just about a hundred years of servants you'll need to hunt down. In the meantime, are you going to let me out of this cage?"

I looked over at Eleanor and shrugged. She returned the gesture. I looked back at Maurice and nodded. "Sure."

"The key's on the peg, next to the stairs," he said, pointing with a small, bony finger.

CHAPTER 27

A few minutes later, as we were all heading for the cars, I turned to Charles Victor. "The way I see it, we've got two problems to solve: one big and one small. The big one is getting our hands on William Pelley."

"Agreed," he said. "And the small problem?"

"Well, if we let Wilmer go, there's nothing stopping him from tracking down Olie Scharf and turning him into you-know-who again, or maybe even the Angry Fur Coat, for that matter."

"Yes," he mused. "That is a problem."

"You-know-who?" Maurice said, joining in the conversation. He was swaddled in a blanket and carrying a suitcase that we had found in the house. "You mean, Offenbach?"

I stared down at the tiny demon creature and raised an eyebrow. "Yes."

"I can fix that problem for you, if you'd like," he offered.

"I'm not up for watching you eat Wilmer for supper," I said.

Maurice looked up at me, horrified, fangs slightly bared. "What kind of savage do you think I am? I'm simply offering to take a stroll through Wilmer's mind and pluck the two particular trigger names from his memory," he said. "Really, you people disappoint me."

"Sorry. I didn't mean to ruffle your feathers."

"I don't have feathers," he said, extending a bat-winged arm. "I'm a mammal – not an earth mammal as such, but – oh, never mind."

We walked with Maurice over to what looked to be a humble delivery truck – no markings.

"But you *can* fly?" Eleanor asked Maurice as we walked.

"It's been many, many years since I've had the pleasure, seeing as I've been a captive in a cage since 1831, but in theory, yes."

I put up a hand. "That flying thing sounds like fun, but I don't suggest you go taking too many pleasure flights in broad daylight around the city," I said. "People might start taking pot-shots at you."

A balaclava-clad New York field operative standing near the truck walked over and opened the back doors to reveal Wilmer, now cuffed at the hands and ankles, on his back having his wounds tended to by another field operative kneeling beside him. At the sight of Maurice, the field operative leapt from the truck and fled to what he guessed was a safe distance. Maurice sighed; then he and I climbed into the cramped confines of the truck. I got around behind Wilmer and put a knee onto each shoulder. Eleanor held Wilmer's feet while Maurice climbed onto his chest. The sight was more than a little unsettling. "Open your eyes," Maurice hissed, raking Wilmer's chest with his bony fingers, "or I will peel your eyelids from your face."

Wilmer's eyes shot open, wide with terror. Maurice bared his fangs, revealing them in their full ghoulish glory, and grabbed Wilmer by the chin. I looked away after that, not wanting to relive the experience, even voyeuristically. Wilmer grunted and gasped a few times as Maurice did his dark work. It was over in under two minutes, but I made a mental note to avoid being around for these kinds of sessions in the future.

His job done, Maurice climbed off of Wilmer, leaving him to his whimpering in the back of the truck.

"Mission accomplished?" I asked.

"Yes."

"Thanks."

"My pleasure," Maurice said, winking and smiling at me in a way that will haunt my dreams to my dying day.

"So, what happens with Wilmer?" I asked Charles.

"That's your call, actually, Henry," he said. "I know that it feels like we're all just making up the rules as we go along, but, if this world is important to us, somebody has to step up and get things done. Arthur Lockwood and I picked you to be our local field operations chief. As such, you get to make the decisions out in the field, and by god, we're standing out in the field, right now."

I nodded and turned to Eleanor Stanton. "Take him to St. Elizabeth's Hospital and cut him loose on the sidewalk."

Fatigue, pain, and some blood loss were taking their toll on me. I wiped my brow and stared around me in a bit of a daze. I used my thumb to point over at the barn. "So," I said in a long breath, "how do we move the Brown Beast?"

Charles Victor raised his hand. "My company has large trucks available. I can have one brought over this morning. But, the hard part will be getting him into the truck. Any suggestions?"

"Trail of meat to the back of the truck?" Eleanor suggested.

"Meat trail," I said in agreement, trying to sound confident.

"Meat trail it is," Charles said with a nod.

"Well, it's been fun," I said to the those around me, "but I need to go home and catch up on some sleep."

"I'll take you," Mohinder said. The full light of day allowed me to finally see that Charles Victor's Stutz was parked about a hundred yards down the gravel drive.

"Just what I hoping for," I said to him with a weary smile. "Thanks."

CHAPTER 28

Truth be told, I fell asleep in the back of the Stutz. I have a vague memory of Mohinder strong-arming me up the stairs to my third floor tenement apartment, like a damn drunk. I think my building's superintendent, Mr. Kirschenbaum, was busy fixing my door when we got there. After that, it was all pillows and blessed darkness until about noon, when there was a knock on my newly-restored door.

I worked the lock on the door and swung it open, revealing a man I'd never seen before. Standing there in his white shirt and rumpled suit, the guy looked like a door-to-door salesman. He nodded slightly as I stared at him through my bloodshot eyes, but he didn't speak up or extend a hand.

"Whatever you're selling, I'm not buying," I growled, trying to project my voice with enough force to send the average salesman jumping back a couple feet. This guy didn't budge.

"You're bleeding," the man said.

I looked down at my undershirt and saw he was right. Where the shirt hung along the side of my rib cage, there were three large blood stains, spaced evenly apart.

"Cut myself shaving," I said.

"I'm glad to see that you survived your ordeal, Mr. Hollis," the stranger said in a dull, monotone voice.

"Ah." I shook my head and smiled. "The Sphinx, I presume?"

"Yes."

"Is this the real you, in the flesh, or are you still sitting on your living room couch?"

"Very astute, Mr. Hollis. I'm actually sitting at my desk in my study right now. This manifestation of me is also flesh and blood, but it's more like a..."

"A robot?"

"Well, yes, but more organic in nature."

"Well, does your manifestation want a cup of coffee at Jeanette's Diner? If I have to be awake, that's where I'm headed."

"No coffee, just water."

"Suit yourself."

After a wardrobe change we headed over to Jeanette's and made ourselves comfortable at a window booth.

"You know," I said to the Sphinx as he stared calmly at me, "right here is where all this madness began for me – sitting in this very spot."

"For me, all this madness as you say began more

than twenty years ago, when I first learned about the windows that open between universes."

"The what?"

"The oscillating orbits of the celestial wave-rings, technically," the Sphinx explained patiently.

"Is that what passes for cocktail party talk where you're from?"

If the Sphinx's "manifestation" had been built for smiling, my guess is that it would have cracked a smile right about then. "In my circles, yes."

"So, those oscillating orbit things are important, I guess."

"Oh, very. Tens – perhaps hundreds – of billions of lives are in the balance, depending on how those wave-rings are used. For some, they could be conduits for planetary salvation – or alternately, enslavement. For others, they might very well be pathways to tremendous power and material wealth. There are almost limitless outcomes, really. Those outcomes bring profound opportunities and profound risks."

"So, these existentially important celestial wave-ring things of yours – what are they?"

The Sphinx studied his water glass. "Have you ever cast a stone into a lake and watched the ripples propagate out from the point of impact?"

"The splash and the little waves? Yeah."

"Well, the current iteration of the entire universe was started by an at least somewhat similar event, though on an almost infinitely larger scale. That massive event gave birth to the current universe and sent shockwaves out through space-time. Those shockwaves collided with other shockwaves that had been generated by other, earlier universes, and that were bouncing off whatever lies at the farthest reaches of space. And where those echoes – or, rings – collided, a new physics was created, profoundly different from the kind that your scientists here on Earth are even now just beginning to understand."

"You done yet?" I asked.

"Not quite. The places where these wave-ring segments overlap cut mostly through the empty void of space, but not entirely. There are times when they pass through or near stars and planets, as well. More importantly, the fact that these crystallized segments are combinations of echoes from many universes means that they create brief opportunities for these universes to connect, particularly when they pass near – or through – planets."

"Okay, stop," I said, holding up a hand. "You hitched a ride on a vibrating wave to send your walking radio transmitter here from your home planet, which existed sometime in the wildly-distant past?"

"Well, yes," he said.

"Is there any more to this gripping yarn of yours?"

"Much, much more," the Sphinx said.

"I'm sure it's all very important, but can it wait for another day?"

"Yes."

"Please tell me that I'm not the first human you've told this stuff to."

"No, of course not. But I've chosen who to tell this information to very carefully. At least one man is likely dead already because of this information. There are secrets, Mr. Hollis, and then there are world-ending secrets. Do you fully grasp what I mean?"

"I doubt it. But if you're asking me to keep my mouth shut about it, then, yes, I grasp what you mean." I looked down at the cup of coffee in front of me and studied it for a while. Nice thing about the Sphinx – he doesn't interrupt people who are just sitting quiet and thinking. At last, I looked back up at him. "So, how do you do it? How does Pelley do it? Hell, how does Offenbach do it?"

The Sphinx straightened up in his seat and gazed at me for a few long seconds. "You mean, how do we manifest ourselves in your world?"

"Yeah, I guess that's what I mean."

He nodded once. "There are three ways – that I know of – to enter your world from another world. The first way is what I call *Stepping Through*. This is when a sentient being physically comes here by simply stepping through a wave-ring segment. The disadvantage of this being that there is no known way back – stepping through is currently a one-way street."

"So, Maurice is stuck here?" I said.

"Currently, yes, until science or luck finds another path." The Sphinx took a sip of water. "The second way is what I call *Imprinting*. How shall I put this so that you can understand the concept?" He paused for a moment. "It is a process by which you take the entire contents of your consciousness and transform it into something that is essentially a very dense and compact code, or shorthand, if you will. That coded information is then imprinted permanently into a host body, here, on Earth. The down side of that option is that you must forever abandon your original physical form back in your home world."

I raised an eyebrow at that. "And that's what Pelley and the kid on my roof did?"

IIe nodded again. "Exactly."

"What about Offenbach?"

"He is using the third way: *Projection*. This is when you use a sophisticated radio device of some sort to transmit thoughts and sensations from your body on your home world to a host body on Earth, as was done with Mr. Scharf – or Offenbach, if you will. This option is similar to what I'm using, except I'm providing my own host body. The primary benefit of this method is that it doesn't commit the person to a lifetime spent on your planet. There are several problems with this option, however. First, the person who is projecting their consciousness must be attached to a transmitter of some sort. Second, it's mentally straining and can be physically difficult to sustain for more than a few hours. Third, in Offenbach's case, it seems that his technology is limited by the onset of sleep. Fourth, once the wave-ring dissipates, the connection is lost, thus limiting the connection to a few months or years."

"Sounds like you have a tough gig," I said.

The Sphinx gave his best approximation of a shrug. "Yes, but my work is important to me."

"I'm sure it is. What the hell is it that you do for a living, anyway?"

"Well, I..." the Sphinx's poker face suddenly went from blank to slightly confused. "Mr. Hollis?"

"Yeah?"

"Do you know who those men are, walking up to your building?"

CHAPTER 29

I looked out the window and grunted at the sight of a uniformed police officer and a plainclothes police detective mounting the stairs to my tenement building. "Well, shit," I mumbled. "That would be Detective Aemon Bettis, and a beat-cop."

"Why are they here?" the Oracle asked.

"Judging from the presence of the beat-cop, Bettis is here to arrest me."

"What will you do?"

"Get arrested, I suppose." I finished the last of my coffee and stood up from the booth. "Could you do me a favor?"

"Yes, of course."

"Wait here until I am safely shoved into the back of the police car, then head up to my apartment and wait for me. It might be a while – maybe until tomorrow morning."

"Yes, I can do that," he said. "I'm good at waiting."

I hunted in my pocket for change and paid for the coffee, then headed to the phone booth at the back of the diner. The phone call took less than a minute. With that done, I went and grabbed my hat from the table and nodded to the Sphinx. "I've got a feeling that Pelley is behind this. His little world is caving in and he needs to make a dramatic play to save his bacon."

"Good luck, Mr. Hollis," the Sphinx said, in his usual monotone, but now somehow with a hint of sympathy.

"Thanks. I'll leave the door unlocked."

I got to the third floor landing of my tenement building just in time to stop Bettis from kicking my door down. "Hey, boys. What brings you to the neighborhood? Collecting for the police pension fund?" I said cheerfully.

Bettis and the uniformed officer swung their heads my way. "Welcome home, Hollis. You're under arrest," Bettis replied in his usual brusk way.

"Oh, yeah? What'd I do this time?"

"Kidnapping," he said, gravely.

"Well, at least it's not murder," I said, then asked, "Not that it matters, but who did I kidnap?"

"Cute," Bettis said. "Do you happen to have an old man by the name of Archibald Flood stashed in your bathtub?"

I frowned at that news. That old man didn't deserve to be in the middle of this mess, but I was starting to get a picture of Mr. Silver Hair's play. "No, not that I remember, but you're welcome to have a look."

Bettis and the beat-cop gave my apartment a good going-over, which took all of about a minute.

After that, they put the cuffs on me and walked me out to the police car. I tried to make small talk as we drove down to police headquarters, but Detective Bettis wasn't biting. He knew I was in deep, but into what, exactly, he couldn't figure. That wasn't my problem. Getting sprung from jail in a timely manner, however, was.

When they were walking me to the processing room, I caught a glimpse of two people who made a few more pieces fall into place: there, in the waiting area, was the friendly receptionist I'd chatted with at the New Eden Home for the Elderly and Infirmed, and standing nearby was Mr. William Pelley, himself. I couldn't wait to hear the story.

"Take a seat, Hollis," Bettis said, pointing to a metal chair in the processing room. "I've got a couple people for you to meet."

I should explain that most police departments don't function exactly the way they do in the movies. Perpetrator identification, for instance. At the New Eden PD, when they want to do a perp ID, they simply handcuff the perp to a heavy iron ring attached to the wall in the processing room and walk witnesses into the room to give the accused man a good look over. That's the treatment I got.

"Stand up," Bettis instructed. I got to my feet just about the time that William Pelley and the nice receptionist lady from the retirement home walked into the room. Pelley gave me the faintest hint of a smile but didn't overplay it. The nice receptionist lady looked genuinely upset and scared. "This the guy?" Bettis asked each of them.

"That's the man I saw, without a doubt," Pelley said, his voice confident yet somber.

"Yes, that's him," the nice receptionist said, her voice and hands trembling.

Bettis walked the witnesses out of the room while two officers got to work processing me. Thirty minutes later, I was cuffed to a chair in an interrogation room. Detective Bettis soon graced me with his presence.

"You're a busy man, Mr. Hollis," he said, circling the room. "The receptionist at the retirement home says you came in just a couple days ago, looking for Archie Flood. She says you had dinner with him and then went on a stroll with him. That sound about right?"

"Yeah, sure," I agreed.

"Then, this morning, the old man goes for a walk but doesn't return. An hour later, a concerned citizen claims to have witnessed an elderly man being accosted by a man fitting your description. The old man, the witness says, got shoved into the trunk of a older-model Ford coupe. He even gives me a plate number," Bettis explained, tapping a notebook in his hand. "The Indiana Bureau of Motor Vehicles says the car is registered in the name of the Lockwood Law Office. Imagine my surprise when I call them this morning and they confirm that you're a contract worker for them, and currently in possession of said Ford coupe." Bettis settled into the chair across the table from me and leaned back, putting his hands behind his head. "So, Mr. Hollis, where is the car?"

There are only so many things you can control in life. You can control your own actions and you can control what you say to others. After that, it's pretty much out of your hands. I didn't kidnap Archie Flood, but someone did – someone named William Pelley. I could say that I didn't kidnap the old man, and so could Pelley, not that anyone was asking him. A denial of guilt doesn't magically change reality. The reality was that Pelley had kidnapped Archie, and Pelley was now in the process of framing me for it. I first knew that Mr. Silver Hair was working on framing me an hour earlier, when I watched Detective Bettis lumber up the front steps of my tenement building. I just didn't know the details. Running isn't my style and I knew I had a couple minutes before Bettis would be making his way across the street to the diner to slap me in cuffs, so I made a phone call to Abner Dodds. That's when I got the news that Bettis had called about the car. Where was the car now? Well, Dodds informed me that Eleanor Stanton and her men had moved it to the underground garage below Lockwood's office. That didn't sit right with me, as I didn't want to put too much of this mess on Lockwood's doorstep, so I had Dodds move it.

"It's parked at 1202 North Park Court. The keys are on top of the driver-side front tire."

Detective Bettis blinked at that and flipped through his notebook. "That's... where the witness, William Pelley, lives," he said.

"Well, then, maybe you should check his house for Archie Flood."

"You play too many games, Hollis. How'd the car get there?" Bettis asked.

"You ever been to Pelley Park? It's very nice – flowers, benches, a weeping willow. I can just sit there for hours, like I did this morning," I said, hamming it up. "Sometimes, I get so caught up in the beauty of the place, like I did this morning, that I just forget where my car is parked and end up walking home."

"That a fact?" he said, not even remotely buying it.

"My memory's bit fuzzy. Maybe you should ask Mr. William Pelley if he saw me sitting across the street from his house this morning for an hour or two."

And Bettis did just that. While he was gone, my attorney, Cornell McKim, was shown into the room, with a look of genuine concern etched on his face. "Kidnapping?" he said, taking a seat.

"I'm as surprised as you are."

"I don't doubt it," McKim offered, sounding guarded.

"I'm almost as much of a victim as Archie Flood, in fact."

Cornell leaned in and looked at me gravely. "Is this going to become a habit with you – getting arrested?"

I was about to laugh at the question, but then the answer dawned on me. "Maybe, yeah."

"Theo Brown hinted as much," Cornell said.

"Yeah? Well, he's hinting too much."

"You've made quite an impression on him, and your wellbeing is now very important to him. I'm intrigued at the bond that's been made between the two of you, but I will try to respect your privacy."

"Glad to hear I've got his vote of support."

That was as far as we got with our conversation before Bettis walked back into the room. He nodded and grunted in the direction of Cornell McKim before taking a seat at the table. Once seated, he let out a breath through clenched teeth. "He's gone."

"Gone? Who?"

"Pelley," he said, shaking his head. "I told him what you said about your car and he said he had no idea what you were talking about. He then... uh... excused himself to use the bathroom and then he uh... he was gone."

Now I had Pelley on the run, all from the comfort of a police interrogation room. "You think that's a little suspicious?" I asked.

"Yeah, a little."

"You track down my car yet?"

Bettis nodded. "We have officers there right now."

"Any bodies in the trunk?"

"No."

I was pleased to hear it, but kept that to myself. "So, what's your next move, Detective?"

Bettis gave me a sour stare. "Getting a warrant and giving Pelley's house a once-over."

"And?"

"And?" Bettis parroted back. He rolled his eyes and nodded. "Oh, I get it." He stood up and snapped his fingers at the officer standing guard at the door. "Gimme the key."

Bettis took the small key and walked around behind me. "Yeah, you're being cut loose – for now."

CHAPTER 30

The Sphinx was sitting perfectly still in my comfy chair when I got back to the apartment, just around sunset. "You miss me?" I asked as I entered, chuckling to myself.

Nothing.

"Hello? Anybody home?"

Nothing.

"You in there?"

Finally, he sparked to life. "Yes. Yes, I'm here. Sorry about the delay. The system I use to manipulate this body remotely is rather more complicated and involved than the simple transceiver I use at Red's Roost. How did it go?"

"No beatings and no prison food. I call that a win."

"So, all is well?"

I shook my head. "Not even close. Pelley tried to frame me for kidnapping an old man by the name of Archie Flood. And now Pelley has the poor old guy tucked away somewhere, and I don't see much chance of Pelley letting Archie live to see tomorrow. I've got Pelley spooked, but I'm not sure if that's a good thing or a bad thing."

"Do you have a plan?"

"Nope. But I know where to start."

"Oh?"

"The Essex Hotel. You up for a drive downtown?"

I always enjoy visiting the Essex. It's a fine example of what the hand of man can create, when it's not preoccupied with more destructive pursuits. Someone actually gave a damn about how the etched floral patterns of the glass sconces blended seamlessly with the art deco stylized Garden of Eden tableau on the walls. The alternating black and white marble stairs seemed to ascend organically from the checkerboard marble floor of the lobby. The sunburst pattern on the elevator doors was echoed in the sunburst design of the massive etched glass lighting fixture that dominated the center of the lobby. Even on a bad day, the main lobby of the Essex Hotel always catches me off guard and makes me a little more sympathetic toward the crazy, mostly-deluded residents of this little planet of ours.

The main lobby of the Essex Hotel that evening played host to more than the usual assortment of well-heeled guests: there was a square-shouldered gent standing a few steps from the elevators and conveniently close to the house phone, clearly a plain-clothes field operative from the Wildflower Society's

New York office. He raised an eyebrow at the sight of us entering but did not interfere when we went to the elevators. I nodded to him and escorted the Sphinx into the elevator. I assume he called up to Lockwood's suite as soon as the doors had shut.

When we got to the top floor, we found another plain-clothes field agent standing guard in the hall. Nobody was taking any chances tonight.

Arthur Lockwood's wife answered the door. "Welcome, Henry," Ellen Lockwood said, warmly. "And this would be?" she asked, extending a hand to the Sphinx.

When the Sphinx failed to grab ahold of her hand, I stepped in. "This would be an alien from another planet – or at least his personal radio transmitter, that conveniently comes with legs, arms, and a head to store a Panama hat on."

Ellen Lockwood stammered for a moment at that, but soon found her hostess instincts and ushered us toward the living room. "You and your friend should join the others."

"Thanks, ma'am."

There was a sort of buffet table set up in the living room, around which was gathered the whole gang. Arthur Lockwood was adding a slice of cheese to his plate while Eleanor Stanton dipped into the potato salad. Charles Victor stood near a window with two finger sandwiches and some cucumbers on a plate while Miss Amelia Knobloch leaned over the buffet, making a close study of the cold cuts. Abner Dodds was in the process of delicately balancing a deviled egg on a rolling mound of cold noodles and Olie Scharf sat on the arm of the couch admiring a plate of tea cookies. Everyone turned to greet us.

"You hungry?" I asked the Sphinx.

"Just water, thanks," he said.

Judge Lockwood walked over and shook my hand. "So, how do things stand, Henry?" he asked.

"Just fine, boss. A psychopathic alien is out there plotting to do us all in as we speak; a crackerjack police detective is about to put enough pieces together to put me in jail for a few lifetimes; your old friend, Archie Flood, has about twelve hours to live, best as I can tell; and the one man who can tell me what rock to look under for William Pelley, well, he's sleeping off a few pints of blood loss over at St. Elizabeth's Hospital right now. So, like I said, things are going fine. Thanks for asking."

"Do you have a plan?" Charles Victor asked, filling a crystal tumbler half-full of what looked suspiciously like scotch on the rocks.

"No. Inspiration hasn't struck, just yet," I confessed.

"Well, maybe this will help," he said, offering up the tumbler.

I accepted it with a smile and grabbed a few slices of Swiss cheese from the buffet. I found a spot on the couch and gave my concentration over to studying the ice cubes in my glass. Somewhere around my tenth sip, Eleanor Stanton took a seat next to me, a small plate of food balanced on her knee.

"This town sure gives New York a run for its money when it comes to trouble," she said.

"I'm starting to get the picture that this town has always been trouble – and a damn strange place, to boot." I shook my head in wonder. Olie Scharf lowered himself on the couch, on the other side of me. I raised my glass to him. "I'm glad to see that they're keeping you safe and sound up here, until all this blows over."

Olie nodded and finished chewing a finger sandwich before speaking. "Your friends have been very nice to me. I sort of wish I knew more about what was going on, but then again, maybe I don't want to know."

"Don't sweat it. The less you know, the better. But having *you-know-who* in your head with Pelley still stalking the streets puts you at risk."

"Couldn't you just ask him to leave?" he asked.

I laughed out loud. "Pelley?"

"No. Ask *you-know-who* to leave."

"I doubt he would agree to that on his own, but... say... you just got the gears turning in my head." I stood up and paced a bit, then stared into my Scotch. "Hey, everybody, help me think this through," I called out.

All eyes were on me. "Yes?" Judge Lockwood said.

I began to pace the room, still keeping my eyes on the glass. "We're on the lookout for William Pelley, an alien from another planet, and he's on the run and presumably alone, except for the company of an old bushy-browed man he's kidnapped. Right?"

"Agreed," Eleanor chimed in.

"He had some local muscle helping him, but they are all either dead or toes-up in a hospital bed, right?"

""Yep," Charles said.

"But his number-one buddy has been *you-know-who*, the alien that's somehow stuck in Olie Scharf's head. And, since they were such close pals, there's good odds that he knows where Pelley is holed up." There were nods all around. I continued. "But there are two funny things about about *you-know-who*: the first is that he's currently sitting here, on the couch, and second, he doesn't know anything that's happened since he took a snooze at the farmhouse last night."

"So," Charles said slowly, "you want to wake him up and get the information out of him?"

Olie gasped at what Charles had said. I waved my hands at him, trying to stave off a full-blown panic. "I don't want to scare Olie unnecessarily, so just hear me out."

The folks in the room gathered around me as I came to a stop by the couch, looming over Olie. "Now, there's not much reason for *you-know-who* to cooperate with me, as he can't be directly harmed by me, as far as I can tell. But," – I raised a finger into the air – "what if we could trick him somehow?"

Eleanor began nodding eagerly. "You're saying we have someone he doesn't know ask him for the information, but in a way that doesn't make him feel like he's spilling the beans exactly."

"Yeah, right. But who? And what's the gimmick?"

"Gimmick?" Judge Lockwood asked.

"You know, the play – the con." I looked around the room, frowning as I gazed into each person's face. Then I began to smile. "Yeah... I got it. We can do 'the fixer.'" I said with a satisfied nod.

"The fixer?" Eleanor asked.

"It's a con that you play on hard-nosed criminals who are in a jam – or at least who *think* that they're in a jam," I explained. "You put the idea in their head that they have one way out of their bind, but only as long as they do exactly what you tell them to do. In the meantime, you scam them for money or information." I gave a satisfied nod, then frowned again. "But..."

"But... what?" Charles asked.

"I don't think anybody in this room has a reasonable shot at pulling it off – except for me – and it can't be me." I went deep into thought and absently put a hand on Olie Scharf's shoulder. All of a sudden, I gave Olie's shoulder a squeeze, which made him let out a stifled yelp. "Holy hell!" I shouted. "I'm an idiot. I already know a real goddamn fixer!" I smiled a devilish grin and looked down at Olie.

Olie began shaking his head, almost hysterically. "I can't do it. Don't make me do it, Mr. Hollis. Please!"

I put both of my hands on Olie's shoulders and stared down into his twitching panic-stricken eyes. "You want your life back, right?"

"Y... yes."

I furrowed my brows at him. "There's a fellow out there who knows the magic word that turns you into his evil sidekick. If we take him down, tonight, he will never be able to get his claws into your brain again. There's someone – or something – in your head that knows where Pelley's hiding. All I need to do is get the information I need and then..."

"Then, what?" he asked, looking lost and forlorn.

"Well," I started to say something, but just couldn't bring myself to say it.

Olie began to give a slow nod of resignation. "Okay, I'll do it. You get the information from him and then you have my permission to... to... punch his lights out."

I gave his shoulder a sympathetic pat. "You're the biggest innocent victim in all of this. I want to make things right by you, and this is the best way I can think of to do just that. I promise I'll take good care of you."

Everyone descended upon Olie, patting his shoulder and giving him gestures of moral support. He seemed to appreciate it. Eleanor Stanton soon turned her attention to me. "Let's say you get a good tip on Pelley's whereabouts. What then?"

I nodded thoughtfully. "Yeah, I've been thinking about that, too. I have bits and pieces of a plan, but they all revolve around offering up a victim to the cops – someone other than Archie Flood." I scratched my chin and walked over to the window, staring out into the night. Then, out of the corner of my eye, I caught a glimpse of the Sphinx taking a sip of water from his glass. "Hey, Mr. Sphinx," I said.

"Yes, Henry?"

"Is that walking radio set of yours a flesh-and-blood human?"

"Why do you ask?" he said, flatly.

"Humor me."

"It's an artificial construct, but it's made of organic material patterned after the human body."

"So," I said, taking a step closer, "if someone were to, say, perform an autopsy on the body, would it pass muster as human?"

"No. But..."

"What?"

Something like a cough erupted from the Sphinx. "Well, it certainly wouldn't pass muster in my world, but in your world... yes, I think it would."

I leaned in close, staring into the eyes of the Sphinx. "If something very violent were to happen to this body, would you feel any pain, back in your living room, on your planet?"

The Sphinx raised an eyebrow, a veritable torrent of emotion by his standards. "I would feel strong simulated sensations, but not pain, specifically."

"So, if this body were to, say, be shot or stabbed to death, you would ride it out, safe and sound on your sofa? No harm done?"

"Essentially, yes. Why do you ask?"

"I'm thinking somebody might kill you tonight – maybe Pelley or maybe me, even – not sure which yet. How attached to this body are you?"

Again, the eyebrow raised. "I spent a good deal of time and resources fabricating it... but I suppose I could do it again, if absolutely necessary. I could even send you the components and have you fabricate it – once you're done using the incubator."

"Incubator?" the room said in unison.

"Yes. The device I gave you, that you're watching over right now."

I raised my eyebrow at that. "You mean the green, glass coffin?"

"Green silica? Yes. Coffin? Not even remotely."

"Whatever. We'll get back to that topic later, tomorrow, maybe," I said, walking back over to the couch. "In the meantime, Olie and I need to go find somebody. Right, Olie?" I pointed toward the door.

Olie Scharf glanced up at me and then at the door. "I, uh, I..."

"Now's the time to decide, Olie."

I need to give the poor guy credit. He bit his lip and started to nod. He put a hand on either side of himself and pushed up off the couch. "Alright, I'll do it."

I turned back to the Sphinx. "I've already asked you to cool your heels once, today. Could you indulge me again and make do with some good company, here, for a few hours? – until I come to collect you for your big exit, that is?"

"Yes. I'll be here."

CHAPTER 31

Nick Palmieri was the manager at a small nightclub called the Firefly, which was one of the clubs owned by "Two-Ton Lou" Rosen. Nick also happened to be one of Lou's top lieutenants in his happy little family of mobsters. Nick was a friend of mine and probably the smartest guy on Lou's crew. What's more, he fancied himself to be the next great discovery in Hollywood, so a chance to try out his acting skills would probably appeal to him. As a bonus, it just so happened that Nick was called in from time to time as an honest-to-god fixer – a guy who cleaned up messes for other dumb mugs who were in a bind and in deep with Lou. Nick wasn't a killer, as such, just good at turning a very bad situation into something that a guy could more or less live with. I found him at one of the tables in the club, chatting up a martini-soaked blonde and her gin-sipping date.

Nick caught sight of me as I took a seat at the bar. A

minute later, he was at my side, summoning the bartender. "Get the man whatever he wants, Mike," Nick said, grandly. "Long time, no see, Henry. How's the new job working out?"

"Job? What job?" I said said, shaking my head. "People keep saying I have a new job. They're nuts."

"Whatever you say, Henry," Nick said, giving me a conspiratorial smile.

"I don't mean to be rude, but how sober are you right now?" I asked.

Nick put some lighthearted effort into looking serious for a moment. "It's barely nine o'clock, Henry," he said. "I had a glass of wine with dinner but I try to stay away from the hard stuff until closer to midnight. I'm on duty, you know."

"So am I."

"Oh?" Nick shook a finger at me and flashed his winning smile. "What are you up to, Mr. Hollis?"

"I need an actor for about an hour, tonight."

"What's the role?"

"Fixer."

Nick smiled and grabbed a handful of peanuts from a bowl on the bar, then turned for the door. "Mike," he said over his shoulder, "I'll be back in a couple hours."

Olie Scharf had refused to enter the club. He was standing on the sidewalk outside the Firefly, looking like a sulking kid who had been left on the curb by his rummy dad. Nick looked him up and down and started to laugh. "Didn't you fix the heel on a pair of brown Oxfords for me?"

Olie shrugged and said nothing.

Nick looked back over at me. "So, who's the mark?"

I pointed to Olie. "Him."

Thirty minutes later, the three of us were standing on the front porch of William Pelley's farmhouse. The place was dark and dead-quiet, with the emphasis on *dead*. I gave Nick a pat on the back. "You know what to do?"

"Sure, I got it. Piece of cake."

"Olie? You ready?" I asked the little man.

Olie looked up into my eyes for a moment, then nodded. "Let's get this over with."

Nick took Olie into the house and up to the second floor, while I retreated to Nick's Studebaker, parked in the driveway. From what Nick told me later, things upstairs went something like this:

Olie and Nick found the bedroom where we had had discovered Olie the night before. Olie kicked off his shoes and lay down on the bed, then Nick cuffed him to the frame. He put the key in the top drawer of a small desk on the far side of the room. After that, Nick turned off the light, pulled a flashlight from his pocket, and retreated a few steps into the hall. Finally, he took a deep breath.

"Offenbach!" he shouted, swinging the flashlight around in the hallway wildly. "Offenbach! Where the hell are you?"

"In... in here!" came a distinctly non-Olie voice in the bedroom.

Nick went into the bedroom and let the beam from the flashlight dazzle Offenbach's eyes. "Get up! We gotta go!"

"Go?" Offenbach said. "I'm... I'm handcuffed to the bed."

"Why the hell would they do that?"

"I'm not... it doesn't matter. Who are you?" Offenbach asked, sounding panicked.

"Name's Nick. Your boss, Mr. Pelley, sent me. He has me on retainer."

"Retainer? For what?"

"Fixing problems like this, when everything goes to hell." Nick gave a yank at the handcuffs and shined the flashlight back in Offenbach's face. "Any chance you know where the keys are for these cuffs?"

Offenbach used his free hand to shield his eyes. "Top drawer of the desk over there. And get that flashlight out of my face!"

Nick dashed over to the desk and rummaged for the key, returning to Offenbach's bedside a few seconds later. He worked the lock frantically and yanked the cuffs off of the prone man's wrist. "We need to get the hell out of here, now!"

Offenbach got out of the bed and shoved his shoes on his feet, then stumbled through the dark room. "What's happened?"

Nick hustled him to the stairway. "I got a call from your boss about thirty minutes ago," he explained, guiding Offenbach down the stairs. "Pelley said it was time for me to earn my retainer money."

"Is he alright?"

"He was, thirty minutes ago, but..."

"But what?"

The two of them made it to the front door and Nick shoved Offenbach ahead of him, shepherding him out into the night. It always helps to keep the mark moving and a little off-balance. At that point, I could see a dim outline of the pair from my spot in the back of the Studebaker. I quickly ducked my head.

"Your boss called me a half hour ago, saying he needed my help," Nick said. "He sounded pretty worked up. Once I got him talking sense, he asked me come here, to this farmhouse, and get you. Then he said I should take you to him." Nick pushed Offenbach toward the front passenger seat of the Studebaker.

"Take me where?" Offenbach asked, as Nick put a hand on his head and shoved him into the car.

Nick left him hanging while he jogged around to the other side of the car and jumped in. "You see, that's a problem. Right when he was starting telling me where to take you, he let out a yell and then the line went dead."

"The line went dead?"

"Yep. You know where he would be hiding out?"

"His house?"

Nick shook his head. "No. He said his house is crawling with cops. So he said he was about to head to some other place that was supposed to be safe enough to give him time to hatch a plan. But, like I said, the line went dead before he could tell me where." In the cramped darkness of the car, Nick summoned his full gangster persona and leaned in nice and close to Offenbach. "We're fifteen minutes from town and I'm not a goddamn cabbie. I'm contracted to help Pelley, but he owes me five hundred bucks and you've got fifteen minutes to give me an address that leads me to a paycheck."

"I understand," Offenbach said. Nick put the car into first gear and started down the gravel driveway.

I was hunched down in the floorboards of the back seat of the car, listening to the whole thing – waiting for the magic words.

"So, where are we going?" Nick said.

Offenbach took a few breaths. "Hmmmmm... I would say...the crypt," he finally said.

Those weren't the magic words I'd expected.

"The what?"

"The Pelley family crypt, at Riverview Cemetery," he explained. "William once mentioned that he used it now and then, when he needed to be away from prying eyes. I've never been there myself, though, and I don't know exactly where the crypt is on the property, though."

"Don't worry. We'll find it," I said from the back seat, even as my fist went flying.

There's a story behind that punch. In the winter of 1918, I was still serving in the United States Army in newly-occupied Germany. I had become a military police trainer by then. In early November, the Army told me to pack up my bags and get ready to ship out for Manila, in the Philippines, where I would be a trainer for the occupation forces there. I went from the November chill of Berlin to the December swelter of Manila. Nobody was shooting at us, but malaria and raging influenza was giving the US military garrison in Manila a real beating. There was one other thing putting a beating on the troops – a dangerous game called *isa sumuntok*, which roughly translates to "one punch," in English.

Our garrison was stationed along the Pasig River, near Fort Santiago. To the east of us, along the river, was mile after mile of shanty town neighborhoods, crude homes stacked one on top of the other or built on stilts over the water. Each humble dwelling was made out of whatever the wind and waves would bring them. My MPs were always chasing American sailors and soldiers out of the bars, brothels, gambling halls, and opium dens that were the main industries of that downtrodden stretch of Manila riverfront.

For generations, the young toughs of the shanty town would prove their mettle by playing isa sumuntok – the idea being to run in packs through the narrow, crowded alleyways and cold-cock some innocent stranger. They had a very specific kind of punch they would use, called a "pok," which was delivered to a spot about an inch above the ear. If the victim fell unconscious to the ground from that single blow, the attacker would yell, "Isa sumontok!" and run on, with his compatriots all laughing and cheering, as they sought out their next victim. The roving gangs took particular pleasure in knocking American soldiers and sailors senseless. That was just one of the many interesting things that the alleyways of Manila taught me in my six months there, but those stories can wait for another day.

I landed a clean "pok" of a punch just above Offenbach's left ear and his lights went instantly out. I took a little too much joy in it, frankly, considering I was also punching poor old Olie Scharf.

"Sweet dreams, you alien bastard," I whispered.

Nick looked back at me from the front seat. "Well, this has been fun, but strange – and I've had some strange nights," he said with a crooked grin.

I patted Nick on the shoulder and handed him a hundred bucks, then leaned back in my seat. "The Essex hotel, please, cabbie. And take the corners slow. My friend isn't feeling very well."

CHAPTER 32

The mood in Lockwood's penthouse suite had changed when we arrived just about midnight. The food was gone, the lights were lower, and Abner Dodds was asleep in an overstuffed armchair. Nick and I were on either side of Olie Scharf as we guided him into the living room. He was conscious, but decidedly weak in the knees. Eleanor Stanton was the first to greet us as we entered.

"What happened to him?" she asked.

"I punched him," I said.

"It's true," Nick confirmed.

Nick and I helped Olie over to the couch and laid him down. Hearing our voices, Ellen Lockwood came to look in on us. "Does he need anything?" she asked.

"An ice pack might be good," I said. She nodded and disappeared into the kitchen.

"So, how did it go?" Judge Arthur Lockwood asked.

"Surprisingly well, all things considered. Nick,

here, did a great acting job. I'm sure Hollywood will be calling any minute. And Olie took his knocks like champ."

There was a brief exchange of greetings between Nick and the others. "Well," he said, after a round of handshakes, "it's been nice meeting you all. I gotta go count the night's take at the Firefly before someone gets sticky fingers at the till. Stop by sometime," he offered warmly to us, as he flashed a toothy smile and headed for the door.

"Thanks, again, Nick." I said as he pulled the door shut behind him, then I turned my attention to the people remaining in the room. "So, I think I know where Pelley is holed up."

"Oh?" Charles Victor said. "Where?"

"Riverview Cemetery, in the Pelley family crypt."

Charles snorted in amusement at the news. "You plan on skulking through a cemetery in the middle of the night?"

"Yeah, that's pretty much it," I said. "I was hoping to have some company, though. "Mr. Sphinx? Eleanor? You ready to hunt spooks and aliens with me?"

Eleanor grinned at the invitation. "My pleasure."

The Sphinx nodded once. "Do you need anything?"

"A good length of rope... and some coffee," I said.

The Riverview Cemetery is on the lower slopes of the rise going up to Olympus Heights. It is the oldest operating cemetery in New Eden and covers close to three hundred acres of land. The eternal residents are a broad mix, but many were the early movers and shakers of the city – at least during their years above ground. It's quite pretty, really, if you visit it during the day. At night, however, it is as dark and forbidding as any place filled with dead bodies and gloomy, hulking monuments to the deceased. The south end of the cemetery is dominated by an impressively large rough-hewn limestone arch, flanked on either side by limestone pillars anchoring long stone walls, disappearing off into the night. We parked about five hundred feet down the road from the entrance, at a darkened gas station.

Just inside the gated limestone arch sat a small brick building that served as the business office for the cemetery. We hopped the wall and made for its back door. Eleanor Stanton dropped to one knee and pulled out her lock-picking kit, and we were soon prowling about in the small building. At the front desk, I soon found what I was looking for: the plot map. It was gridded and next to it was an alphabetical list of the residents. I found the entry for the Pelley crypt and dragged my finger across the map – M 23. "Got it," I whispered, without really needing to. "Either of you see a phone?"

Eleanor and the Sphinx glanced about. The Sphinx pointed his flashlight to a small ledge behind the front desk, where a phone sat bathed in the pale beam of moonlight.

"Perfect," I said and made a quick phone call. Once that was over, I looked at my companions. "We have maybe fifteen minutes – tops – to find the crypt and rescue Archie Flood, if there's anything left to rescue."

We filed out the back door and headed into the night. "Flashlights off," I whispered.

Dropping into crouches, we headed north up the main gravel road, which shone a pale bluish-white when compared to the darker mounds of grass and brooding headstones on either side. I counted off the gravel cross-streets that intersected the main road, and when we got to the right one, I pointed to the left, moving more slowly now. Long rows of family crypts dominated this section of the cemetery. Silhouettes of weeping-angel statues loomed over us as we moved from crypt to crypt, with me counting silently as we went. "That one," I muttered at last, pointing ahead of us.

The Pelley crypt was rather small, by the standards of its peers in the cemetery. It was also clearly very old. The iron bars of the gated entrance were covered in flaking rust and sagging in their fittings. On either side of the gate were stone urns, devoid of flowers and now playing host to thickets of tangled weeds. The whole effect of the crypt was to remind the casual observer of the lonely fate that awaits us all, once we shuffle off into eternity. But I smiled anyway, because on top of the crypt were two carved gargoyles crouching in an eternal vigil. They were Pelley's little inside joke, and I was one of the very few people on Earth who was in on it. Eleanor made a cautious survey of the outside of the crypt while the Sphinx and I crouched about twenty feet away in the deep shadows of a nearby crypt.

Eleanor came skulking back over to us after a couple of minutes. "It's a front. There's a larger structure underground," she whispered. "The old gate smells of grease – it's been oiled and maintained better than it looks. The bronze door behind the gate has a new lock – but I can pick it."

"Looks like we're in the right place," I whispered back to her. "Time to tie me up." I handed her the rope I had brought. "Make it good and tight, but make sure I can walk."

"You're the boss," she said.

It took Eleanor a couple minutes to properly truss me up; then I gave her the go-ahead to pick the lock. The gate swung open nice and quiet, and Eleanor put her little tool kit on her knee and set to work. The Sphinx and I crouched on either side of her and waited.

"The bolt is moving... got it," she said.

"Good. I want you to lead the way in with your weapon out, but no heroics and no gun-play. The whole idea here is to set Pelley up to take the fall, not have him die a martyr or take us with him."

"I need to ask a favor, before you go in there," a voice said from behind us. Needless to say, I nearly jumped out of my skin.

The three of us spun in a panic and were greeted by the sight of a long-haired boy of perhaps ten, standing in the cemetery lane just a few feet away.

"Christ! This is a hell of a time for you to stop by for some chit-chat," I said in the loudest whisper I could manage.

"You know that kid?" Eleanor hissed, reaching for her sidearm.

"Yeah. Let me introduce you to the Oracle of Dalton's Bluff."

"What do you want?" the Sphinx asked.

The boy came closer, his innocent face and ancient eyes coming out of the shadows as he neared. "I want to save a man's life."

"You mean Archie Flood?"

"No, actually." the Oracle said. "I'm talking about William Pelley – or, rather, the innocent man he was a century ago, before he was infected with the consciousness of another being."

"Infected?" I said in a hoarse whisper.

"Yes. I can't banish the alien inside his human body, but I can give the human another chance at a life free of mindless bondage."

"I can't say I follow you, but I'll take your word for it right now. Stay behind us and get ready to run like hell when I tell you."

The Oracle nodded, then asked, "Why are your arms bound in rope, Mr. Hollis?"

"I've got a bad plan. Now, stay quiet."

Eleanor looked at me and I gave her a nod. With that, she heaved on the heavy bronze door, pulling it aside, and plunged into the crypt, a Colt .45 in one hand and a flashlight in the other. We all piled in, close behind her. The first thing we saw of the interior was was a limestone sarcophagus. It took up the center of the small room but was turned or dragged and now sat at an angle across the space. On the floor, where the sarcophagus would have rested normally, a narrow set of stairs was visible, descending into darkness. Eleanor raised an eyebrow at me and I nodded. She took a breath and rushed down the stairs, gun and flashlight at the ready.

There was soon the sound of something sliding, and light flooded up from below. I started down the rough hewn steps, awkwardly, as my arms were tied to my sides. My two new alien friends were close behind me.

A couple seconds later, we heard Eleanor call out, "Don't move a damn muscle!"

We quite literally tumbled into the larger space below. It was maybe twenty by twenty, made of poured concrete. Two naked lightbulbs hung overhead. The bunker was full of shelving, a couple tables, a sleeping cot, and several metal chairs. William Pelley was seated at a work-table, his hands in the guts of some kind of machine. A few feet away from him was Archie Flood, bushy brows and all, on the cot, trussed up in rope.

"Well, don't you look a fool, Mr. Hollis," Pelley said, with surprising composure.

"I'm worried about the results, not the looks," I said, struggling to my feet.

Then Pelley saw the Oracle. "Ah..." he said, sounding more concerned than he had a moment before. Mr. Silver Hair and the little alien boy entered into a brief conversation – in their native tongue. The volume of their voices ramped up pretty quick and it was clear by the tone that they weren't quite ready to kiss and make up.

"Mr. Hollis," the Oracle finally said, in English. "It's critically important that I have a moment's access to Mr. Pelley's arm. Can you and your friend make that happen?"

"His arm, huh?" I said. "Eleanor?"

Eleanor braced her pistol with both hands and walked cautiously toward Pelley. He raised his hands slowly and turned in his chair to face her. "Put your hands on your head," she said to him, then placed one of her own hands on his two hands. "Kid," she said to the Oracle. "Do what you gotta do. Make it quick."

The boy approached the man in the chair. As he walked, he pulled what looked like a very small, silver pistol from his pocket.

"No. Wait!" I called out, but it was too late. The Oracle put the tiny gun to Pelley's arm and pulled the trigger. There was a muted thud and a hiss, like compressed air escaping. Pelley flinched, but there was nothing more dramatic to see.

"I'm done," the Oracle said, stepping back. Eleanor stepped back, as well.

"Good, then, get the hell out of here. You, too, Elcanor. Beat it." I looked over at the Sphinx, who had been standing silently off to one side of the room. "Tie up my legs."

Eleanor walked slowly backward, toward the narrow stairway, with the Oracle at her side. "You're a crazy bastard, Henry," she said.

"Yeah, I know. Just follow my plan."

"Don't worry, I will."

The Sphinx busied himself with binding my legs while Eleanor and the boy started up the stairs, leaving me and Archie Flood, both bound and helpless, with two aliens in a crypt. An awkward minute or two passed without anyone speaking.

Pelley decided to break the silence. "So, what happens now, Mr. Hollis?" he asked.

"That's up to you," I said, leaning up against the concrete wall.

"So, you'd be happy to have me just leave, then?"

"I can't stop you. I'm tied up. Whatever you do, I suggest you do it quick."

William Pelley rose slowly from his chair. Neither the Sphinx nor I moved a muscle. Pelley seemed to be feeling slightly more comfortable with the situation because he began to walk sort of sideways across the room, keeping his eyes on me the whole time. He took a chance and glanced to his left, at a shelf, then back to us. We still didn't budge.

"What's your game, Mr. Hollis?" he asked, taking a couple more sideways steps.

"No game," I said, calmly. "Like I said, you're in charge, now."

"If I walk out of here right now and leave you alive,

with Archie for company, would you continue to pursue me?"

"The odds are pretty good," I said, nodding in agreement.

"You understand that leaves me little choice but to kill you, don't you?" he asked.

"Shame you didn't bring a pitch fork, huh?" I said, then grunted a laugh.

"Oh, I've got better," Pelley said with a savage smile. He took one more glance at the shelf to his left; then his right hand darted toward it and came back sporting a snub nose .38 revolver. The Sphinx and I still didn't budge.

"You can leave, you can shoot me, whatever you want," I said, trying to play it calm and cool.

Pelley started laughing and shaking his head. "You really have been a thorn in my side, Mr. Hollis. Considering all the trouble you've been, it's probably best that I just shoot you."

"I hear that a lot."

"There's an irony to it, really."

"Oh, yeah?" I said.

"Well, this would be the second time I've killed you."

"You mean Adam Smith?" I said.

"Oh, you know about him?" he asked, raising an eyebrow. "Yes, of course. Mr. Flood must have given you that little piece of history." Pelley waved the revolver casually at Archie. "I was going to pin his death on you, but now I'll just satisfy myself with killing you both... and I suppose I'd better kill that strange, quiet fellow, in the corner, too." He glanced at the Sphinx.

"Yeah, about him..." I said, making a failed attempt at a shrug, being that I was tied up. "You see, he's a... well, I don't really know what he is – but the point is, he's not gonna let you kill me."

"Oh?" Pelley said. "And how is he..."

Right then, the Sphinx took a long step toward Pelley, followed by another, accelerating as he went. Pelley leveled the snub nose .38 on him and began firing. The first two slugs buried themselves in the Sphinx's chest, spinning him a little, but he just kept coming. The next slug went through his outstretched forearm and then kept going until it found its way into my upper left thigh, sitting as I was on the other side of the room. Two more shots rang out, each a head-shot, but to no avail. The Sphinx kept coming.

The scene was as just as gruesome as you might imagine. There was blood, some bone and maybe even some brain. It also happened to be the first time that I had ever been shot. It hurt – a lot. The Sphinx – or what was left of him – finally careened into Pelley as the last bullet went wild, into the ceiling. The Sphinx's shaking arms wrapped around the shooter, sending both of them crashing to the floor.

Pelley screamed in fear and fury for a few seconds and then concentrated his efforts on getting out from under the corpse that had now gone limp on his chest. It took him a while, but he finally shook and shoved himself free. He got to his feet, on shaking legs, and looked over at me, wide-eyed. His face was twisted in blood-spattered rage. "You're utterly mad!" he said, spitting. He stared at the revolver and threw it at me, sending it glancing off my chest. Then, he went running for the stairway.

I could hear Pelley pull aside the bronze door in the upper crypt. Almost instantly, there were other voices shouting. I heard the shuffle of many feet on the stone floor and a scuffle and screaming. Finally, the voice of Detective Aemon Bettis rang out, telling William Pelley to stop squirming and lay still. Things got a little fuzzy after that, as my leg was leaking blood at a pretty good rate by then.

CHAPTER 33

St. Elizabeth's Hospital sits on a slight rise, about a half-mile north of New Eden University. If you get shot in New Eden, this is the place to be taken. It opened a year ago and is full of the best medical science that 1934 can offer.

Arthur Lockwood got me a private room and was the first to come visit, right after my mother and father. "How did the conversation go with your parents?" he asked.

"They know I take risks," I explained. "I dropped a few hints that I have some kind of business relationship with Charles Victor. I played it that he hired me to pay on an old gambling debt of his, but things went south and I got a slug in my leg for my troubles."

"That sounds reasonable," Lockwood said.

"Yeah, but they know there's more to it. They won't ask any questions, but they know."

Lockwood nodded solemnly. "It's best they don't

know too much."

"Yeah, that's what I was thinking." I winced at a wave of pain as I adjusted the pillow under my wounded leg. "Any news from the county prosecutor's office?"

"You're in the clear. That little rope trick of yours convinced the prosecutor that you were just another one of Pelley's victims. Detective Bettis isn't buying it, but he doesn't get to make that call."

"I'll work on him," I said, smiling. "So, how are things at the island?"

Lockwood's face warmed at the mention of the island. "Clarence Boyette is making great strides. We've changed the plans a bit, due to the need for more permanent housing for your new... associates," he said.

"Oh?"

"I met the Brown Beast."

"The Brown Beast?" I asked, amused.

"Yes, the large, hairy creature that attacked you – twice. It turns out he's quite tame, and gentle. Maurice has taken him under his wing, so to speak."

"You met Maurice?"

Arthur Lockwood grimaced. "Yes. It was, um... awkward... at first, but I soon warmed to him. He's really quite clever, and it's clear to me that he is good at heart, once you get past the macabre exterior and gruff demeanor. It's also a fact that he has nowhere to go. I think we will be playing host to them both for the foreseeable future."

"That's quite the motley crew."

"More than you know," Lockwood said, with a chuckle. "Clarence has been dutifully watering the box the Sphinx left you, and as best we can tell, it just finished cooking this morning."

"Oh yeah? What is it?"

Lockwood shook his head in bemused wonderment. "I don't really know. I'm not sure how to describe it, to be honest. Maurice says he thinks it might be something called a *golem*."

"A what?"

He shrugged. "You'll need to see it for yourself, and then perhaps have a chat with the Sphinx about it."

"I'll do that," I said.

Lockwood walked closer to my bedside. "I want to congratulate you, by the way," he said, extending a hand.

"Oh yeah? What for?"

"Why, for completing your assignment, of course – finding out who destroyed that statue in Children's Park, and why. It turned out to be much more involved than I expected, but you rose to the occasion." Lockwood gave me a warm smile. "I... we... thank you for your efforts."

I gave a good-natured shrug. "No problem. But..."

"Yes?"

"I still have a lot of my own questions – important questions – that I need answers to. I don't feel like I'm anywhere close to being done."

"You're absolutely right, Henry," Lockwood said, giving me a sympathetic smile. "But that feeling you have is something that you – and we all – will need to get used to for the foreseeable future. For our own sanity, we all need to be patient and approach our jobs one assignment at a time."

"Easier said than done, but I get it," I said. "So, what's my next assignment?"

"I've been thinking," Lockwood said, slowly. "What you are doing is important – not just to me but to the entire world. History will want to know about what's happening here in New Eden, during these desperate days."

"Yeah? So, what are you suggesting?" I asked.

"Well," Lockwood said, reaching over to a leather satchel he had placed on my bed-side table when he first entered, "I picked up a little gift for you. It's your choice what you do with it – but whatever you do, keep it safe and secret until the world is ready for it." With that, he pulled a notebook and a fine pen from the leather satchel. "I thought that since you're laid up for a few days, you could use this to pass the time."

"Why, thanks, Judge. It just so happens I've been kicking around an idea or two."

"I'm sure you have, Henry."

My time with Arthur Lockwood was interrupted by a nurse, who politely but firmly asked him to leave and give me a chance to rest. She then gave me some kind of medication for the pain, and I spent the next hour or two in dreamless slumber. Just about the time that I was able to lift my head off the pillow again, there was a soft knock at the door.

CHAPTER 34

"Come in," I said, surprising myself with the sound of my own shaky voice.

The door swung open to reveal two people standing in the hallway. The taller of the two was a complete stranger to me – an older woman of perhaps seventy, dressed in a very faded flower print dress. The other visitor was none other than the Oracle of Dalton's Bluff. He gazed at me and smiled, almost shyly. His eyes held the wisdom of the ages, but there was still a youthful spark to them.

"Don't just stand there gaping at me. Come in," I said, in teasing gruffness.

Both of my visitors stepped into the room. The Oracle had been holding the hand of the older woman, but now he lifted her hand slightly and patted it reassuringly. "Thanks, Rose. If you could wait down the hall for just a few minutes?" he said. She nodded and left the two of us alone, closing the door behind her.

"Who's the lady?" I asked.

The boy smiled. "She's an old friend."

"So, how old are you, anyway?" I asked.

"Four hundred, give or take," he said, casually.

"I met another one of your kind, the other day. He goes by Maurice."

"Maurice?"

"He said William Pelley held him in a cage in his basement for a hundred years."

The Oracle shook his head, visibly frustrated. "Yes... I know him by a different name. I saw him several times, but never had the opportunity or resources to rescue him."

"Yeah, he's a bit sore about that," I said. "There's also a big, brown fringe-covered beast in town, too. Pelley had him imported from the homeland more recently, as best as I can tell. They tell me he's more bark than bite, though."

"I know the species. They're semi-intelligent and slow to anger, but dangerous when threatened."

"I'll keep that in mind, seeing as he will be calling my new work-space his home for a while – at least, until we can figure a way to send him back to wherever it is that you folks are from."

The Oracle frowned. "It could be a while. I've been working on solving that riddle since I arrived here."

"Great." I stared at the boy for a moment. "Do you have a name, by the way? I hear that the folks up on Dalton's Bluff used to call you the Oracle, but I'm betting you picked another name for yourself, back in the day."

"It's true, the child before you did have a name, before I... came into his life. I adopted his name, and was eventually accepted by his community."

"You took over his body is what you're saying, right?"

"Yes," the boy said, looking pained. "And I hope to give him his life back one day, when my work is done here. I made a very difficult choice many years ago, Mr. Hollis. I left a place engulfed in centuries of death and war, seeking a way to stop the bloodshed. I could have come here looking much like Maurice – who was sent here against his will – or, I could take possession of a living form that was already here and try to blend in."

"Like William Pelley did?"

"Yes, like that. He and I are on opposite sides of that fight, however."

"Are you two looking for the same thing here?"

"Yes and no. We've both been looking for a certain very special insight into the universe, but he wants to use that knowledge to find weapons. I want to use it to do something very much the opposite."

"Well he did nearly kill me last night."

"I'm glad to see that you're alive. I wouldn't want to lose you again."

"Ah, right. Adam Smith."

"Yes, it's true."

"So, what's true, and how, exactly?" I said, sitting up a little in the hospital bed, wincing as I rose.

The Oracle walked over to the chair next to the bed and hopped up on it. "You were *originally* born somewhere around 1796, in Connecticut, I think. Your original name escapes me now. You went west sometime after 1820, seeking to make a fresh start in the new state of Indiana. I first met you in the Assinowa Valley when you came to visit the native village in the summer of 1830. I had been living amongst the Assinowa for three centuries by then." He paused and pointed to the white pitcher on the bedside table. "Water?"

"Sure, thanks."

The Oracle poured me a glass of water and continued his tale. "And then, in the spring of 1831, the stars aligned and a window of sorts opened."

I interrupted him. "Are you talking about that 'celestial wave-rings' stuff that the Sphinx gave me a primer on?"

The Oracle raised an eyebrow at that. "Well, that exact term is new to me, but I suspect he and I are talking about the same thing." He briefly paused and gazed out the window. "Semantics aside, multiple small portals started opening in 1831 – some of them between my home world and this world. They continued to randomly open and close in and around what we now call New Eden – and other places on Earth – for the next 19 years. It's a 95-year cycle and the portals are open again, right now. They began to open in 1926 and will keep appearing and disappearing until the summer of 1945."

"So, what happened to Adam Smith?" I asked.

"When the portals began opening again in 1831, I was able to communicate once again with my people, back on my home world. They agreed with me that circumstances were changing here, in what would soon be New Eden, and that I would need some help in carrying out my mission."

"Things were changing here?"

The Oracle nodded. "As I said, I've been here for centuries, waiting for your world to catch up with its potential – for good and evil. Not much changed for centuries, then the white men arrived." The boy poured a glass of water for himself. "It was decided that we would bring the consciousness of another volunteer over from my home-world. I chose you – or your former self – to be the host."

"So, my – his – life essentially ended that day?" I asked.

"Essentially, yes. But you were reborn in 1896, with the hope that you would finally get to live the full life that you were entitled to. Your wife made your rebirth possible, as a matter of fact."

I spat water across the room and gaped at the little Indian boy. "What?"

He nodded. "Once my colleague assumed your identity, he aided me in my work here for more than sixty years. In 1845, we made contact with another alien visitor to your world. She had assumed the identity of a human, but was from a far different and much more advanced society from either yours or ours. Over the years, we grew confident that her mission here was much the same as ours, and an alliance of sorts blossomed. Much to my surprise, a romance blossomed, as well – between her and Adam Smith. Then, using assumed names, the two of you were wed in the spring of 1851, which was shortly after contact with our home worlds was cut off."

"That wasn't me," I said. "That was an alien who hijacked my body."

"Well, that may be true, but Adam Smith and Evelyn Smith were happily married for decades – until you were murdered, that is."

"Evelyn?" I gasped.

"Yes, Mr. Hollis, *your* Evelyn. The woman who had married Adam Smith – alien though she may be – deeply grieved the loss of her husband and used her knowledge and technological resources to put the breath of life back into a few drops of his blood – your blood – and from that, an orphan infant was born," the boy said, his voice crackling with emotion.

I stared at him, looking stupid and confused.

The boy pointed a finger at me. "You, Mr. Hollis. You were that orphan infant. She made you, and then, as Evelyn Fabré, she waited for you to grow to manhood, hoping against hope that the two of you would find love together with once again."

The tears started flowing down my cheeks. "It was all a setup?"

"It was a love story more than seventy years in the making," he said.

"And now she's gone."

The Oracle reached out a child's small hand to my arm. "She chose to leave."

"That's a lie," I said, pushing his hand away.

"It's true. I don't know much about it, and I don't know where she is. Things were happening fast and she sent word to me that she had made a breakthrough in her work. Evelyn also said that she was being pursued and had to make a drastic choice in order to safeguard the lives of every person on Earth – and countless other worlds, as well."

"She went into hiding? With my daughter?"

"Exactly. But you won't find her anywhere on this world."

"Where, then?"

"I don't know. It was part of her plan to withhold that information from me – from everyone."

For once, I was silent. I couldn't find any words. The world was falling away from under my hospital bed. The air went out of my lungs and I just laid my head back on the pillow, my eyes staring a million miles ahead, up into the stars beyond the ceiling and the sunny blue sky above.

"You need to rest," I heard the Oracle say quietly. I found myself nodding in agreement.

The boy climbed off the chair at my bedside and took a step toward the door. "I'll get in touch soon. There's much more to talk about, and we both have much more work to do."

END

Stay tuned for the next exciting Desparate Days installment: King Jim

ABOUT THE AUTHOR

Matt can't remember a time when he wasn't conjuring up imaginary worlds and telling stories. He's always loved breathing life into characters and places that existed only in his head. By the age of ten, Matt was writing fantasy stories. By the age of thirteen, he was deeply involved in storytelling games, a pastime that continues to fire his imagination and keep him in good company. After growing up in South Bend, Indiana, Matt went off to spend his undergrad years at the University of Iowa, then he did his graduate studies at Indiana University. After that, Matt spent a solid decade learning about adulthood and himself and the real world. Eventually, and for more than twenty years, he came to live and work in Bloomington, Indiana, where he owned a property development company. These days, Matt lives in Arlington, Virginia, where he dedicates his work-time to writing and the rest of his time (and heart) to his wife and two children.

You can learn more about Matt and his work, on-line at:

authormattpress.com
facebook.com/authormattpress

Made in the USA
Middletown, DE
31 December 2018